PUBLISHER: Margaret Obank
EDITOR: Samuel Shimon
FRONT COVER PAINTING: Mahi Bir

CONTRIBUTING EDITORS
Fadhil al-Azzawi, Issa J Boullata,
Frangieh, Camilo Gómez-Rivas, Marilyn Hacker, William M Hutchins,
Imad Khachan, Khaled Mattawa, Anton Shammas, Paul Starkey, Mona Zaki

CONSULTING EDITORS
Etel Adnan, Roger Allen, Mohammed Bennis, Isabella Camera d'Afflitto,
Humphrey Davies, Hartmut Fähndrich, Gamal al-Ghitani,
Erdmute Heller, Herbert Mason, Hassan Najmi, Saif al-Rahbi,
Naomi Shihab Nye, Yasir Suleiman, Susannah Tarbush, Stephen Watts

EDITORIAL ASSISTANTS:
Charis Bredin, Maureen O'Rourke, Nisreen Ghandourah

PUBLISHING ASSISTANT: Agnes Reeve

INTERNS: Caterina Pinto, Ceren Cano

LAYOUT: Banipal Publishing

CONTACTS:
TEL: +44 (0)20 7832 1350
WEBSITE: www.banipal.co.uk
EDITOR: editor@banipal.co.uk  PUBLISHER: margaret@banipal.co.uk
INQUIRIES: info@banipal.co.uk  SUBSCRIPTIONS: subscribe@banipal.co.uk
ADDRESS: 1 Gough Square, London EC4A 3DE
PRINTED BY Short Run Press Ltd
Bittern Road, Sowton Ind. Est. EXETER  EX2 7LW

Photographs not accredited have been donated, photographers
unknown.

BANIPAL, ISSN 1461-5363, is published three times a year by Banipal
Publishing, 1 Gough Square, London EC4A 3DE

We thank the Abu Dhabi International Book Fair
for their support for Banipal 46 – 80 New Poems

معرض أبوظبي الدولي للكتاب
Abu Dhabi International Book Fair
24th-29th April 2013 | adbookfair.com

Supported using public funding by

LOTTERY FUNDED  **ARTS COUNCIL ENGLAND**

BANIPAL
Magazine of Modern Arab Literature

## www.banipal.co.uk

Taha Adnan

Amjad Nasser

Hassab al-Sheikh Ja'far

Salah Faik

Heind R. Ibrahim

*Philip Metres*

*Dunya Mikhail*

*Khaled Najar*

*Lorand Gaspar*

*Latifa Baqa*

Read all these authors online with a digital subscription from iTunes or Exact Editions

For Saif Ghobash Banipal Translation Prize and Banipal Trust, go to www.banipaltrust.org.uk

# WERNER MARK LINZ

## 6 April 1935 – 9 February 2013

On 10 February, I received news that Mark Linz, who had directed The American University in Cairo Press for over 25 years, had passed away the day before. He had been battling with cancer, but when I met him at the Frankfurt Book Fair in October, although he looked gaunt, his broad smile and twinkling eyes were still there, and I was reassured of victory over the disease.

Images of him over the years that I have known him immediately sprang to mind. He was gracious, open-hearted, encouraging, charming and supportive, almost always smiling and in good spirits – a friend who will be so missed.

I will never forget the countless chats and discussions, the emails, we have had with him since *Banipal* started in 1998, not to mention the sharing of a booth at MESA, the advertisements in the magazine, the meetings at Frankfurt and London Book Fairs.

He had not long ago retired from the Press that he had seen become – in his own words in *Banipal 43*'s celebration of doyen translator Denys Johnson-Davies – "recognized as the world's leading publisher of modern Arabic literature in translation". It is ironic that the headline Mark Linz gave to the work of DJD in that article – *A unique and lasting legacy* – must now, with his passing, become his own.

Humphrey Davies concurred when he added his tribute: "Mark Linz was ahead of the curve in recognizing the interest in Arabic literature for readers of English. Among his many achievements, this may be his most significant."

*Margaret Obank*

# EDITORIAL

We are pleased to open *Banipal 46* with the debut novel, *Land of No Rain*, of well-known poet Amjad Nasser. Set in the future, the protagonist struggles to understand his past in an unnamed Arab country and his present life in the ruined City of Red and Grey. It is followed by an excerpt from Faris al-Shidyaq's 1855 Rabelaisian work *Leg over Leg*, translated by Humphrey Davies for the new classical Library of Arabic Literature.

The main feature, **80 New Poems**, takes the pulse of new poetry with works by 14 poets who reflect the diversity and dynamism in Arab life and society today. It begins with Kurdish Syrian poet Hussein Habasch's ode to Edith Piaf after a visit to Père Lachaise Cemetery, and is followed by Moroccan Taha Adnan's tender appeal for more than "a tattered flag" or the sounds of what "the people want". Philip Metres, an award-winning Arab American poet, reclaims his Arab heritage in a magnificent toast to my Iraqi friend Nawal Nasrallah, who spent years researching ancient Iraqi/Mesopotamian recipes.

We introduce Hassab al-Sheikh Ja'far, an award-winning Iraqi poet never before in English – we need more of his existential immediacy. After him is Tunisian intellectual Khaled Najar who asks many questions and remembers his youth. Then two more Iraqi poets – the young Heind Ibrahim who now lives in Washington DC and writes in English, and Kirkuk-born Salah Faik, settled in the Philippines after living in London in the 1970s and 80s, writing epigrammatic shorts. Grande dame Vénus Khoury-Ghata never ceases to inspire with her rich prose poems from the pen of a "doyen" of French poetry translation, Marilyn Hacker. Turn the page and this time Amjad Nasser is foxing readers with a brilliant philosophical work of hope and death, a contradiction of senses, of pain, dread – and acceptance.

Libyan poet Khaled Mattawa, master of experimentation with the English language, pays homage to his native Benghazi and invites readers to consider a Heaven that is "terribly cold", while Palestinian Musa Hawamdeh, living in Jordan, invites us to defeat death and look for life in its variety. Dunya Mikhail, from Iraq and now settled in Detroit, looks back and forward, needing a "second life" in order to forget. Mohamed al-Harthy, from Oman, gives us an epic tale of a car mechanic in the 1970s, while Berlin-based Iraqi Fadhil al-Azzawi opens his imagination and teases us with a British Airways flight to Gomorrah, then hawks, apostles, strangers and policemen.

We are proud to feature as Guest Writer the major French poet Lorand Gaspar, whom Samuel Shimon first met in Tunis, many years ago, then later in Paris. Just recently we were greeted by both Lorand and his wife Jacqueline in their flat there. Somehow, very little of his extraordinary work has been translated into English. His explorations into the intricate relation of the natural world to the emotions and physicality of human beings are profound in their simplicity and we thank Mary Ann Caws for the excellent translations of his poetry.

This Spring there is also a special section of excerpts from the six shortlisted novels of the 2013 International Prize for Arabic Fiction. And we present a searing memoir, *The Day the Olive Harvest was Stopped*, by Palestinian writer Mohammad Khashan. I think our friend was right when she said each issue of *Banipal* is a book of wonder.

MARGARET OBANK

# AMJAD NASSER

# Land of No Rain

## AN EXCERPT FROM THE NOVEL
## TRANSLATED BY JONATHAN WRIGHT

Here you are then, going back, the man who changed his name to escape the consequences of what he'd done. It's been a long time since you left, and that was an event that mattered only to the few who took an interest in your case. As usual, those few are constantly declining in number. You're not sure what's left of the flame that burned deep inside you in the days of youth and hope. Your feet have worn out so many pairs of shoes, roaming the streets, walking along dirt paths and paved roads. How many more steps must they take? How much more emotion can your heart muscle handle? What's left that will still excite you? Does the smell of coffee still promise mornings that haven't come? After looking in different directions for so long, will your eyes ever finally converge on the same point? Can you still believe that lie about how cute your cross-eyes are, a lie uttered one day long ago by rosy lips that you were the first to taste?

Your eyes are like you. Whenever you look, you have to force them to work together. You were about to ask yourself: on the spiral, or circular, pathway that leads back to the start, who lost and who gained? This question nags you. Another question nags you too but you've never given it a chance to take shape in your head: did you take the wrong path?

It's hard not to ask such questions in a situation such as yours, although you learned in your long exile how to suppress questions you don't like or how to dodge them by procrastination or equivocation. But from now on there can be no more procrastination or equivocation. There was a time when you didn't notice time creeping along the ground and through your body, but now the sound of it is clearly audible.

Everything is endless but nothing remains as it is. That's a lesson your hand has learned, right down to the bones and the nerves; the hand that no longer shakes the air like a fist of bronze, but hovers uncertainly – with bulging veins – over the table, the hand that has to reassess dimensions and sizes, heaviness and lightness. Have you noticed how unsteady it is when you shake hands with people, give directions or touch things? Perhaps not, because against the background noise of flesh and blood, you cannot hear that mysterious and perfidious pickaxe chipping away, as the stones of the fortress start to work loose from the inside. But the rasping noise of that pickaxe comes straight from the lungs. It cannot always be muffled with the palm of a hand or a pocket handkerchief.

Where will you begin your long story, or rather your many stories that overlook each other like the rooms of an old Arab house? You don't know exactly, because the years and events, the faces and voices, are mixed up in your memory. The officers who questioned you at the National Security Agency imposed a sequence of events on you, one that might be better organised from a chronological point of view. But you cannot use the records lying in the drawer assigned to you in that star-shaped stone building. Besides, those cold bureaucratic records are not interested in your inner world, your motives, in what lies between the superimposed layers of yourself. Those records contain no monologues, no waking dreams, no nightmares, no echoes, no convolutions; only uniformity, a regularity, a linear sequence of events and names. Where among them can you find your mother's soft footsteps at night, as she hovers over the blankets spread on the floor, covering this son or that daughter, opening or closing the windows, rising before anyone else in the morning so that they can wake to the smell of coffee and fresh bread? Where is your father's tall, lean frame, a cigarette hanging from his lip, and his inks, pens and calligraphies that explore the expanses of creation? Where are his leisurely footsteps as he descends the twelve steps to his underground temple? Where are your noisy brothers and kindly sisters? Where is your grandmother's winged shadow, and your grandfather, sitting up straight as a bolt, who stopped writing out those proverbs and sayings when his eyesight started to fade? Where are the faces that somehow imprinted their features on your memory forever, and the faces whose details have been erased and whose ghostly passage across the screen of your memory keeps you awake at night? Where are the smells that mysteriously preserve the images and feelings you secretly treasure? Where are the pavements, the cold, life when it became just a lucky coincidence, the skies as low as a wall of grey, the long sleepless nights, the cough, the stubborn hopes, and the dancing lights of return? There's nothing of all that in those reports, so dry that the paper crinkles, because these are things that don't interest them. These things are useless when the accounts are settled and the harvest is weighed. You didn't answer some of the interrogators' questions, or you responded vaguely and coldly to the questions that no longer interested you. In short, that was the version of the story they wanted, to fill the gaps in their files, not your rambling, tangled story.

So begin here, although it may not be the right beginning, but every story needs to have some beginning.

It came to pass that a plague, reminiscent of an ancient pestilence, swept the City of Red and Grey. You recall the panic that gripped that great conurbation, built of red brick under grey skies. The anarchy, the breakdown in law and order, the great convulsion that affected everything because the plague had come almost without warning. Some people attributed it to the large numbers of immigrants, especially those from impoverished countries, and to the crowded slums or asylum camps. Others said the plague was latent in the fabric of the city itself and needed only a catalyst for it to spread. The plague's black wing touched your wife, whom you had met on the Island of the Sun.

You almost perished at the hands of outlaws more than once. Most of your neighbours fled the working-class area where you lived. You don't know what happened to them. The doors of their houses were pulled off their hinges. Some houses were set on fire, some were looted. You found the immigrant grocer who used to sell you goods on credit – although such a practice was unknown in this city – lying in front of his looted shop, his mouth agape as if screaming. So many perished in that unexplained plague, including some of your professional colleagues and some of your drinking companions.

Images of those struck down by the plague – in the streets, in the quarantine centres, at bus stops and on the underground – recur from time to time: of your wife looking at you with weary eyes from behind a glass screen, of the cough that tore the lungs, spitting blood, the almost primitive emotions and behaviour that people exhibited, the face masks that made people look like highwaymen, the X-signs written on walls in thick black ink to distinguish one house from another, the codes used in conversations, none of which you understood, and the weird way that people spoke, as if from the guts and not from the throat.

This memory, or nightmare, recurs time after time. You took backstreets to visit your wife in quarantine in the city centre, which was orderly compared with the suburbs where things had slipped out of control. Three masked men had pounced on you out of the blue. You were carrying a bag with some food in it. They brandished knives and the sharp blades glinted in the tense space between you and them. They told you to put the bag on the ground, that if you wanted to escape with your life you should leave the bag and step aside. You did so. What they found in the bag didn't satisfy the savage eyes behind the masks. They ordered you to give them all the cash you were carrying. You threw your wallet at them from a distance. It seemed there wasn't enough money to make them leave. They saw your wedding ring on your left hand. They gestured to you to take it off. It was hard, not only because you were loath to do so but because your fingers had suddenly swollen. Fear had made your blood flow and your hands were as thick as a couple of fresh peasant loaves. You tried to budge the ring but you couldn't. One of the masked men came forward cautiously. He brandished his knife and you saw the blade. Another man coughed with a sound that seemed to rip his lungs to shreds. It looked like he had to spit. He spat blood on the ground. You could see the colour of his face behind the mask.

'I'm the same colour as you!' you said in the local language to the masked man advancing toward you. That was naïve but you couldn't help saying it.

'Shut up! Just shut up!' he barked. He put the tip of the knife between the ring and the flesh and started to lever it. It hurt. You saw drops of blood but you suppressed the pain. The ring didn't come off, so the masked man patiently changed his plan and was about to sever your finger when a police car appeared at the end of the street, saving your finger from amputation.

When you reached the quarantine centre they gave you a tetanus shot and bandaged the wound. Your wife's dull eyes looked at you from behind the glass screen in hope, or despair, or reproach. You couldn't understand how her look could be so changeable, but you will never forget it. You weren't allowed inside the glass enclosure, where dozens of victims were lying. You stood outside it. You spoke to her. She couldn't hear you. She seemed to understand what you were saying from your lip movements, because she nodded. Every now and then she had a coughing fit. You couldn't hear it but you could judge its intensity by the way her thin body shook when she turned her head aside. You told her everything would be fine. You weren't sure about that but it's what one has to say in such situations. She moved her head slowly and looked you up and down with her dull eyes until they came to rest on your bandaged hand. You told her it was nothing, just a scratch.

Night had fallen. The night held unpleasant surprises in the City of Red and Grey even before the plague spread, let alone after! You always avoided the night. The night when people fell asleep and talked to themselves on the last buses and trains. The night when drink brought their dark secrets to the surface and they vented the anger that was hidden behind their daytime masks – the masks that made them appear so composed to those who could be taken in – or jabbered in strange languages that sounded barbaric to ears that did not know what they were talking about.

The masked staff at the quarantine centre kept you in the hallway. There were others like you who had nowhere else to go. In the morning you crept out. The new-born day was a dome of grey. The city centre, usually crowded with pedestrians at all times of day and night, was almost empty. Few shops had opened their doors. Guards stood in front of them on the alert. The cafés where youngsters would drink coffee, smoke and shout at each other in high spirits were mostly closed. Mannequins gazed out from the shop windows like frozen idols, displaying the fashions of a hypothetical summer. The air was so thick you could touch it. The tall trees crouched like mythical creatures about to pounce. In the street the manholes that led to the nether world were uncovered, and foul smells emerged from them. Soldiers armed with strange devices stood guard in front of critical government facilities. Intermittently and cautiously, spectres crossed from one pavement to the other. Police cars and ambulances ploughed through the streets that were almost empty of cars, the sound of their tyres amplified in the muteness of the morning.

There had been a time when faces from all corners of the world had cut a path along the city's narrow pavements and down the subways, when young men and women had embraced with a physical freedom that was sometimes embarrassing, when buskers had played music, sometimes cheerful and sometimes sad, in front of the big shops and at the entrances to the gloomy nether world, in this grey-skied Babel crowned with the gold of the colonial era. It never occurred to you, even in your worst nightmares that this city would descend into ruin and see the reappearance of primitive weapons, obsolete symbols and emotions you thought you had left behind in your long journey.

In the great square and the cobbled streets that radiated out from it in all directions, the desolation reminded you of an old film of the area, deserted after some disaster you don't recall. But you do remember the hero of the film running through the empty streets, crossing the bridge with the two stone towers, entering one building and emerging from another, being ambushed by a wild gang, getting away and being on the run throughout the film. It's as if the film was a terrible warning, except that in reality, but not in the film, people were moving about – some wearing masks on their faces and gloves on their hands, covering anything that would give away their colour, their features or their identity. Masked against the raging storm of fear and danger. Was it similar to what happened in the City of Siege and War? No. Maybe. You don't know, because your nightmares have merged with reality. Your ability to judge has diminished. You can no longer be sure. Time has dissolved, and the events and the faces have merged together.

So you've returned. It's been twenty years since you fled Hamiya. Of course, you don't need anyone to remind you how many years it's been, but you believe, as you put it during casual conversation on the balcony of your family's house, between coughing fits, that time has unexpectedly played a cruel trick on you – how is it that things that should have disappeared have survived, while many faces have lost their details? That's just a roundabout way of talking about time, because instead of saying time, you said things and faces. But the name doesn't change anything, because time, as you know (do you really know?), does not defer to hopes, however fervent they might be, nor to resolutions, even if they are as firm as steel. Time has its own ways, direct or cunning, of achieving its purposes, and it never fails to hit the mark. No glancing blows, or blows outside the line. Time is also a train that does not prefer any particular station, even if it lingers here or hastens there. Maybe you can't hear its whistle until it's left, but its effects are visible on faces, on hands, in the way people stand and in the pictures hanging on the walls. The people who waited for you saw the whole map of your long journey on your face. Twenty years is not a number. In fact, in a case such as yours, it might be a life that has run its course. But do you know what's good about it? That the days roll on, impervious, for everyone. They hone, erode and level everything they touch. Even your double, the person you used to be, the one who was frozen in his twenties by some mysterious disease, knows what that means.

Once upon a time you were considered a hero, or a conspirator. A brave young man who either – in the eyes of some abroad – took part in a heroic act, or whose head – in the eyes of others here – had been poisoned by imported ideas and who was implicated in a reckless act. You and your double, the man you used to be, both paid the price for what you did. While he survived as a ghost or a freak, growing no older and no younger, preserving a name and a life that had been nipped in the bud, you had to tramp the pavements and face the cold – battered by winds that blew your tattered sail far away. Now that matters have changed, the names and the acts balance out on the scales of insubstantial oblivion. You're no longer a hero or a conspirator. Just an old man, half-forgotten, coming back after twenty years of struggle, pursuing ideas that did not bring about much change in your country, and perhaps nowhere else either.

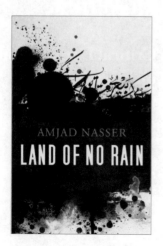

*Land of No Rain* [*Haithu La Tasqut al-Amtar*] will be published in 2013 by Bloomsbury Qatar Foundation Publishing ISBN 978-9992194584, 264pp.

# Fāris al-Shidyāq

# Leg over Leg

or
### The Turtle in the Tree
regarding
### The Fāryāq
### What Manner of Thing Might He Be
otherwise entitled
### Days, Months, and Years spent in Critical Examination
### of The Arabs and Their Non-Arab Peers

*The writings of Zayd and Hind these days speak more to the common taste*
*Than any pair of weighty tomes.*
*More profitable and useful than the teachings of two scholars*
*Are what a yoke of oxen from the threshings combs.*

## Translated by Humphrey Davies

# From Book One, Chapter 18

**Here the Fāryāq (the author's alter ego), following his conversion to Protestantism, news of which is poorly received by his family, debates the claims of the Catholic Church with his local bishop. That spiritual dogma are "goods" over whose sale to the public religions compete is a conceit that runs through the first half of Leg over Leg. In this scheme, the bishop is called a trader because he is a "Market-man", or member of the Maronite Clergy, who enjoy the comforts of a permanent marketplace, presided over by a "Market Boss". The American Protestant missionaries (who arrived in Lebanon in the 1820s), on the other hand, are itinerant "Bag-men", who are forced to go from village to village hawking their wares. *Translator***

When his family and neighbors found out, however, they erupted in rage against him, saying, "By the Lord of Hosts, it is not our custom in these lands to change, barter, mend, or dye goods" and soon thereafter the news reached the bishop of the district, one of the big-time fast-talking market traders.[1] You would have thought a knife had fallen on his wind-pipe or mustard got up his nostrils, for he fumed and frothed, thundered and lightninged, surged and thrashed, roared and bawled, conspired and plotted, jabbered and prattled, wheeled and dealed, remonstrated and reproached and jumped up and down, braiding his beard, in his fury, into a whip, and trying to inveigle every other bilious beard-plucker like himself to rise up with him as he cried, "God's horsemen against the *infidel*![2] They shall *roast in Hell*![3] How dare this accursed rascal, this raving *lunatic*, choose a path other than that laid down for him by his masters *ecclesiastic*, that followed by his very own patriarch? How dare he, in his impertinence, brazenness, and *infamy*, have dealings with that miserable traveling peddler and barter away to him what's been passed down to him from his ancient *ancestry*? Are there in our land no *roods*, no stocks or leathern *hoods*? Bring him to us in *disgrace*! Flog him in the nude! Throw him in the *fireplace*! Feed him to the *fishes*! Make him eat *ashes*! Cut out his tongue and make him drink camel *snot*! Bring him to me while the iron's *hot*!" At this, one of those present leaped forth and said, "I shall bring you the little squit 'before ever thy glance is returned to thee'."[4] Then he hot-footed it over to the Fāryāq, whom he found pouring over the ledger in which were written the prices of the goods and set upon him with his sword and injured his scalp, after which the Fāryāq was handed over to the aforementioned butcher.

When the latter set eyes upon him, his jugulars swelled, his nostrils flared, his brow knotted, his lips turned *blue*, his mustaches quivered, his eyes turned red, and from his teeth smoke *flew*, and they proceeded to engage in the following dialog:

The Trader: Woe unto you, you sucker! What made you barter away your goods?

The Fāryāq: If they're my goods, as you have just admitted, what's to stop me?

The Trader: Misguided man! They're your goods in the sense that you inherited them from your forefathers, not in the sense that they're yours to do with as you please.

The Fāryāq: This is against custom and truth, for a man may do whatever he likes with his inheritance.

The Trader: Liar! You inherited them precisely so you could preserve them, not so you could squander them or exchange them for something else.

The Fāryāq: It's my inheritance and I shall do with it as I wish.

The Trader: Accursed one! I am the warden of the inheritance and its preserver from all that might sully it.

The Fāryāq: That's the first time we've heard of someone being put in charge of someone else's inheritance, unless the heir's incompetent.

The Trader: Dupe! You are incompetent and I am your guardian, your trustee, your sponsor, your agent, and the one who will hold you to account.

The Fāryāq: What proof is there that I'm not competent, and who made you a trustee and a guardian?

The Trader: Deviant! The proof of your gullibility and error is precisely that you traded in your inheritance for other goods. As to my being a trustee, everyone else in my position attests to that fact, just as I attest that they are the trustees of others.

The Fāryāq: Exchanging one thing for another isn't evidence of error and deviation if the thing exchanged and the thing it is exchanged for are of the same kind, especially since I'd observed that the color of the old had almost completely faded and that the material had worn through. That is why I exchanged it for something more attractive and stronger.

The Trader: Blasphemer! He blinded you so that you couldn't distinguish among the colors.

The Fāryāq: How can that be when I have two eyes to see with and two hands to touch with?

The Trader: Blind man! The senses can be deceived, especially sight.

The Fāryāq: If my senses were deceived, how come you've been able to preserve yours from being deceived too when you're a human being just like me?

The Trader: May you perish! Though I was once a human being just like you, I am now an authorized agent of the Market Boss, who has let me in on the amazing powers that God has bestowed on him, which include my being able to see through any false claims or dishonesty that may come my way, because he himself could never cheat.

Said the Fāryāq (who had a speech defect involving the letter f): And where is this "Boff of the Market Difgwace"[5] (then he corrected himself and said) "I mean 'the Marketplace'? Shouldn't the addition of these eighty require the eighty-lash penalty?"[6]

The Trader: Curse you! He is far away and between us lie seas and mountains. But his holy spirit courses within us.

The Fāryāq: What happens if he falls sick or goes mad, or is touched by some wandering jinni or afflicted with pleurisy? In such a state, how can he distinguish low-quality goods from high?

The Trader: May you perish! He is never afflicted by such attacks, for he is the keeper of a mighty gate and he has in his hand two mighty keys to close the door tight, one from in front and one from behind.

The Fāryāq: That's no proof, for any person in the world could become a doorkeeper with two keys.

The Trader: Depraved sinner! He alone has sole charge of this plot of land, for it was entrusted to him by its All-commanding Owner.

The Fāryāq: When was that?

The Trader: May you be crucified! About two thousand years ago.

The Fāryāq: You mean to tell me that this "boss" has been around for two thousand years?

The Trader: Atheist! It came to him by inheritance.

The Fāryāq: From whom did he inherit it? From his father and grandfather?

The Trader: You should be punished as a warning to others! From a person not considered to be a member of his family.

The Fāryāq: That's odd! How can a person inherit anything from a stranger? If a stranger dies without leaving an heir, his money goes to the public treasury, which has a better right to it than any individual.

The Trader: May you be tortured! It's a sacrament that you have no right to discuss.

The Fāryāq: And what proof is there that it's a sacrament?

The Trader: Now you've gone too far! Here's the proof (and he got up in a hurry, fetched a book, and started leafing through it from beginning to end, looking for what he wanted—for he hadn't studied it at any great length—until he found a passage that said, in summary, that the Owner had once loved a man, so he'd given him a number of gifts, among which were a cup, a basin, a stick with a carving of two snakes on the end, a robe, a pair of shorts, a pair of sandals, and a door with two keys, and had said to him, "All these things I give unto you. Use them and enjoy them.").

The Fāryāq: I swear there's nothing in such a donation to prove it's a sacrament, not to mention that both the benefactor and the beneficiary have died and the whole gift has been lost. How can just the keys be left, when the door's gone and they're useless without it?

The Trader: May you be shown up for the liar you are! The keys are all we need now.

The Fāryāq: By the power of these two keys over you, My Lord, if you can show me just once in my lifetime the cup—that's all—you can have complete authority over me from that day on.

Faced by this resolute attitude, the trader burned with ire and was on the point of bringing the Fāryāq the door and the cup when someone called him to table. Rising energetically, he appointed a few of his knaves to see to the Fāryāq, for at that moment he was so con-vulsed with hunger that he believed the sight of the bottom of the pots in the kitchen would be more appetizing to him than that of the Fāryāq's face and he pretended to forget about him. Thus the Fāryāq escaped from that sticky situation and set off at a run to the Bag-man and told him, "I lost by my trade with you, for the goods almost landed me under the scalpel, so I want to revoke the deal—or if you will not, and you have in your bag a head that will fit my body when the latter's deprived of this one, show it to me now and calm my nerves, for I cannot live without a head. If all you have in the bag is the tongue, it is of no use to me. Here's your property. Take it."

# From Book Two, Chapter 9

**The author sets the adventures of the Fāryāq aside, as he does from time to time throughout the work, to meditate on a theme—in this case, the political, ecclesiastical, or social title.** *Translator*

The definition of a title in the minds of Orientals is that it is an insignificant fleshy protuberance or a flap of skin,[7] or an extra bag hung onto an already loaded camel, that dangles from a man's essential being. The author of the Qāmūs has said, "*'Alāqā* means 'titles', because they are hung onto people (*li-annahā tu'allaqu 'alā l-nās*)."[8] To Occidentals, which is to say Franks, it is a second skin that wraps itself around the body. Our commentary on this is that an insignificant protuberance may be cut off and totally excised with ease, and the same goes for the skin tag and the extra bag, which may be overturned or inverted; the second skin, however, cannot be removed from the body without harm to its owner. Our super-commentary (for every commentary must have a super-com-mentary, however incomprehensible) is that the skin flap is not hered-itary among the people of the east, or only rarely so (and every rule must have its exceptions). Among Franks, on the other hand, the sec-ond skin is passed from older to younger by inheritance. Examples of the former are the titles *Bāshā* ("Pasha"), *Bēh* ("Bey"), *Afandī* ("Ef-fendi"), and *Aghā* ("Agha"); even *Malik* ("King") is limited in its ap-plication to the person so titled and is not extrapolated from him to his son, for the son of a minister or a king may be a clerk or a sailor. Among Franks, however, it is incorrect to refer to the son of a marquis as a "marquisito" or as being "marquisate".⁹ Apart from the fact that the former is finite and the latter infinite, the essential meanings of "skin flap" and "second skin" may converge at a certain point, in that both generally have their origin in an itch that affects the bodies of those in positions of power because of the aggravation caused them by their blood. Such aggravation cannot be quieted and such itches cannot be scratched without creating either a flap or a second skin.

The archetype of this would be a king getting angry, for example, with some man or other for an offense he had committed, that man sending him a naked intercessor to placate him, this intercession soothing the eruption of the king's anger, the aggravational modality then combining with the gymnological quiddity, these two forming a second skin around the one who'd been in fear of losing his first skin through flaying, and he thenceforth flaunting this among his peers as a permanent adornment, never again to fear that fate might one day turn its horns upon him. In general, such second skins require two bodies—a body with which someone is angry and a body interceding on the former's behalf—while, in general, the insignificant protuberance requires just one.

One kind of insignificant protuberance is the ecclesiastical, and such is of two sorts, the earth-bound and the air-borne. The earth-bound is that which has an abode or place of origin in the earth where it grows and bears fruit; such would be the case, for example, of some "catholicos" abiding in a house or a monastery who has authority over the people, who send him tithes and the like and whom he therefore commands, forbids, rules, and judges according to the requirements of the law, or whim. He is bound to have a secretary to keep his secrets off the *books*, to stiffen his backbone one or more *cooks*, a treasurer to hoard his golden *dinars*, a jail to hold anyone who differs from him in opinion or his ambition *bars*, and so forth. The air-borne is the opposite of the preceding, an example being the protuberance borne by Metropolitan Atanāsiyūs al-Tutūnjī, author of *The Leavings Pile concerning Lame Style*, whose master has invested him with it so that he can use it to rule over Levantine Tripoli even though there are none of his sect in that city to send him his tithes, make him his food, or write a letter for him;¹⁰ he has been invested with it, it follows, simply for decorative purposes, in keeping with the custom of certain ancients, who would give the protuberance "emir" to one who raised donkeys and of "king" to the shaykh of some benighted village. The object of all this is to set one individual apart from the rest by the use of some distinguishing mark.

Now that you have become aware of this, know too that the titles Khawājā, Muʿallim, and Shaykh are not to be considered either pro-tuberances or second skins since obtaining them calls neither for in-tercession nor for any pruritic combining with gymnological quiddities.[11] They are merely rags to cover the shame of the naked name that has been given its bearer and are neither stitched, tacked, nor buttoned onto it nor wrapped around it. In fact, they are more like a ticket tied onto the one wearing it to show his value. Frequently, however, the mistake is made of attaching them to persons to whom they have no connection. Thus in Egypt, for example, they apply the word Muʿallim to Coptic Christians, who are neither *muʿallim* nor *muʿallam*, if we are to derive the word from *ʿilm* ("knowledge"),[12] though if we are to derive it from *ʿalāmah* ("mark"), there can be no objection. They apply the term Khawājā to others too,[13] and as its original meaning is the same as that of Muʿallim, the same objection holds true. The word "shaykh" appertained originally to one who had reached old age; then it was applied to someone who had advanced in learning and other things, as a figurative extension of advancement in years, for the minds of the elderly are discriminating and their judgment is sound, even if women will have no more to do with them. This distinguishing characteristic was then transferred to those who engage in scholarly pursuits.

After pondering the matter, it seems to me that these protuberances and skin flaps do great injury both to those whom they adorn and those who are devoid of them. The first argument in support of this is that a person who bears one believes, in the depths of his heart, that he is better than others, physically and morally. Thus he looks at the other as a ram with horns does at one without and contents himself with this external feature instead of seeking to attain praiseworthy qualities and meritorious inner traits, and this allows it to lead him in the direction of moral torpor and vicious pleasure. The second is that should Saturn's noose get caught round his neck one day and drag him into the orbit of its adversities, if he fails to find a woman with a second skin like his, he'll be unable to withstand those adver-sities with any other; and it may happen that he fall in love with a beautiful serving girl who works in his house, in the kitchen or the stable, and his father, or his father-in-law, or his other relatives, or his emir, may tell him to have nothing to do with her, in which case beautiful girls will be left high and dry, which is regarded by Islamic law as reprehensible—nay, the scholars have all asserted authoritatively that it is absolutely forbidden.

The third is that it might happen that he marry a woman with a second skin who is as badly off as he and not well-heeled. Then, if she bears him children, he will lack the means to bring them a shaykh to teach them at home and he'll be too embarrassed to send them to the local school to learn along with everyone else's. Should this be the case, his children will grow up to be unlettered and the process will repeat itself with their offspring for as long as God wills. The fourth is that both protuberance and second skin impose upon those who bear them devastating expenses and catastrophic costs, driving their owner to excessive outlay and *profligacy*, collapse and imminent *bankruptcy*, which may even lead him in the end to the noose of a palm-fiber rope. The fifth is that humans in their native state have neither protuberance nor second skin and to add them to them at a later stage is contrary to nature, or at least a form of meddling or recklessness. Other arguments exist but I have decided not to mention them here for fear of going on too long. At least it must be clear to you by now that the Khawāja in question was possessed of neither protuberance nor second skin, though perhaps, had it not been for his natural inclination toward poetry, he might have acquired one or the other. But everything has its drawbacks.

# From Book Two, Chapter 12

**The Fāryāq has been engaged to work at the "Panegyricon," an institution established by "the Ruler" (of Egypt) to record and disseminate information about his daily doings, just as the author was himself engaged to work on Egypt's official gazette, then newly established by Muhammad Ali. Each day, a flunky brings the Fāryāq two lines of verse to translate into Arabic, providing the author with ample scope for an exploration of the conventions of the praise-poetry of his day.** *Translator*

On the ninth day, another flunky appeared and he wrote
*Time's lips parted to reveal a radiant fate,*
    *the day our prince took a bath and was rendered depilate.*
*His noble nether parts thus appeared less hoary*
    *and poetry, through his pubes, gained in glory.*

These two verses were very well received because of the antithesis, perfect paronomasia, and so on they contain. Except for the words "in glory."[14]

On the tenth day, another flunky appeared and he wrote
*The prince coughed (*qaḥaba*), and what glorious and gallant*
    *gentleman of his ilk, among the human race, has never had a cough?*
*It's a habit imposed on all mankind,*
    *and any who hasn't should be hung on a cross!*

Fault was found with the word *qaḥaba*, to which the response was made that it is a chaste word meaning "he coughed".[15]

On the eleventh day, another flunky appeared and he wrote
*The prince sneezed, so tears of blood we wept, one and all,*
    *while both globe and celestial sphere recoiled in horror.*
*God protect his brains from another such sneeze*
    *lest it so scare the angels that they die of terror!*

On the twelfth day, another flunky appeared and he wrote
*The prince let off a string of silent farts, and what heady odor*
    *within the universe was spread, what musk unpent!*
*Would that the limbs of all mankind*
    *into noses might turn, to inhale that scent!*

Fault was found with the word *fassā* ("let off a string of silent farts"), since the repetitive form[16] has no meaning here, to which the response would be that even what is little becomes much when attributed to a prince; a similar logic applies to the words *ẓallām li-l-ʿabīd* ("a (re-peated) oppressor of mankind"),[17] since the least degree of outrage (*ẓulm*) against what is due to the Almighty Creator in terms of the ruler's dealing justly with His creation is too much.

On the thirteenth day, two flunkies appeared and he wrote
*The prince at mid-morn this day let off an audible fart,*
    *the sky being dark, no hint of sun revealed,*
*And all parts of our land with its perfume were scented*
    *for t'was a fart (*ḥabq*) that the scent of basil (*ḥabaq*) concealed.*

This was well received because of the paronomasia that it contained.

On the fourteenth day, two other flunkies appeared and he wrote
*The prince's bowels this day were loosened (*ushila*) and as one*

> *did all rejoice, for his looseness* (ishālihi) *brought him ease*
> (tashīl).
> *They purchased some silk-wool for him, embroidered,*
> *and rushed to claim that constipation's a fatal disease.*

The first verse was well received because of the paronomasia but fault was found with "embroidered" since there's no call for embroidery in this context; indeed, it would cause pain—to which the response was that it follows the original and a good translation neither adds to nor subtracts from the original from which it is taken, especially where important and significant matters are involved. Fault should have been found with the words "as one did all rejoice" (albeit he does go on to explain what he means, by saying "for his looseness brought him ease"), for one's natural first reaction is that the looseness of the bowels will lead to the death of the object of the panegyric; the paronomasia, however, may be considered to draw a veil over this solecism.

Notes:

1  One of the big-time fast-talking market traders" (*mina l-ḍawāṭirati l-kibār*): see Glossary.
2  "God's horsemen against the infidel!" (*yā khayla llāh ʿalā l-kuffār*): the first half of the cry used to assemble the first Muslims before battle and subsequently used as a pious invocation to action on behalf of Muslims in danger.
3  "They shall roast in Hell!" (*innahum ṣālū l-nār*): Q ṢĀD 38:59.
4  "I shall bring you the little squit 'before ever thy glance is returned to thee" (*anā ātīka* etc.): the wording evokes the *Qurʾān* (Q NAML 27:40), when a member of Sulaymān's council volunteers to bring him the Queen of Sheba's throne
5  "who had a speech defect involving the letter f" (*wa-kāna bi-hi faʾfaʾah*): the defect called *faʾfaʾah* is defined as "repeating and over-using the letter *fāʾ* in speech" and causes the Fāryāq to say *shaykh al-fusūq* (literally, "the Boss of Disgrace") for *shaykh al-sūq* ("the Boss of the Marketplace").
6  "Shouldn't the addition of these eighty require the eighty-lash penalty?" (*fa-lā takun ziyādatu hādhihi l-thamānīna mūjibun li-ḥaddi l-thamānīn*): the addition of *fāʾ* to *sūq* (see preceding endnote) produces *fusūq*, the numerical value of the letter *fāʾ* in the counting system known as *ḥisāb al-jummal* is eighty, and eighty lashes are the penalty specified in the *Qurʾān* for the *fāsiq* ("committer of *fusūq*" or depravity) (cf. Q NUR 24:4).
7  "flap of skin" (*zanamah*): the author appears to have in mind the following among a number of definitions of this word given in the Qāmūs: "something cut off the ear of a camel and left hanging, done to the best bred."
8  "The author of the *Qāmūs* has said": *Qāmūs* 3/268.
9  "it is incorrect to refer to the son of a marquis as a 'marquisito' or as being 'marquisate'" (*lā yaṣiḥḥu an yuqāla li-bni l-markīzi muraykīzun aw markīzī*): i.e., it is incorrect to refer to the son of a marquis with a diminutive noun or a relative adjective derived from "marquis," meaning, perhaps, that European titles, being, unlike oriental titles, hereditary, can be applied to only one holder at a time.
10  "none of his sect": the Melkites of Tripoli numbered "barely ten" (Graf: *Geschichte* 277).
11  The author's distinction recognizes the fact that such titles are informal terms of

respect rather than titles awarded by an authority.

12 "Muʿallim . . . *muʿallim* or *muʿallam*": *muʿallim* means literally "teacher" and is used as a term of polite address to Christians and others; read as *muʿallam*, the same word means "taught."

13 "they apply the term Khawājā to others": i.e., to other Christians (from Persian *khōjā* ("teacher")).

14 "Except for the words 'in glory'": *tanawwarā*, repeated at the end of each hemistich of the first line ("to reveal a brighter fate" and "was made depilate"), is an example of both "perfect paronomasia" (identicality of form with difference of meaning) and "antithesis" (the use of two contrasting ideas in one line); *al-shiʿr* ("poetry") and *al-shiʿrā* ("pubic hair") are examples of near-perfect paronomasia and antithesis; *mafkharā* ("in glory") stands out as neither paronomasia nor antithesis.

15 "the word *qaḥaba*": this, in the unchaste or vernacular language, means "he whored."

16 "the repetitive form" (*al-takthīr*): i.e., *fassā* versus *fasā*, the former indicating repeated performance of the action indicated by the latter.

17 "*ẓallām li-l-ʿabīd*": the phrase occurs several times in the *Qurʾān* (e.g., Q ʾĀL ʿIMRĀN 3:182); *ẓallām*, from *ẓālim*, is the nominal equivalent of the verbal intensive.

---

**Leg Over Leg** is the semi-autobiographical account of (Aḥmad) Fāris al-Shidyāq, a pivotal figure in the intellectual and literary history of the modern Arab world. This edition is the very first English translation of the work and reproduces the original edition, published under the author's supervision in 1855. Akin to Sterne and Rabelais in his satirical outlook and technical inventiveness, al-Shidyāq produced in **Leg Over Leg** an unprecedented sui generis work. It was initially widely condemned for its attacks on authority, its skepticism, and its "obscenity," and later editions were often abridged.

The above excerpts were selected by Humphrey Davies from Volumes One and Two (of an eventual four). Both volumes are due out with New York University Press in June 2013.

## LEG OVER LEG

Volume 1
by (Aḥmad) Fāris al-Shidyāq

Edited and translated
by Humphrey Davies

June 2013 • 368 pages
$35.00S (£25.99) • Cloth
• 978-0-8147-2937-3

Volume 2
by (Aḥmad) Fāris al-Shidyāq

Edited and translated
by Humphrey Davies

June 2013 • 336 pages
$35.00S (£25.99) • Cloth
• 978-0-8147-6984-3

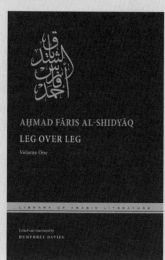

AḤMAD FĀRIS AL-SHIDYĀQ

LEG OVER LEG

Volume One

LIBRARY OF ARABIC LITERATURE

Edited and translated by
HUMPHREY DAVIES

# 80 New Poems

## HUSSEIN HABASCH

### PÈRE LACHAISE CEMETERY

I saw not one dead person,
in Père Lachaise Cemetery.
I saw only
lofty tombs
raising their heads
to the sky
and a small squirrel
worrying Balzac's shoulder
and listening with sharp ears
to the sorrowful singing
coming from
the Piaf family tomb.
For a moment, I thought
I heard Edith Piaf moaning.

*Translated by Allison Blecker*

# TAHA ADNAN

## YOUR SMILE IS SWEETER THAN THE NATIONAL FLAG

### TRANSLATED BY ROBIN MOGER

*To Sanaa*

Your mobile's dead
your landline's not responding;
on Facebook your picture's gone away,
the national flag draped down
over your smile,
over the gleam in your eyes.

I move along the wall: your wall,

I scrutinize it, clicking and updating,
I brush from it the dust of grief
and stillness.
The clouds above the country could clear;
the wall might split open
on your captive face.

As though it truly mattered
I brooded fretfully and weighed it up:
has revolution swept the land?
Has spring, a whirlwind, passed through
for your absence to flourish
in autumn?
Or have I missed the train
to remain right here:
an indifferent witness?

I lit up Al-Jazeera
where coddled Arabs
set revolutions ablaze
in sister states,
frame hearts
and impetuous scenarios
and compose ad lib laments
sung by a turbaned chorus
to the strains of an orchestra coached
to mourn.

Nothing new in Arabism:
killing is the order of the day
and blood up to the knees.

There, on the revolution's stage
tragedy is comedy,
rulers vampires,
and the people a clutch of fools
careering after a tattered rag
they think a flag
and like a crowd of extras

chanting: "The people want . . ."

With trembling fingers I pluck up
the remote
and put out the revolution
that your smile might flutter in my mind
and I rally, sleepwalking, to your banner.
You are my flag and my revolution
and I am your loving people,
your beloved leader.

I take up the receiver
(the heart wants it so):
your mobile's dead
and your landline's ringing,
Ringing . . . but no answer.

On Facebook
the homeland's colours hide
your smile.

Your smile is sweeter
than spring,
than all the seasons;
your smile is more magnificent
than the crowds in full cry,
more radiant than the people when they rise up
and sing, "My country";
your smile, a joy
at every gathering,
your smile, God's protection settled
in my heart,
your smile –
O beat of my heart –
exalted above every banner,
sweeter than the national flag.

Published in Arabic on www.kikah.com

## PHILIP METRES

# Selected Poems

## A TOAST FOR NAWAL NASRALLAH AT THE ARAB AMERICAN NATIONAL MUSEUM

Chair legs screech across the banquet floor
    above us, a wedding feast
of people pulling themselves closer, closer
    to the constellation of tables

while here, underground, alone with our ears,
    we can't get close enough
to Al-Azzawi reciting "A Toast", and laughter
    in two languages marinates

the hunger of this room, and now you lean
    to hear him, who has not lived
in your homeland for most of his days on earth,
    like you who have lived

your country in kitchens, far from your country,
testing the tastes of the ancients,
citizen of this implacable state and its armies
pitching their permanent tent

in the dictator's palaces; you, who out of grief's
    maw, the daily shipwreck of news,
translate the alien clay of cuneiform relief
    into Mesopotamian stews,

a toast to you, Nawal, at whose Mesopotamian
    table I have been honored to sit
& be sated, not with fried eggplant but buran
    not with drumsticks baked in fig

but with Afkhadh al-Dijaj bil-Teen, your homeland
    transfigured by flame, Baghdad
now spiced with coriander, now stewed in the skin,
    a toast to you, for my insides

have not forgotten, even now I can taste
    how qullupu means "whole"
and "wheel" and "cardamom circle," and dates
are the cake of the poor,

and now the people above us are dancing,
    they cannot help themselves,
they are wrapping themselves in a song,
    stuffed like grape leaves,

they have no room for us in the light, so below
    in our rootcellar of words,
here in the underland of exile, a toast to you,
    the country of your tongue.


## BEL CANTO

You tilted my wells, dizzied my head
wings.  Now tender my bell.  Blend my word

hoard with your sing sing. You
taught me the tunes of Katyusha

& Uzi, now mend me in tidal pool
hiding Aprodite.  Baby please.

A sniper's souvenir: ringing in
the chambered brain.  Bloom from no bud.

Though my skull has no memorial
for ears, you breathe in their bowls, you love

lure, you dulcimer stream.  Anvil
you hammer pneumatic, year by year,

come to drown everything.  Trumpet
you play and play me by inhaling.


## THE BROKEN GHAZAL OF QUESTIONS
*(for William Stafford)*

How can I breathe in the close
margins of this life?  All day
plans take off and land.

Deep in the night the runway
stills to black.  Dreams are a second
life.  The soul rattles in that happy

old man, like dried seeds
in a gourd that has sweated out
its milky life.  What is this child in our bed

dreaming of, just hours in this life?
On the train the man growls
to no one at the far end of the car

a report on the war of his life.
My infant scans the shoreline
of my hair, ebbing from temples.

Is life from body, as lief is to lib,
then is swallowing libations
a folding of body into body?

Swallow the book, the prophet
advised, it's sweet to swallow, but
bitter in the belly.  Epigraph:

next
issue
Fiction
in
Kuwait

what hovers above the body
of each day?  Epitaph: what did you
make of your life?

## SALAAM EPIGRAMS
  *– after Nahid Dukhan*

\*

You trail a comet's tail.
Everything you do quotes you.

\*

O well overflowing, tell.
Broken vessel you, don't heal.
Stream of grief: blessing.

\*

You awaken in the wake
Of a sentence half-written,

The missing past tense
Cordoned by comma.

\*

Star jiggered from sky
To green ground you
Beeline toward its bloom.

\*

Apostrophe of a womb –
Fetal you – and the line you will become.

# HASSAB AL-SHEIKH JA'FAR

*From the opening to*

# Collusion with Blue

## TRANSLATED BY CAMILO GOMEZ-RIVAS

## I AM NOT THAT WRETCH

Buy me a cognac
fifty grams
I am not that dissipated woman, that wretch
so I'll have more.
The night is long
so where to? Suspicions buzz (as do the police)
I won't stay more than a few minutes
I am not that fearful woman
Closing time is soon and
the office is close.
In the lobby, the hotel is full
so if you need company
I'll come back.
We just need the bottle
I have fruit
and savory slices
and songs.
Music cradles us with tenderness
The world, to me, is all
noise and monkeys.
Who disturbs us and changes our course?
Who staggers under the load?
What time is it? Ah!

I run
and return and return.

## CLARITY

Maria reminds me of one of the women
in novels, Maria
at eighty.
Little remains:
the pitchers and the pension
On eid nights, she'd share
a bottle, joking
and repeating the details:
A dancer, married to a wealthy man, and a storm
overwhelming the water-logged ships
and the rider alighting at the sanatorium, the madness.
The year ended
as she recounted these details.
It made me suspicious at first,
apart from her calling me Victor
"You look like him, his features, his fingertips",
"the eyes, the eyes," she insisted.
And then I returned from a trip,
after the break,
to find her in my bed, asleep.
I asked the maid for help. She proposed
I sleep next to Maria
"And if she turns over?"
"Just hold her and be very quiet!"

## THE MASK

On the way to the end of the night
or the end of the bridge
a raindrop
still swelling
where shadows drift
and the cemetery rustles the buckthorn

Apparition,
whether ghost or empty jubbah,
be my companion until dawn
be Desdemona on her black wedding
in her wasted youth,
shroud or sail
Be snow over her closed quarters
I will pull off the mask
from your devastating quicksilver face
before the roosters crow
in the empty yards


## GYPSY

Night of rain
wake the hands of the rock
(maybe in the letter there is help for wakefulness)
She wrapped her abaya around her, clumsy and hurried
A falling banner spurring on the wind and the tree
She didn't forget either shoe or cup or slipper
a handful of piastres under our hands.
So I said what once some of our brothers said:
Shunning has become the reward for those who were honest with
    us.
And I said: "There is no good. For the world lends a hand
in either case. Hens or crabs."
Angry night,
wake my warbling mouth!
Maybe in the letter there is attachment to the traces of the camp
and the wandering king wears his robe
at the crossroads
fearsomely filling the hands of the wind and the trees,
night of the gypsy

## EXCAVATIONS

By which wall is the treasure hidden?
I had rented a room in her house
and every time she treated me to a glass of tea;
she would return and propose the excavation
(She wasn't crazy or joking)
Let's dig up the floor, I said,
at the north wall
but the pickaxe found nothing but dirt.
So we dug in front of the south wall.
Bottomless pit!
Stairs upon stairs
in a maze, in which we saw
nothing but steam and fog
Still, I led us down with a faint pocket torch
and all at once (the eye had not seen before)
Carthage? Babel?
On the balconies, in the corridors,
no one could be seen but a frail old sheikh,
leafing through a tattered manuscript
"Our next steps
may lead us to the treasure," I said.
But everywhere we went we met the scrawny Tatar
bent over, wary
of who we were,
scouring his empty files

## BAIT

The hour the light turned pale and the furniture swung back and
    forth
and thick rope dangled from the ceiling
the hour the walking started, deliberate, suspicious,
no passersby to be seen
the woodwormed stick prodded the blind man into the corner,
algae climbing over his bony shoulders.
The hour the books flew from their places
crashing in a pile
The hour the plate was filled with worms
and the spinster's swing brought down the clown
The hour the chicken hatched the fox's egg
and the creditors split
what was left of the fuel in the heater
(In the end, as usual, litter is loot
in the hands of amateurs)
The hour wall split from wall
waiting for guests
and the goat was content with dance and carnival,
brass rings clamped around its neck in the act of begging
leaving with its shadow swinging between shadows

## KHALED NAJAR

# Selected Poems

TRANSLATED BY KHALED MATTAWA

## THE POEM OF QUESTIONS

*After Pablo Neruda*

Are birds born out of the sea
or do they bloom out of the rocks of Guatemala's mountains?

And the butterflies
do they arise out of night's latest hour
or do the winds of September give birth to them?

Do they emerge
out of the Sporades Islands in spring
or from a poem by Georg Trakl?

And the steamers, are they, too, bred in seawater
or do they arise from the poetry of Saint-John Perse?

How many horses are neighing
on the steppes of Asia?

And do church bells
gleam with redundant silver?

And is it true that the sparrows of Amsterdam
sing Jacques Brel's songs in their sparrow tongue?

How many seeds do the winds of Provence carry
when they blow on Marseille?

Photo by Annet Haak

And this rabbit
did he just come up through the rain
with all this gold?

And where are they now, those who dream of sparrows
   swimming in the sea
and fish flying over church roofs
and the rabbit who comes visiting from Cairo?
Did they now, or have they ever lived, in Arles
or were they a dream of another dream?

## GOLD SEA

I said I will go to the sea
to see the sea's gold
And I to the sea did go
   and I found the gold of my childhood


## DESIRE

I said I'll go
to see the gardens of the sea
their bees
and butterflies

And I said I will go, as well, to see Canterbury Cathedral
in the light of Britain's dusk
and explore its dark corners
and look through the stained glass of its Gothic windows
and touch the stones that Milton touched

And I'll also go to Athens, Izmir, Alexandria and Cartagena
and touch their stones in the spring
between the shores and their mimosa trees


## POEM I

I see the birds of Venice in the shadows
        that the lamp makes
Or maybe it's Apollinaire standing on a balcony somewhere in Italy
Oh, dear lamp,
you who used to light up the dreams of a child
in his eleventh year
Once Tagore sang about you
and now you no longer have a country to illuminate

## POEM II

When the star shone brightly in late September
when you heard the echo of the sea
                    in the conches
when the rain hid among the trees
and a lantern lit our home
and our school books were blank pages

## POEM III

September brings back the hours
when Georg Trakl
used to read his poems in the Minerva Club
between white roses
in the Vienna of the early twentieth century

## POEM IV

The silence of Wednesdays,
the cry of a bird coming through the centuries,
a man in the observatory of the Shah of Isfahan –
I listen to it all

## POEM V

When I was young
The wind's shadow was my home
The school bells my songs

I used to wander,
mysterious as the north
and conspiratorial as spring,
I walked and walked
to reach the springs of midnight

The world bathed in my first mirror,
and the yew trees grew taller in my sleep
than they did on their islands


## POEM VI

Valerie,
when I remember your name
the bird of Bologna that Borges spoke of returns to me
and Alexandria's nights return
and the Euphrates gardens return
and I hear rivers
     as they pour into the sea


## POEM VII

When I was young
the horses looked out to sea
and the rain
   and cities
and butterflies bouncing outside windows
came to me in summer
    They brought the keys of season
      and the flowers of Damascus


## POEM VIII

No lights out at sea
no flute for the dust
no sparrow for the well
no evening rose
no horses in Damascus
no summer for the butterflies
no thimble for the fishes
no ships for Wednesday
no silence in Germany

POEM IX

After midnight
herders trudge on southward,
a fly buzzes past my window

My doll is in the bay
my summer is without insects
and I belong to dust

There is no well in the courtyard of my house
no waves in the sea
and I am as cold as a polar bear

A north with calendars
or hours

No lightning at dawn to light my house
no wheat in my winter
And I am forgotten like a heath

North without a star
South without sweet clover


POEM X

A star lit up my bed,
O rooster of the springs
a Wednesday made of ashes,
my notebook was filled with scribbles
a blue mare
of graze in my sleep,
the summers of Damascus

# HEIND R. IBRAHIM

# Three Poems

## EPITAPHS ON THE WATER

Blossoms on the collar,
sawdust inside:
you were born right.
Chasing lines
in your deserted palm,
gasping you arrived
to find yourself merely a rumor:
awareness dented your shape.
Of you not much is left.
Still "wrestling the dragon", you said,
"everything, everything comes to an end."
You died near a clock in the midst of town:
small wishes
foamed around the lips.
No one claimed you.
No one read your letters of thanks:
Remnants of youth on your black shoes,
a fake ID in the pocket,
and a swing in the skull,
a hundred splinters on your limbs.
On which side will you rest tonight?

## UNTIMELY NOVEMBER

Frightened, he squats in a corner of his head
and pushes the wall.
Perhaps the hung paintings would finally fall.
Some autumn inside him

and a wolf —
such are the chords of the song.
He wears coldness as a coat
and takes off reason.
Amulet in his mouth
and the remains of his teeth.

Terrified by a thought
he lies to her right

with a cocoon in his eyes.
Her thighs remind him of a staircase he descended rapidly.
His ominous silence wakes her.
He sweats himself in the corner,
he sweats the maps.
He leaves his head dangling from a window
hoping for a thief to steal the face
or the mind.
He walks in with a dianthus, thunder and demon's prayers,
> *"darma darma mai*
> *darma darma xafa mei.*
> *Darma darma mai"*

He has been pending since the dawn of time.


## EXPRESSION OF INFORMAL RULES

*To Ludwig Wittgenstein*


Patches veiling him from the chills,
exhibiting the poor eon, too,
are his eyes.

Useful nonsense whistles in the mind,
and nocturnes of silence.

He follows a misleading linguistic event,
and a nameless private sensation.

A broken universe glistens in the head,
he writhes and groans.

SALAH FAIK

*From*

Flashes

TRANSLATED BY RAPHAEL COHEN

## SALAH FAIK

**1**

Descended from the age of the Ziggurats am I.
I attended the banquets of Gilgamesh. Hard he was on philosophers,
generous with lovers.
He grew his hair down to his knees
in memory of an old friend of his.

**2**

I swallowed my wedding ring.
I often mixed with the jokers at funerals.
My thoughts collapsed onto pavements.
Since that time
I have shown no mercy to clerics.

**7**

The voice here is asleep in a hotel tower
bare-headed, and in this head is a handsome thief
who steals the wages of the maids.

**9**

This waterfall is the mountains' gift to the ocean waves
swelling towards
a volcano where my room is.

**12**

The solar eclipse delighted me.
I saw the red wings of the sun.
Gilgamesh stood close by, he was watching too.

**18**

At the weekend he puts his many scandals
into alphabetical order.
Afterwards he heads to a bar to sweet-talk the pianist
or annoy despairing workers.

**19**

I am an expert in myths, known for desecrating graveyards.
At night I creep into the vaults of museums
and implicate their dead in unforgiveable crimes.

21
Astronomers must be saved from their observatories.
Scattered dreams and scattered friends must be saved.
Rain settling over the ruins of houses must be saved.

A wounded wordsmith must be saved
at the start of this poem.

22
Tolling bells pollute my clothes.
My friendships, time has given  cancer
so I retreat into the past
to drown my remaining hopes in black ink.

23
On Portobello Road
I trade my poems for old books
I need for a collage.

Sometimes, just for a loaf, a kiss.

26
Every city is a prison.
I nourish my poems with the singing of the fruit sellers.
Sometimes I cheat my neighbours.
I work like a woodsman from morning to night.

28
He finds a rabbit that has fled one of his poems
waiting for a ship at the harbour.
—— Sir, are you travelling or emigrating?
—— I am emigrating. I am fed up with this country.
—— Did I do something wrong to you? Why did you forsake my
    poem?
—— Instead of treating me like a rabbit, you treated me like a
    servant or a dog,
or at times like a woman. That annoyed me.

## SALAH FAIK

34
My presence roused some hornets.
They swarmed around me so I rushed over to some trees that hid
    me. They said:
This is the last time.
I promised them I would never return to the mountains.

41
I bite the hand of my servant
if my morning coffee is late.
My talents are limited:
I dress better than my neighbours
I smile when I come.

42
From the sea I borrow the slap of the waves
for the sake of my old city.
I know I will end up as a flower seller there
and in its alleyways loiter in pity.

45
I tricked my youth with lots of promises.
Shakespeare met me at Heathrow airport.
On the way to Hampstead, where I live,
he kept insulting the television and the newspapers.
He was harsh.

46
I danced at my friends' parties.
They died, one after the other.

56
Night with its phosphorus seeped spiders
is not here or there, but in his head,
whereas the rain on every occasion fulfils his wish
and stops.

57

When he sleeps, he leaves the front door open.
Those who come into his dreams are friends
the world no longer holds.

62

No, you are not alone.
You are hidden, nothing more.
You bite your lips sometimes and jump from image to image
tasting the admonitions of lovers.
You give directions to a ghost seeking water for ablutions.
You take the umbrellas of guests and see the river has a mouth
so you sit and listen to the advice of its polluted waves.

63

He takes a night walk by candlelight.
He is in dispute with these stretches of territory
because they lack any animal or bird
and because their trains have aging drivers
who have stolen out of spy stories.

64

Defeated workers assemble by a bridge.
I create this image to leave my imagined exile
for a suburb where I stand in solidarity with them
with insults against their run-away leaders and their statues.

65

He lives in a cellar. His bedspread sheets of newspaper.
One has photos of thieves who have lost their teeth.

66

I look in the mirror and see myself looking in the mirror
I would see you in every mirror:
because I write your absence
and because I live on an island.

SALAH FAIK

67
It's high time for the man of exiles to take off.
His days have lengthened in the margins
and in the vestibule of those who have split with the gods.

74
Weeks spent setting up barriers
and a few barricades.
I donated piles of my diaries to a fire,
a poet antagonising his past by degrees.
Who will you turn to now that your friends have been scattered
    among the pages?

75
A city, even a small one, would be enough
for me to lose my faith in everything.
That's why I've lived years in an imaginary countryside.
I look through the eye of the needle
and see my long-lost brother picking grapes in a vineyard.

76
From time I borrow a friend who died.
We linger on the shore, discussing cafés and friends
He likes my banquet and his new shirt
that I stole from someone on a plane.
I have brought him books, my latest poems, and a wristwatch
I inherited from my dead father.
Suddenly time forecloses on him.

83
Year after year, I toil here and there.
Now dressed as a chef, now with gypsies sharpening their knives.
I take no interest in the rectangular moon above
or the gangrene that's been in wait for years.
I toil here and there, year after year.

Translated from his collection *Wamadhat (Flashes)*,
online edition, Cebu, Philippines, 2012

*VÉNUS KHOURY-GHATA*

# Six Poems

TRANSLATED FROM THE FRENCH BY MARILYN HACKER

## The tree that got loose from the forest can't mend our fence

Can't fill the silence of our beehive

A worried loaf of bread has seized our table

The cricket's rusty wings no longer make a sound

And yet yesterday the house walked in the same direction as the road and the trains

Followed the smoke's black breath as it divided the forest into two clans

Yesterday

The oak, oaken as he was, weighed himself down with our roof when the shutters left for the season

House that's still a house despite its door creeping along the ground and its furniture narrow as hermits' tombstones

Pebbles lined up on the threshold are landmarks for lost walls

House which conjugates war in every tense

The mad brother ate the windows and belched up glass slivers

The mother imprisoned in a cube devoured the snow down to its roots

Deaf grass grew along the moulding

We would reap it in September after the noise-harvest to stock up for winter

After the harvesters departed, leaving us their arms but taking summer away in their armpits

At least that's what the mother said in her cube of stones, and no one contradicted her

The harvesters, she would cry, plant their red sweat at the crossways of women who can be read in darkness

Open to hands that pull out, replant, hoe, far from pitchforks, stakes and ploughshares

From their sewn pockets fall muticolored grains which will grow into children

A house, she would cry, needs four cardinal points, while we only have one opening on the interior

A house needs a spring while we only have a basin in which to

soak our faces and our garments shrunk with grief
A house should be able to go to town whenever the spirit moves
it
Brush up against those who make pitchers out of clay instead of
eating it


## We went through the whole forest without meeting one friendly tree

Without touching the smallest scrap of God's robe or His bark
Malicious moss sowed discord between resident trees and those
vegetating alongside stagnant ditches
The sun was growing old
And the flammable conifers kept their distance from the last
sparks that could turn into torches

When winter had come
And the sun was double-locked into its circle
The forest migrated under our roof with its horde of braided
lianas like horses on parade
Scrambled our reflections in the mirrors
Our shadows on the wall fought like ragpickers when the mother
lengthened the lamp-wick
Daily battles that left the house battered
The crumbled plaster was our acknowledged grief


## The sun came between us in all of our squabbles

We would come to blows over a scrap of shadow
A pebble with two faces
A Mohican bird feather
The brother swore on the family's honor never to have undressed
in front of a stream
Or stepped on a bee's foot
The mother stayed in rank among the honorable casseroles
Our pantry overflowed with copious chatter

We were opulent   needy
Sad   mischievous
Stingy and lordly
We went to Mass one Sunday out of two to save our knees the
   wear and tear
And only traveled when absolutely necessary to spare the donkey
   on duty hired for public transportation
We aged despite our smoke that blew backwards


**Strangers passing through the town mistook the mother
   for a garden**
Their children climbed over her wall
The men bared their heads before her knees rubbed with forget-
   me-nots
A hodge-podge of down and wing-beats   the lark's nest when she
   weakened with winter
The mother was buried in all her leaves with a padlock and a
   triple-grooved key
The train departed for more cosseted gardens
They refused our names to the fence-posts that knew us by chance

Fence-posts they'd say
Dead men cramped in their bark who emerge between fields and
   hillsides clothed in fog
They're sometimes mistaken for warriors sometimes for
   conquistadors
For widows dressing themselves in smoke and mourning
The houses that cross their paths dare not greet them
The fence-posts struck blind are inconsolable


**Reading wastes words and makes concentration boil
   over like milk on the stove**
The mother would repeat
And she sharpened the cypress like a pencil

For lack of books we read her intentions
Sure that she would leave us at the juncture of sleep as soon as it
  gave her some children that were hers alone
Would leave us
As soon as she had swept our fears under the table
Gathered up the crumbs of her huge fatigue
And our shoes lined up in order of size like good scholars
Would leave us without going away
Sewn into her sheet
Her children become pebbles in her womb

## How to find the mother when her face disappeared behind the hills

Leaving us a body without contours
Two packets of cold for the armpits
White grass for the pubis

Gone off with her friend the fire
She spoke to us in flares and sparks from behind the hill's
  shoulder
Her voice became brambles loose stones broom bush
If a storm broke she collapsed in soot

Whole nights spent down on the floor sniffing a sketch of her
Looking out for her rages in lightning
Lips split by sun and frost

We called the mother till the closing of the last field

Selected from the author's collection *Où vont les arbres*, Mercure de France, 2011. The English edition, translated by Marilyn Hacker, will be published by Curbstone Press, USA, in 2014.

# AMJAD NASSER

## THE EDGES OF DAY

TRANSLATED BY FADY JOUDAH

I

Because I've never survived one hope without succumbing to
    another, and because whenever a mask smiled to me I took it as
    my confidant, I died, though not as one who walks with gaiety
    among his vigilant friends dies, but as one who has died over
    and over, so that when death came laughing in his green plume
    and drooped my eyes over the gentle light of the valley I didn't
    believe him. Because I used to think death was a clamor, "a
    great scream that deposits all we've surrendered to, grows rich
    and abandons us", and not a mere dozing off in an arid bed
a lonely bed
in white nakedness.

There are those who die of despair and I died because hope
continued to hop around me, and hope, that hunter of feeble
    souls,
will guide you to the water springs and bring you back thirsty,
and play a game of rock-paper-scissors with you.

I did not know
hope had
snuffed out so
many lives.

I have died a lot and persisted in dragging myself
under the long arm of promises,
and all who know me know how death becomes a dream
for which the most vicious nights ornament their beds
incense their sheets
call to him by the sweetest names
and yet he doesn't come.

It isn't easy to seduce death over a glass of wine or toss it a moon
under whose light lovers have wasted their fortunes of tears.
For whoever sees death's hands as I have
knows how difficult it is for the absent one
to return to his mother's palms and drink.
No one returns as he left

and water has no memory
that preserves the faces of the absent
and no one dies when he wants.

Don't believe the suicides who throw themselves in rivers
or from the tops of buildings packed with the sleeping.
It was another thing, beside their fates, that had slunk its strand
   of hair
out of the night's dough
and let its curtains down over them.
I did all that the others did
but the one who toys with the hours
and feeds scorpions the sugar of absentmindedness
put nothing in my hand.

Once I swallowed a sleeping pill
ate berries ad nauseam
then threw myself across the railroad tracks
the hum shook my body
from the right jugular to the left
and I aimed my fist toward my heart
which was hanging by a thread
in the emptiness of the core
before springing up with all my might
but nothing fell from the bough
that was dangling by the edge of day;
only the leaves yellowed and mummified
in the long autumn of hope.

## II

And when I tired from dragging myself among you I slept.
Then I saw a passerby who resembled me,
he was leaning to one side and hoofing it on a slow afternoon.
I tried to discern his features but couldn't
and each time I tried I kept sinking in some puffed up wool;
I heard mutterings and retreating footsteps
and the world got cloudier in my face, beacons

over some mysterious citadels went out
and buckets were raised from wells whose waters had dwindled;
I heard the creak of pulleys and pulled ropes
and the knocking of empty buckets
raucousness
movements
shouts
that were
van-
ish-
ing.

I must have died
or how else could I have seen all this through my sutured lids
and remained still in the cotton mountain I had slipped into.
My mouth was completely dry, my throat
a hollow cork, and what I thought was my voice
was an echo reverberating in a dry arroyo;
what need have I, at any rate, for speech where my parents dwell.

It suffices to shake my hands free from what I despised
and had rotted my blood
or
from what I crawled to
on all fours
to make my offerings.

I am now without a name for calling,
I left him to pick up his own load;
in the partition of water and dirt
shadow does not ask about its roots.

So let the one who toys with the hours and raises scorpions under
    sturdy towers place his biggest scorpion in the vineyard, the
    wind has frozen in the flute's reed and the feather that kept on
    falling from the bird of mortality has arrived. I am so touched I
    thank you so much for sending me, in my striped suit and lilac
    shirt, to my parents. And I would have squeezed your hands if
    I'd known what it felt like to touch the hands of the dead.

## III

Naked I left and I shall return in my best clothes.
My mother, hostage to her longing, waits, and mothers weave a
    waiting whose cottons have no likeness; and my father, the
    failed acrobat, balances cancer, with dread, on his most robust
    vocal chord. My days are up in a city whose men mate with
    nursemaids of lightning and feed on inductors.

Once a utility worker
came and found the electricity
meter disconnected
and didn't understand
how my room was pulsating
with volts!

I did love and did exit from the other side with more than one rib
missing; love's claws are no shorter than hope's.

Just ask my heart which I left
boisterous as a slave freed from the stranglehold of the night
on a road that loved others more
even when I ripped for its sake
a vein.

I left no Metro barrier unjumped,
or no street whose memory my feet hadn't stored,
I wrote stories about love and madness
my demanding friends didn't like
because I wasn't as concerned with craft as I was
with classifying the levels of deception.

I have nothing to do here or anywhere else,
that's why I leave to you my books, the fires of harvest
in my paintings on the walls of my room,
and the promised days that never came,
so give them away to a passerby

leaning to one side between two starless nights.

Autumn is a perfect season to bid Paris farewell.

Dice are falling heavily on nacreous backgammon squares.

Sleep-walkers are returning to their beds.

The mighty are free from the grating of their teeth.

The sun of serum bags inundates the hospital,
while metaphorical friends are outside smoking with a boredom
their frowning faces cannot hide; or they are pecking
the ground with the tips of their shoes.

There are wolves that don't see with the naked eye
silently squatting behind bends and on streets corners.
And there are those who hear what you cannot hear.

But life
is hope's
slack
saddle
on the back of an indomitable horse
It venerates its promises
It gives
and takes
from the bushels
of the wind.

Translatd from the author's collection *Kullama Ra'a 'Alama*,
al-Muassassa al-Arabiya lil-Dirassat wal-Nashr,
Amman–Beirut, 2005

## KHALED MATTAWA

# Selected Poems

### SONG OF THE DISSIDENT

*A Homage to Benghazi*

Because old skin can't be shed,
because one life is only one life,
everywhere you go, a hemorrhage of dread,

always pushed back, your aim far ahead,
because no sweetness to your strife,
because the old weight can't be shed.

The sky a hole at your feet, the earth overhead,
you stray and the roads pull out their knives,
everywhere you go a hemorrhage of dread.

Your face is a familiar stranger, silent, unread,
because you can't live another life in your life,
because the old story has been torn to shreds.

Because you aim to defile the purebred,
their smugness calcified, self-deception rife,
everywhere you go, a hemorrhage of dread.

Because you seek light and the shadow's widespread,
because you've given up child, husband, wife,
because old skin can't be shed,
everywhere you go a hemorrhage of dread.

## GHAZAL: IN THE DARK

All those organs working in the dark,
the kidneys siphoning, the liver dredging, the stark
heart tightening and flinging, all the secretions dissipating in the dark,

and the brain's primordial muscles almost bursting,
flashing their proverbial tungsten,
their dim fibers beaming a darker dark.

I can't believe this unneed,
this foregoing of light, this dimwitted greed,
each of us a bundle of machinations in the dark.

Or shall I say dark machinations? their fumes
wafting into the lungs' smoke-filled rooms
that are already dark?

Of course the air does not know its colors,

even when it's dyed or discolored
into rainbows of dark.

Even when it brushes against
the clouds' brows, and no matter who paints
it rose or green, the air is made of dark

bubbles
rising from impossible
depths which have known nothing but dark,

colors that only ears and tentacles can detect,
which is what I've been holding inside the deep reds of blood,
a spectrum of crimson lava thinning and coagulating without my
   knowing, dredging their own dark.

That's where I see
a luminous tree –
could it be the soul? – growing deep inside a well of dark.

Your words to me
tunnel a plea
into burrows of dark

growing in heat, in throbs,
steam valves busting and hissing their sobs
deep inside my dark.

All the books I've read
in the dark tossed, as if torn into shreds
into another dark.

The stories I wished to take down,
the ships from where villains at last fall and drown
irretrievable dark.

O poets of Carthage, pity Khaled, his errors;
his regrets, his failings have grown bones and spurs.
They prod and poke him, headlong into the dark

## AFTER SHAHID

Splendid silks of Central Asia, O how their finery glows
in patterns like plumed rainbows!
Why is it hard to believe that such finery is worn by nomadics.

You'll never know the end of the story. Enjoy phrases then and
   trot along
its caesuras and diphthongs.
Let meanings wander nomadic.

A piece of bread, a few dates, a glass – No, a skin! – of water.
You've found your way to the truth, but your belly is ready to
   barter:
Eating like a nomadic.

The world is upside down, Heaven is terribly cold.
Whether Hell's ash is hot or frozen, the angels have put me on
   hold:
My faith flutters nomadic.

How oppressive these brick buildings in the fog!
A sole crow on the ledge panting in the smog:
you too want to fly off nomadic.

But then you walk the lush field and dream of seeds,
green flames bursting into speed
razing your urge to be nomadic.

You read, and from each page you extract brick and mortar.
Soon you're walled in your thoughts deeper and farther.
You are fortress lost to itself, your soul gone nomadic?

Twilight and Hager paces "a valley without a single plant".
Her milk is all dried up, her baby kicking at the sand.
Abraham, why have you let our mother scurry about like a
   starved nomadic?

She oiled her hair with ghee, smelled like a sack of soot,
calloused hands, gleaming eyes, anklets ringing from her foot.
Once, I loved a nomadic.

What have you got to say for yourself, other than nomadic, nomadic?
Your knees, Khaled, grind, their pain almost ecstatic.
Unfortunate for a nomadic.


## SONNET

Are they
'waiting' for
a new light?

a false hope
so seamless,
it soothes.

Will love
reshape the bones
of their chests?

A lizard
adjusting, its
stone body spun.

Yes, their lives
are this waiting
for flight?.

Is it suscept-
ability or eaves-
dropping, this glow?

A new alphabet,
a new reach,
a rugged crest.

Loves like
sunflowers
turning with sun,

A lizard
sinks in an
ocean of dark.

'waiting' like
radars, like
beggar bowls.

Your feet devour
A road in
pace with truth

Even on
streets narrower
than cribs,

At night the
sunflower, its
dismay stark,

love, a coin
ricochets between
their ribs.

*MUSA HAWAMDEH*

# Two poems

TRANSLATED BY ALLISON BLECKER

## WHEN DEATH COMES

When death comes,
I'll spit in life's face,
I'll persuade myself that the world is wretched
and people, all people, are yellow worms.

When death comes,
I'll sow sunset in the garden of farewell,
I'll announce the defeat of man
and cast Palestine
into the notebook of absence.

When death comes,
I'll throw the flower of immortality
in Gilgamesh's face

and mock
the doctors' advice.

When death comes,
I won't bargain with it
to induce loved ones
to gather and mourn.
The fewer my final escorts,
the whiter my conscience.
The fewer the tears,
the more beautiful my sins.

Let those offering condolences leave
before the consecration of whiteness.
Let them leave –
I'm in no need of an incomplete elegy.
My good deeds are not a peg on which to hang their hypocrisy.
Let the lowlifes leave –
What use are sighs to the heavens?

Let the beneficent,
the good hearted,
the well-intentioned
leavedepart.
My past,
present,
and future are all dead,
and I  have no desire for salvation

When death comes,
I won't apologize to the air I breathed,
nor to the threads that touched my body.
I won't apologize to the water I drank,
nor to the delusion that enveloped me,
or that I imagined,
nor to the country that clung to my back like a turtle shell.

I won't apologize to anyone
or any country.

Perhaps I'll liberate my soul from the universe's corruption.
I'll detail to myself my perfect goodness
and spring's elegance in the book of summer.
Perhaps I'll caress my mother's face with clean hands,
hear my father's cough,
and smell the scent of his chest, even without a miracle.

When death comes,
I'll cross the distance between life and death
with a passing, lustful tremble,
exactly like that first resounding gasp
on the haunches
of the virgin earth.

Mountains oblivious to a prayer
and supplications oblivious to my calls
die with me,
walk in my funeral procession,
and perform the final ceremony with all their might.

When death comes,
I'll escape to my mother's bosom
and her soft face,
to her slender hands
and her strange gaze.
I'll bring her all of my heart
and confess my many faults:
my inability to free myself from the impurity of my desires,
my past indifference to encounters with wisdom,
the good nature of figs and olives,
the muddle of memory,
the death of people, all people,
upon the waning of grace.

I won't shout out of regret for my birthplace,
I won't die out of sorrow when I'm not buried in my country's clay.
I have enough imagination
to grasp the world's soil in my hands.

My body dwells
in each particle of the universe.
I won't die a stranger anywhere,
my corpse in its entirety lies in every corner.

I hear the creeping fear
in the limbs of creatures.
I won't cry out, trembling,
I'm neither more courageous than myself,
nor am I a coward hastening after the train of lost chance.
I'm incapable of fleeing the game.

I grin from ear to ear.
If my jaws were to rescue me, I would laugh
at those who cry over death,
considering it their only enemy,
while they pretend to forget that mortality
is an ancient language of physics.
They pretend to forget that death does not come from the transcendental,
nor from hell's mistresses,
but from their attachment to life
and from their broken bodies.

Sorrow's journey is complete,
I was willingly routed
despite all my heroism and courage.
I was defeated in all my existential, lifelong battles,
and that was my virtue.
The fewer the final escorts
the more complete my freedom.
My faith in God bore me as lightly as angels,
I'm in no need of the mulaqqin or the Qur'an reciter.
I'm in no need of elegies or mourning
for I'm not attending a deceitful ceremony there;
I am
returning
from myself
to
eternity.

## PREOCCUPATIONS

Today, I am preoccupied with the preoccupations of those bereft of
   silence.
To the flowers I babble about the biography of the rain,
to the soil I relate some of the larks' tales,
to the gazelles I confide a love story belonging to the swallows.

Today, I am preoccupied with the preoccupations of those unable to
   speak.
I dream of the countries of butterflies,
a paradise of rivers and birds,
a wide, green meadow,
a homeland with no roadblocks or detours,
mountains with no settlements,
and enemies who neither spill the blood of olive trees
nor rip up the roots of pride.

Today, I am preoccupied with the preoccupations of the bellows
   worker.
I blow my days into hope's embers,
heat defeat's ore,
burn time's rust,
roast a sliver of the heart of the ages,
and sharpen salvation's saw.
I am satisfied with fire,
with the wisdom of smelting iron.

Today, I am preoccupied with the preoccupations of the muezzin.
I shout into the darkness:
O black night, who am I?
O silence, who am I?
O drunken cave, who am I?
And who are you, thief of the sorrowful chords?

Today, I am preoccupied with the preoccupations of the photographer.
I print my country's life as forgetfulness
and wipe my forefathers' words from the face of dust.
In the camera of nostalgia, I capture

a face of ululation that never ascended to the heaven of living creatures.

Today, I am preoccupied with the preoccupations of the sculptor.
I chisel the years of exile,
I carve from the phoenix's defeat
a statue befitting the myth.

Today, I am preoccupied with the preoccupations of the prisoner.
I smash through the iron bars of the jail cell,
fly over the authority of history
and the balance of power,
tear down the walls of captivity,
break open the sun's shackles,
and cast the jailer into the abyss of defeat.

Today, I am preoccupied with the preoccupations of the miller.
I prepare my wheat for the mill,
pour the grain into the quern,
and arrange my days as bread for exile.

Today, I am preoccupied with the preoccupations of the genius.
I sit with my head beneath the apple tree,
waiting for one of the stars to fall
so I can uncover the heavens' secret.

Today, I am preoccupied with the preoccupations of the astronomer.
I survey my days from the observatory of mistakes,
and pour drops of nostalgia onto the clouds that pass.
I observe the shifting of galaxies
and whisper the name of my Romanilover to the dawn.

Today, I am preoccupied with the preoccupations of the pagan.
I worship the idol of freedom,
and turn my gods around in nature's hands,
now certain that you are my path to faith.

DUNYA MIKHAIL

## Four Poems

### AT THE MUSEUM

A small Sumerian goddess
stands behind glass,
her upright hands
touch the sky.

On my second visit
the goddess has grown
leans forward a little,
her hands point down
to the earth.

On the third visit
she is lying down,
her hands to her sides
ready for sleep.

On my last visit,
she her eyes are closed
her hands are folded across her chest
hiding a secret?

## IN THE AQUARIUM

A fish
comes across another
and lays eggs.
As its fins signal to the seaweed
its colors come forth
one after the other.
They mouth empty bubbles,
speech meant for no one.
The world rises and falls
every day
through the eyes of a fish.

## A SECOND LIFE

After this life
we need a second life
to apply what we learned
in the first.
We make one mistake after another
and need a second life
to forget.
We play marry-go-round
and need a second life
for love only.
We need time
to finish our prison sentence
and then live free
in the second life.
We learn a new language

and need to practise it
in the second life.
We rush
all over the place,
and need a second life
to take pictures.
We write poetry and move on,
and need a second life
to know the critics' opinions.
Pain takes time
to dissipate
we need a second life
to know how to live
without pain.


## THE AIRPLANE

The airplane coming from Baghdad
carries American soldiers
rises up
over the moon
reflected on the Tigris
over clouds accumulated like corpses
over an ancient harp
over skin stroked with hands
over the kidnapped
over ruins growing with children
over long lines at the passport office
over Pandora's open box.
The airplane
with its exhausted passengers
will land six thousand miles away
from that finger
amputated in the sand.

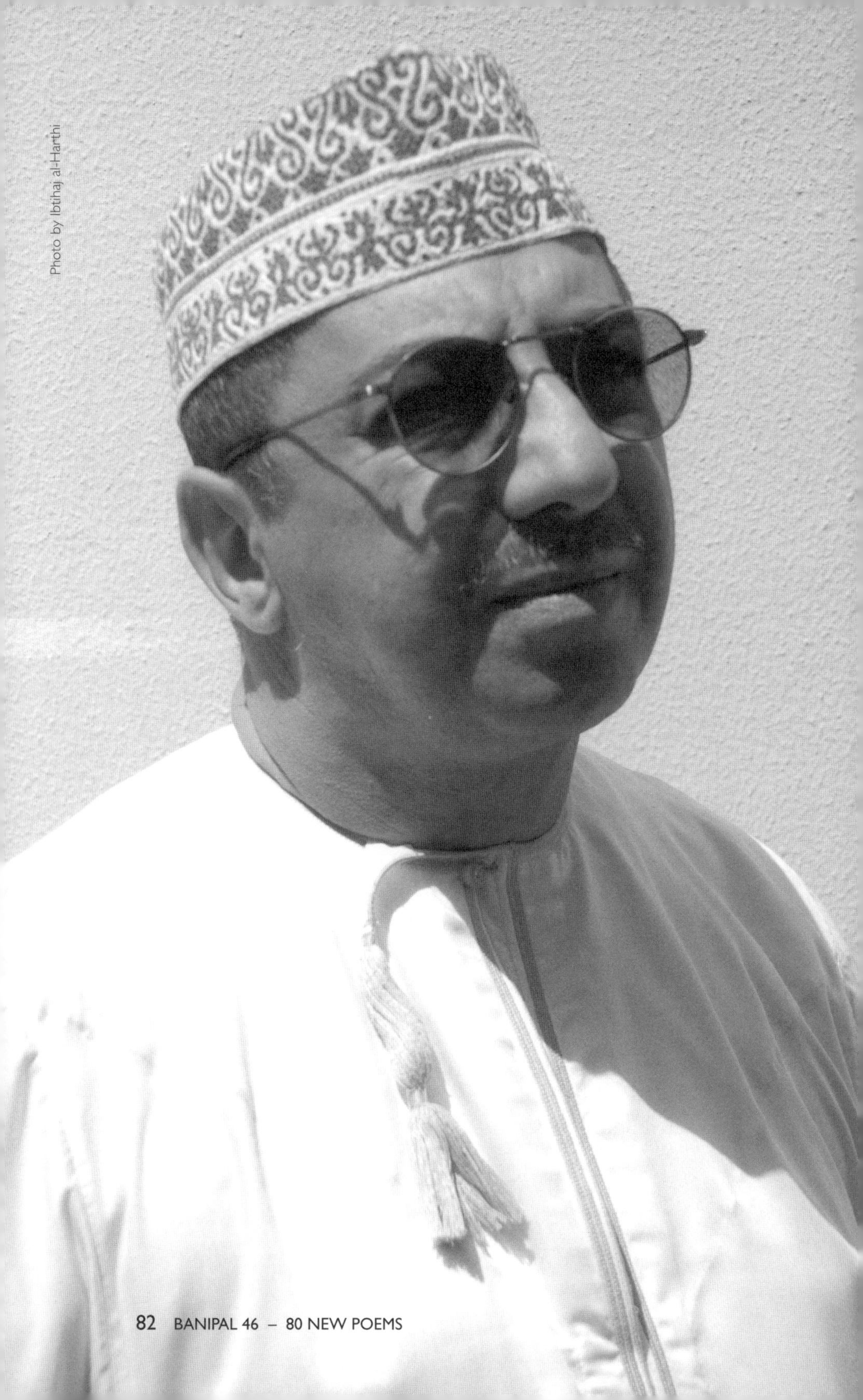

Photo by Ibtihaj al-Harthi

# MOHAMED AL-HARTHY

## A FAILED MECHANIC
## AT THE ONSET OF THE SEVENTIES

(*A memoir retrieved from
a teenage autobiography*)

TRANSLATED BY IBTIHAJ AL-HARTHI

In my early teenage years, I busied myself with the innards of the
    Land Rovers of that time
(the 1967 models and the ones that followed) . . .
With their enigmatic innards under the bonnets, I busied myself
with the cacophony of their four-cylinder symphony, as well as
    mechanical defects
with the ones that did not end up in Muscat, Calcutta or Zanzibar
and on top of them a body speeding on four
so I could dream of inventing the patent for the childhood of the
    age that was about to shed its skin anyway:

In the future, I will become a mechanic in the valley of al-Jardaa[1]
    fixing the defects of vehicles under the Muqaihfa acacia tree
    before reaching the mouth of Wadi al-'Aqq[2] which was rocky
    with the boulders of Imru' al-Qais and Abu Muslim al-Bahlani.

I started dreaming, after witnessing, in the midst of tiresome
    journeys in Bedford trucks, the mechanic Hassoon dismantling
    the innards of the vehicles of that time, piece by piece, with his
    simple tools in his improvised garage under that acacia tree.
    While he worked, he drank from a bottle in his dishdasha
    pocket, a liquid that he pretended was medicine for his chronic
    cough. He drank out of sight of the turbaned travelling sheikhs
    to whom he never paid much attention, with their calling for a
    decayed Imamate and the five prayers, which Hassoon did not

pay much attention to, either, still busy repairing the innards of
vehicles on those burning hot afternoons.

No, I did not become that mechanic, not in this garage of words,
nor in the midst of his memoir that I retrieved,
though once, on one of those journeys, I dared to ask:
"And what about the Land Rovers, Hassoon?
Are they more complicated than the Arabiyya trucks?"
(the local nickname for Bedford trucks back then)
His response was as it always was in the darkness of memory
    under the acacia of his improvised garage:

Oh, don't bother yourself with it, my boy, don't bother. The
    English beat Hitler and the Axis powers while we were still
    suckling our mother's milk. So I think they can fix the defects
    of Bedford trucks and these Land Rovers. It is their
    craftsmanship, and we learned it from them, then mastered it
    in Baluchistan and in the garages of the Sultan's Special Forces,
    which would not have won over the imams if it hadn't been for
    those vehicles, despite their numerous defects.

This is something you might not comprehend, my boy, but I will
    tell you another secret
that only an expert mechanic would know,
a secret that that even the Shah and the canny English never
    knew.
If you know it, my boy, you will gain high status in our world.
    Do you know what it is?
It is the German cars with their meticulous craftsmanship and
    luxurious velvet seats,
their sandalwood, and their golden metal which I bashed with
    this screwdriver in the Sixties,
the Mercedes of Bahraini and Kuwaiti Sheikhs . . .
This metal which, if you ever weighed it on the scales of a sheikh
    of mechanics, would, I'm sure, leave you dissatisfied with
    repairing Land Rovers; of course, this is if you'd want a noble
    job, my boy.

Memory is as treacherous in its straightness as enthusiasm is in
   the crookedness of the falajs[3],
yet the boy, in the exuberance of that afternoon,
who had fortunately missed the siskin[4] in the acacia with the
   pebble from his slingshot, said:

I will not become a mechanic like you, Hassoon, I will be a poet
   instead, singing like the siskin in the acacia tree . . .
A poet, whose memory might serve him to write a poem in his
   fifties about the magic of a golden screwdriver, rusty Land
   Rovers and your days as a lucky mechanic in Sixties' Kuwait,
   buying seven sardines from your fishermen friends with your
   Indian rupees
(seven sardines, in which you wouldn't find any of the pearls of
   the Omani poor)
so you could have a lentil dinner with your fellow workers in the
   yard of the Kuwaiti oil refinery

No, I wouldn't become a mechanic like you, sheikh of
   mechanics,
because life might change in the blink of an eye.
I might stay home doing nothing, or travel around the world,
the siskin of the acacia accompanying me to more than one
   chosen exile
so that I could return to my bittersweet homeland with a flute
   nobody can hear . . .

I might sit on the patio entertaining myself
by rewashing my already ironed dishdashas
but I will not, like you, look for a pearl hidden in the sardines of
   my days
I will not be content, even with my geological knowledge of
   digging a well, with milking the oil's tears

There is enough wasteland, master of mechanics

I will not become a mechanic like you
but I might willingly let go of rhymed verse
and willingly take the time to pen free verse

And who knows?
In the workshop of the future I might learn to make a bed for the
    "renaissance"
so that it can wake from its years of somnolence
in case it might want to clip a few wings of that crowd

And who knows?
I might eat fish not cooked with rice but steamed with what is
    there – seaweed,
just to follow the Japanese tradition.

And who knows?
I might finally like sushi sometimes and hate it at others
O Hassoon, you siskin of the sardines, dried with nostalgia for
    the 1960s.
I might be wrong if I ever tried to challenge their master poets
    with a haiku
or a Zen poem
but a poet follows the dusty road
following it to the end like a grammarian monkey towards the
    certainty of doubt . . .

A poet might not have, like al-Mutanabbi[5], a luxurious Mercedes
    in his middle years
and he might not have the nation rise up for law and order
or have Sayf al-Dawla[6], Hassoon,
but he might pretend and show off in a Volkswagen
Beetle, swanning off with a humming engine
to the deserts of mankind and djinn-kind
just so he can park it near the acacia tree,
this acacia tree and no other.

When the bulldozer swept away that last rock in Wadi al-'Aqq,
in the 1970s they built a road for God's worshippers,
for the children riding their little bikes and

picking the ripe and the bitter acacia fruit,
for the donkey's master, ascending to his valley farms,
praying, as it ate grass, to remember its piety,
for the taxis, followed by other taxis,
for the Volvo, the BMW and the popular Corolla,
for the bus overcrowded at times with its human passengers
and at other times with some djinn passengers,
for brave soldiers waving at a reclining camel
in the truck of a cheerful Bedouin as it passed through the valley,
for the sun washing itself in what is left of light in the fort,
for the taxis arriving after three days from Jalan and Sur[7],
for the Volkswagen dream
and for the fuel trucks being raced by speeding cars
I wonder:

"Did I tell him it was from that time?"


Selected from the author's latest collection
*(Back to Writing with a Pencil)*,
Dar al-Intishar al-Arabi, Beirut, 2013


Notes:
1  A small desert village in the Sharqiya Region of Oman
2  A rocky valley in the Sharqiya Region on the way to Al Jardaa
3  A system of water channels that were the main source of irrigation in Oman
4  A species of finch. In Arabic, *hassoon*
5  Al-Mutanabbi (c. 915–65 CE) was a famous Arab poet
6  Sayf al-Dawla was a famous Hamdamid ruler of Aleppo who was the patron of al-Mutanabbi (948–957 CE)
7  Towns in the Sharqiya Region

# FADHIL AL-AZZAWI
# Selected Poems

## TRANSLATED BY THE AUTHOR

photo by Ali Ghandschi

# ESCAPE TO GOMORRAH

Tightening my safety belt around my waist,
through the window I saw Bedouins galloping
on their tired camels.
They came from all corners of the desert,
set their tents in the hills
and burned their fires
upon the ruins of their history.

They came and kneeled
                kissing the ground
                               and swearing eternal loyalty.
They wept and beat their chests with chains,
shed pagan salty tears and begged me, their prodigal son,
to forgive them their mischiefs and sins
but I, who wrote his name in the sand,
closed my eyes and listened only to the thundering of my soul.

When their piercing shrieks drowned
in the deafening rumble of our flying carpet,
a blond Scottish stewardess appeared suddenly
like an angel, spreading her kisses left and right,
and taught us how to stay alive and survive
when the veil is lifted
and the world comes to an end –
"The day whereon neither wealth nor sons will avail." *

She said:
Please, don't forget to turn off your mobile phones!
There are eight emergency doors on both sides
and under the wings.
However, there is no reason to fear
so long as God is with us
as we cross the Sea of Darkness
on this blessed bird.

---

* Qur'an, Sura "The Poets", Verse 88

Thank you for making the right choice to fly with us
from Baghdad to Gomorrah.

British Airways
                    is always
                            at your service.


## A HAWK IN THE WIND

Evening falling. A city mourning. Barbed wires.
From the beach a confused hawk flying high into the wind.

A wide flatland, greenish with grass, stretching to the horizon,
    stopped short by the sea.
On the beach, we see three baby dinosaurs playing peacefully. In
    the sky, jet fighters head towards me. In the foreground, a
    clown all dressed up, with a painted face, plays football with
    three plastic dolls.

A high wall, up to my shoulder, crumbling away and darkened
    with the scars of time. From behind it, a man with an animal
    head, blotched with red inside blue spots, gazes at us. There,
    under the wall, is a guitar covered with ants.

Oh, how white is the rock, except for the algae covering its
    surface!
Oh, how happy are nations, except for the blood writing their
    histories!
Oh, how vital is the king, except for the death lying in his heart!


## THE OLD PROPHET AND HIS APOSTLES

The prophet sat under an olive tree and asked:
"Who knows who will live or die next in our story?"
"No one will die here, Master! We came here to live, not to die.
We already burned our boats."

Travelling from one village to another, the old prophet talked to the
living and the dead.
"O good prophet, what shall I do to inherit eternal life?" one asked.
"Nothing at all, my son," said the old prophet,
"for all you need is here in this world."


## A STRANGER AT OUR PARTY

We saw him at our party. Wearing his smoking jacket and bow tie,
he came and preached the word of the New World, talking about
the feast of infidels who leaned their backs on the cold wall of our
past. There was no sun in our house, so we offered him the moon.
He came, followed by his familiar disciples and showed us golden
soothsayers flying through glass corridors. We loved him as a
scarecrow with all our hearts.
The only possible revolution, he told us, is the one that will make
you believe in a god who has never existed. And then he ended his
secret contract with life and died, like all poets with kind hearts.


## THE POLICEMAN AND THE WINDOW

We were 17 detainees in a room not bigger than 3 x 4 metres: it
was in fact not a room, but an underground cell, a shapeless hole
in the ground, a kind of cave. The iron gate to it was black with
only a small opening in the centre. We used to stand at the gate
and piss into a bucket we'd bought from the police guard for half
a dinar. At the back part of the cell, near the ceiling, was a small
opening through which we could see the legs of people walking
past outside. As the cell turned into a real inferno in summer, we
had no choice but to open that tiny window to catch, at least,
some fresh air. We were like fish out of water. Our guard
appeared every day and talked to us through it: "You know it is
forbidden to open this window." One day he went off and came
back with a piece of wood, some nails and a hammer: "It's not

allowed, I'll have to block it from the outside so it can never be
opened again." As his hand stretched through the opening we
put coins into it. When he pulled his hand back and looked at
the cash he said: "It is really very hot in there, how can you
bear that inferno without a window open." But he still came
back next day, carrying his piece of wood, his nails and his
hammer.

## GILGAMESH IN SIDURI'S TAVERN

In the tavern on the shore I watched Gilgamesh approaching,
   hairy-bodied, wearing the skin of a beast. He came and sat
   beside me grieving:
— It's me, returning empty-handed. There will be no immortality
   after all.

Veiled Siduri, the tavern keeper, brought us two mugs of beer
   and sat down. Putting her arm around Gilgamesh's shoulder,
   she intoned like a sacred harlot in Ishtar's temple:
— How many times have I advised you to accept the rules of this
   mortal life, but you haven't even listened to me. And now you
   discover there will be no escape.
Gilgamesh drank his beer in one gulp:
— I'm returning to everyday life again: to eat and sleep and wait
   for death.
Gilgamesh threw some gold coins on the table and left. I said:
— If only there were no snake in this tale . . .

My guide replied:
— My dear, it's a snake in a play.
— Do you mean that everything was planned from the very
   beginning?
— No doubt about it, but we swallow the bait each time.

# GUEST WRITER
## *LORAND GASPAR*

by Mary Ann Caws, Marilyn Hacker,
Khaled Najar, Herbert Mason,
and Ghenwa Hayek

*LORAND GASPAR*

# The Fourth State of Matter
## (Extracts)

TRANSLATED FROM THE FRENCH
BY MARY ANN CAWS

## KNOWLEDGE OF THE LIGHT

Our rivers have caught fire!
A bird sometimes glides over the light –
here it is late.
We shall go through the other end of things
to explore the clear face of night –

I know mornings mad with their stretches
of desert and of sea –
motion reshaping faces
refilling its tracks.
Monastery of life of pulmonary flame
in the smoking thickness of noon –
we teach the algae, the fish
the color of air and the story of man
to set them laughing in the evening in the opaque ink
of the frightened squid

this morning coming so freshly in your eyes
still full of fragile porcelain
the porous day
its long wool kiss
this whole body remaining somewhere for the night.

Light plays in the narrow bodies of birds
brief motions of air where sounds pleat
and reveal the skin     the eyes of women

men heavy with trespass, with sleep,
night arched in their back are looking
at this mesh on the water severed by the slightest things
and over there surely some windowpanes afire

white walls of rested birds
fossils by chance in the layers of day
waters painted with our passing
the depths are still trembling

swaying of wings
rapid chasms under the skin
one leans over smoking beaches
with cheeks burned

•

tender cloths of grey steel
our hands pruned on the slopes
of this light –
and our fingers laugh
at wheels immensely slight
in the most inward house of life
where someone comes
steel
silence
folds.

Sounds swell in the tiles of light.
You've made yourself white night in the white
piercing the net of our sounds.
Distant surfaces devotions
days fritter away in the arena
and the gaze
and the dance –

I have built you from screeches and cries
exhumed then slowly
buried once again.

Blinding slowness
from mineral to the sea
long trips gouged out in time
to find yourself in a plant, a ciliate
the coolness of its nights
all those doors where you are and give up

•

Like those astonished gazes
at being dead
as the drunken birds
tear off their feathers
our gestures were too clear
to not surprise
their weight in shadow.

•

So far off that the smile does not know the eyelids.
Drawn from the long cries of birds in flight
the fluid letter of unremembering things
the day burned you might forget the words.

Over there at the end of the world
over there the suns
the swollen mouth of nights
over there horizons
the wild silk of desire

grave world
where nothing's insulted or ugly
the knife falls
the day walks on the ceilings
in its copper entrails

The port is repainted black
two or three very white boats

where night is lacking –
windows where islands sunken in the eyes
are dreaming.

Oh so much night eaten away to white
we also had a window's fate
where someone cried out with joy –
silence the port at evening
two or three very white boats
where night is lacking –

I wanted to be loved –
exact beggar at the feasts of light
worn out with grey and blasphemies.
From this flesh I keep the bones
of so many stitches –

now the daytime
            the bare eyes
                        and someone
has repainted my ceiling of things
and already I see nothing more in it –


• 


it is raining in the sun
the trees and houses are graver
by the earth weightier I know where you are
when the eyes are emptied
and you see space through them.



## SHELLS

Death where so much life is getting lost
left by our feeble eyes.
Torrent you astonish us
shining and muddy

from mouth to mouth
the sweet and the bitter
pebbles and wood
finished taken back.
These blurry photographs
that time has moved.
The light seeks itself under our hands
and suddenly all is feather
snow snow —

The same wind pulled into the fire
the same night with the same texture of branches
of an unconfessed joy.
The same growth in the gestures
and the bareness of hands under the skin
sudden gaps in the forms
when space hears us —

•

We have just barely lived
the time of this weight
of all that rips itself asunder unlamenting
your view last night
and all these small ports of the eyes
the eyelids repainted.

•

For years we haven't traded
except with stones.
Our steps light up with blind chalk
thin layer between two water points.
My life burned with so many lights
sometimes with immense tenderness I forget
that everything is deaf
and I raise myself up like a melody.

I listen to you

a sound that burrows into the mornings
the very thin bodies
dance on the knives
standing sharp in the weft
of a resurrection –

Our lives ripened in the hottest of our limbs
all our dwellings on the move from now on
the obtuse thickness of our walls
from strand to strand and from sea to sea
porous and frail in the hand
and everywhere these shells
where the day trembles and decays

I say now all is smooth and dismayed
I say by the bald mountains of memory
in the pleats of a great foam curtain
when the sea windows open
that the sky should arrange itself facing the shadow
and the sculls of the passerby be readable –

How far shall I stretch to watch over you?
You teach me to walk when the path is silent.
Don't forget this white wood of windows at evening.

•

Night circulates along its vast nets
its pupils dilate at a constant speed
and never burst –
you'll never reach
the depth of this night

trembling obstinate fevered detail
I read your rigor in the shadow of depths
everything so smooth so clear so rested
no disorder or anger
in the pure snow of laws
beasts with claws and teeth

struggle in silence
between skin and light –

all this grandeur of air
is swallowed in gestures
everything that is not yet
comes so near in the straw
of so many extinguished worlds –

I know your steps wearing out in my veins
I know your steps like the words I make
like what pierces my silence
and undoes itself.
You pour nights into my limbs
and leave me
when day runs into my lamps
to remake yourself from nothing


## THE GARDEN OF STONES

We were living in the coolness of going
bearers of images to the garden of stones
the vast empire spread out, exposed.
What remains in the breadth of years
breaths gone blue, limestone violence
enormous land of mute lives
green crackles in the fingers of chalk
little by little we learned to listen
somewhere to the fall of jasmine –

all these nights in the stones
you sleep your eyes your lungs steeped
with sounds of a wind forever.
The limpid flood of a fugue of bodies
leaning on the hours that harass the bed
of the hasty campground in the light –

to silence the names with enough joy
so that the force lines
show up in the gaps.
See if you can feel the artery
of so much weight –


•


There were nights of crumpled steel
with gestures curved in the fire
the weight of sands and sorrows forgotten.
Patient airhole in the thick of shadow
at each dawn in the heart's granite
you learn again to move the light –

This sound of words
that you came to dry up
on these paths where the wind
readies with cares the minutiae
of an entomologist stooping over butterflies –

what I used to love most of all
the grassy brightness of fragile joy
it was then the invention of the stem
thrust forth bravely, vulnerable
just busy with growing.

That in so sweet a syllable
I can dilute all violence and all gold
this pure wheat  of myself gone quiet.
The crumbling is at my fingers.

I feel you an inflection in my voice
where the evening dusts come to rest.
The crossing will be long said the angel
in the thickness of the stone


•

let there remain just the sole eye of our weight.
We were forever coming back heavier to earth
pierced by space nailed with light
our hands quieted in the fall —


•


your arms fall
in a low-lying purplish forest
your eyes fall
and the scales of your voice
and I listen to myself a thousand centuries on
recomposed sound by sound.


•


I hold my life
a piece of bread
so hard the hundred grams
of the prisoner of war
and often I'm so hungry
that there's scarcely any left
and things are colored
with marvelous fears —

Night again
blast of windows in the bodies
sudden and mute.
The painted flame of the voluble day
its powders placed on the icon of flesh
and each step of the evening to grasp
the exhausted memory how long will we delay?

This fullness almost and the ruins of lighthouses
the waters inside knock against the panes
unmoving I hear my hearing myself somewhere
an unquenchable hunger to be born —

## KHALED NAJAR

# Evenings by the Sea with Lorand Gaspar

Those years brimmed with questions about life and questions about poetry. You were inhabited by a Faustian hunger for knowledge and, simultaneously, by the dreadful feeling that you were surrounded by the unknown. Those were the days when you listened to the global anthem, with all its "h"s, and felt a deeply Nietzschean sensation of belonging in the world, and a finely-tuned Romantic urge that was a combination of sorrow, lust and a deep desire to discover poetry in the world and the world in poetry. Thus, everything was primed for you to discover Lorand Gaspar, that universalist poet whose work centers on the existential experience – not on the bombastically ideological discourses so beloved of our intellectuals. Now, after many years, I have come to realize that our most consequential actions are caused by events that we cannot know yet which rearrange the shapes of our lives into the forms they were meant to take.

\*

I first learned about Lorand Gaspar from a conversation with Ezzeldine Madani. We were strolling down Carthage Street at nightfall. I remember the orange light radiating from the windows of the Central Library, and the pedestrians walking beneath the trees. I don't recall whether it was the end of autumn or the beginning of winter, but I was asking Madani about Lorand Gaspar, whom I'd heard of in a most unusual way following the publication of the first issue of his journal *Alif*, which had been filled with authors from east and west. Madani began to talk passionately about this remarkably cultivated French poet who had recently moved to Tunisia from Palestine and who spoke several languages – in fact, Ezzeldine mentioned that Lorand had just released a French translation of the journals of his friend the Greek poet Giorgos Seferis, which had been published by Mercure de France.

Ezzeldine Madani was a true pioneer, having many years ago been the first to shake up cultural life in Tunisia, making waves in writing, intellectual thought and artistic vision. He introduced the vocabulary and sensibility of contemporary writing into the Tunisian literary and intellectual scene. Before Ezzeldine, literary culture in Tunisia had been delimited by the work of Abu al-Qassim al-Shabi and the Arab modernist poets of the 1950s, as well as by Ali Douagi and Bachir Khraief's realism and the musings of Mahmoud Messadi, which oscillated between the asceticism and tent-pitching of Abu-l-'Atahiya and Schopenhauer's pessimism, laid out in a classical Arabic prose that resembled the language of Abu Hayyan al-Tawhidi, al-Jahiz and the Qur'an. None of which had anything to do with the everyday lives of ordinary people. In a flash, Ezzeldine Madani managed to expose the innovative adventurousness of modern theatre, painting, writing and literary criticism, and he attempted to implant them into the Tunisian cultural scene. He introduced the concepts of historical consciousness and experimental fiction and revolutionized writing for the theatre, the cinema and the short story. He placed names like Marcel Proust, James Joyce and Aldous Huxley into circulation, as well as Michel Butor, René Char and the writers of the Lost Generation. He introduced Tunisia to Paul Klee and Mondrian, as well as to the theories of Heidegger and the writings of the *Tel Quel* group. He also returned to the mystics, repeating the words of Abu al-Hudhail al-'Allaf, Wassil Ibn Ata, and the Pre-Socratics, whose philosophical fragments he brought into Arabic. He also returned to Al-Hallaj and Tunisia's oral folk tradition, integrating them into his theatrical work, where history and historical events were used as stand-ins for the present, and the past intertwined organically and dynamically with the present rather than merely being used as a tool to show off an encyclopaedic knowledge.

*

On that evening in the early 1970s, I asked Ezzeldine whether he knew Lorand, and whether the two were close. Ezzeldine told me he often visited Lorand, adding, a few moments later: "The man knows five languages, and if you were to sit with him, he'd broaden your outlook. He has translated poetry from Greek, German, English and Romanian, his native tongue, and also writes in French."

Those words from that distant evening have remained with me, as has Ezzedine's deep admiration for Lorand Gaspar, the poet, and his humanism.

That evening as well, I set my mind on meeting Lorand Gaspar.

At the time, Tunisia's cultural scene was resoundingly Stalinist, despite Bourguiba's ostensibly westernized and liberal proclamations: the writers' union belonged to the ruling party, and the cultural associations in the villages were overseen by party men. In short, it was a wasteland: a few had sold themselves to those in power and others were forcibly silenced, marginalized and slowly forgotten. And that was the way it was in Tunisia in those days.

Thus, it was inevitable that I would seek out Lorand Gaspar, the individual, and the symbol, who stood in opposition to everything about that terribly stifled cultural moment in Tunisian history.

*

Our first encounter was in Café Tunis, which used to be on the ground floor of the Moorish-style Continental Hotel on the corner of Yugoslavia and Carthage Streets. We had made the rendez-vous over the phone, and on that light summer evening, Lorand Gaspar came to meet me, accompanied by Jacqueline Daoud. He was in his late forties, and wore a light summer suit. His posture was straight, his step light, and, beneath their heavy lids his eyes sparkled with a bright joy that illuminated his face. Jacqueline, who loved to arrange everything, stood beside him, with her short bobbed hair and her elegant movements.

It was a fleeting introduction, and I don't remember anything from that first meeting besides the exchanged pleasantries and the fact that I spoke of my desire to read his poetry. Jacqueline directed me to her clinic on Gamal Abdel Nassar Street, in a third-floor apartment of a French colonial building, and I said I would drop by at some point.

My relationship with Lorand, which has lasted all these years, began that day.

## The Word is a Global Anthem

And so we met, while Tunisia napped, in Jacqueline's radiology clinic. It was July 15th, 1976, which is noted in my copy of Lorand's first book of poems, *Sol Absolu* (*Absolute Earth*) and it was the first time I saw that book I had heard so much about. I remember it well: Lorand sat in front of me on a floral pink sofa in the darkness of Jacqueline's office, in that Italian-style apartment that evoked Tunisia's colonial Mediterranean past. The curtains were drawn to keep out the sunlight and the outside world, and in a smooth gesture, Lorand handed me Sol to show me, in his own writing, the line, "life and poetry are one". That simple sentence opened up a vast horizon of poetic understanding before me. I came from an Arabic poetic climate dominated at the time by song, ideology, abstraction and empty formalism. That sort of poetry was a serialized form unaware of itself, which was the deepest shame, and the tragedy that led us to perform opaqueness for opaqueness's sake, instead of expressing the complexity of articulating the mystery of the human experience. Man is mysterious as he traverses an endless night. That one sentence was a flash of light, a beacon that later opened me up, gradually, and over many years, to the broad horizons of poetic action . . . and to Lorand's poetry, specifically. After long discussions, and lengthy, careful reading of *Sol Absolu*, *Le Quatrième État de la matière* (*The Fourth State of Matter*), *Carnets de Patmos* (*Patmos' Notebooks*), *Corps Corrosifs* (*Corrosive Bodies*) and his memoirs, and after years of his readings and translations of other poets: Saint-John Perse, Cavafy, D.H. Lawrence, his friend Giorgos Seferis, Pilinszky, I began to delve into the poetic world of Lorand Gaspar. I know that Lorand Gaspar had grasped intuitively, from the beginning, that poetry and life are one; yes, indeed, one. He also realizes that poetry begins out there, in the depths beyond language; his distinguishing trait is that he expresses himself not in language, but through language. It's the passing of the spirit in words. For this reason, he does not celebrate the word in itself, the sort of attitude that often leads to vacuous formalism. Since he does not attempt to grip the reader through his words, he does not cherry-pick them. For him, the word is the embodiment of the world, and there is no need for linguistic acrobatics or pedantry. The word is neither sacred nor profane . . . the word is the word . . . and poetry buds from the non-lingual. In

*Lorand Gaspar and Khaled Najar in Sidi Bou Said, 1975*

a conversation with the Tunisian psychoanalyst Khadija Bisbas, he says:

"I try to shape things on paper that don't have a clear shape in my mind. Something within me bubbles up and sends signals that I try to make sense of; this shape may not necessarily be transmissible. I often write under the pressure of an inner compulsion, a flash of consciousness, or deep exhaustion. I feel that if I could only give words to that thing that is brewing inside me, this mixture of emotions and feelings and old forces that have awakened for some reason or the other, I will have relieved some of that pressure."

The poet's problem is how to express that which is outside of language; how to articulate the inarticulable in language? How can you utter the inutterable? It is no coincidence that many think of poets

*Lorand Gaspar at home in Sidi Bou Said*

as qawwals, truth-sayers. The word appears in the folk heritage of the Arab-Islamic world, from Pakistan to North Africa . . . But how does Lorand manage to express all of this interiority so successfully? Perhaps the French he learned at a later age has helped him to express this non-linguistic world more easily. French is not his native tongue, so it was not imprinted in him from a young age, which perhaps freed him of its linguistic habits and chains. He didn't learn French in France, which freed him from that culture's everyday traditions, liberating him from the way it is used commonly, every day. In short, he has no linguistic memory of French, all of which helped him to bend that language to what he wanted it to say, French having been born on his tongue as Adam's language was on his.

This then is Lorand Gaspar, poet of the inspired word, the rarified word, the word that expresses the loneliness inside and outside, the word that expresses his nomadic life, and that celebrates the world; the word that is the anthem of the world.

\*

One now distant autumn evening, at the end of the lecture he had given on Saint-John Perse in Tunis' Charles De Gaulle Library, Lorand invited us back to his house. Myself, the novelist Habib Selmi and the two poets Mohamed Ghozzi and Moncef Ghachem were to meet with Dorothy Leger to talk about her husband who had passed away some months before. Her husband, Saint-John Perse: the legendary poet whose work, back then, was a grail to us, an absolute challenge we could not set aside. That anthem replete with every element in the universe and crammed with every incident in human history from primordial geological epochs, a history whose "epic oceanic passage concludes in man's honour and glory". That's how it was: Perse's work was an unsurpassable challenge, perhaps because for us, the text was the ultimate authority, for us descendants of a culture of revelation that sanctified the letter and the world. Truth came to us in the form of a book. Authority was language.

Looking back, I see Dorothy Saint-Leger sitting with something like a smile upon her face. A tall American with the air and manners of New England aristocracy (a decade later I found out she was a New Yorker), with a gentleness, an elegance of movement and a trace of hauteur in her delivery that was kept concealed, prevented from manifesting and wounding others.

After Lorand Gaspar and his wife Jacqueline had made the introductions the conversation came spontaneously to life. We didn't sit there glowering, with the heavy air of university men turning questions over in their heads a thousand times before they spoke, for fear of sounding like academic bores ("What was the influence of American poetic discourse on Perse after he arrived in the States?" – plus all that stuff on Tzvetan Todorov, text and intertextuality, poetry and poetics, *structure profonde* and *structure de surface*, French constructivism and all the other newly minted humbugs that filled the obscure lectures we attended: translated from the French and stripped of their historical contexts and the Western culture from which they came). That night we asked our questions freely over cups of tea and Dorothy, too, spoke freely and briefly about Alexis her husband.

We were in love with texts, not analysis.

Then the conversation turned to Lorand's tales about Perse. Lorand was our true window into contemporary French poetry and it was with his help that we learnt the ABC of this mysterious world. There was talk of Arabic translations of Perse's poetry and I remember Dorothy looking delighted and amazed: she hadn't known that translations of her husband's work had started appearing in the Arab world in the Fifties.

I told her that his poetry had made a huge impression on our generation, that Arabic was an essentially lyric language and thus had had little difficulty in absorbing and adapting the French lyricism of those poets most suited to it – Lamartine, Rimbaud and Perse. Dorothy seemed much moved and affected by this meeting, which had come only a few months after the death of her husband. She had not expected to find young men so taken with his poetry, and it could be that Lorand contrived the encounter to convey this happy truth.

We also asked her if Perse had known the Arab world.

"No," she said. "We never came to Tunisia and if Leger had ever learnt of all this interest I can assure you from what I know of him that it would have made him very happy."

She was silent for a moment, as though searching for some distant memory, then in her faintly accented French she said: "He loved the poetry of the Georges Shehadeh."

I remember that, that night, she spoke about the Saint-John Perse Foundation which had been set up in his lifetime and to which he had given all his things and private papers.

Perse, Lorand explained, was extremely conscious of his image. He once asked Gaspar to delete a few sentences that displeased him from a brief sketch by the famous Greek poet Giorgis Seferis, who had run into Perse by chance in a Manhattan hotel. The encounter was like something out of a novel: both real and unreal. Seferis first caught sight of Perse in a mirror, sitting behind him in the hotel lobby. He stood up, introduced himself and the pair spent the whole day in each other's company. Seferis had written an account of this meeting in his memoirs and opened the account with a portrait of Perse, describing the poet's face as a cross between Charlie Chaplin and Adolf Hitler. When Perse read the French translation he requested that Lorand remove this line and indeed, after the poet's death the French version was printed in *Alif* magazine (published in Tunisia by Lorand) with all Perse's emendations and shorn of the description.

At Lorand Gaspar's *salon* I met many of the big names of the Sixties and Seventies, among them French novelist Michel Butor, Chinese artist Zao Wou Ki, Henri Michaux's wife Micheline Phankim and Guy de Bosschere. Writers from Russia, from all four corners of the world, passed through Lorand's house, planted on the Sidi Bou Said mountain.

*Translated by Ghenwa Hayek and Robin Moger*

# LORAND GASPAR
# Approach of the Word

TRANSLATED FROM THE FRENCH
BY MARY ANN CAWS

The language of poetry cannot be enclosed in any category, cannot be summed up in any function or formula. Neither instrument, nor ornament, it scrutinizes a word transporting the ages and the fleeting space, founding stone and history, the place receiving their dust. It moves directly in the energy that makes and breaks empires. It is this dilapidated back yard, overgrown with grass, its walls covered with lichens, where the evening light lingers a moment.

No one justifies poetry and it needs no defense: I am only trying to see what in myself advances precisely in such an unchangeable way towards that nightly groping toward the search of another, a rockier precision. Understanding and not, stumbling, breaking, losing oneself, understanding still. I want to assume all the contradictions, to exceed them. For everything in me knows that I am speaking always the same language (that which *speaks me, constructs me* in speaking, in expressing) on different levels. And it isn't a matter of more or less perfect degrees of elevation, higher or lower; what distinguishes them is a particular movement, organization, a relation to the human and to the world. The suddenness of nameless facts and the patient ways of dealing with a fragment.

I see no break between language (or expression), which is matter diversely brought to life, human and social discourse. Levels of emergence, of composition, of vitality and dessication, perhaps of sickness, of an identical word displaying itself in discontinuous signs, caught up in the game of a formidable scheme, a game whose matter, rules and energy, text, syntax and writing it is.

What my ceaselessly interrupted word is seeking, ceaselessly insufficient, inadequate, breathless, is not the pertinence of a demonstration, a law, but the laying bare of a gleam that is ungraspable, transfixing, of a fluidity in turn benevolent and devouring. *A breathing*.

To class, isolate, fix; once these exercises are guided to their sleepy use, we are ready for the sleeplessness of genesis.

All these paths I am following open onto something impossible where only the vertical exercise of language maintains the motion: menace, happiness and loss. And nowhere any term that would resolve, reassure. Nothing but this narrow discomfort, nothing but this excessive width. You cannot close off poetry: its central place collapses upon itself, in an all-consuming compactness, pierced. An unfounded silence where, against any proof, the fragile word, the scandalous word, the crushing word, the useless word still moves forward.


The poem is not an answer to a questioning of the human or the world. It only digs into and aggravates the questioning. The most exigent moment of poetry is perhaps the one where the movement of the question is such – by its completeness, its bareness, its irrefragable progress – that no answer is expected; rather, all reveal their silence. The breach this gesture opens wipes away the formulations. The separate values, duly catalogued, that create the coming and going between opposite shores are, for a moment of lucidity, caught up in the force of the river. From this word that refers to all burning, the mouth lost for ever.

Our meaning and our thought are ceaselessly encumbered with reflections, losing this vivacious fluidity that we sometimes call soul. But someone stops near a dilapidated mud wall, near a stone missing any words. He palpates the seed of an off-white, secreted light. He touches a porous crackled glass, with the rough texture of a voice. Moving through the strata, he works in the very motion and breath of language. An architect of the statute book, he shapes the material of signs at their birth. Ceaselessly taking up again the veins of an order at their source of energy, he leads them to a meaning that disappears. This endlessly thirsty seeker, this eternal inadequate person, this scorner of the impossible is above all a worker of language, a worker despairing and laughing. Going to the very fibers of the weave, to the sources of the chemistry, he wants first of all to wipe off gently the vapor, the vapor of the vapors, to look through this awkward-shaped hole at the slow migration of the landscape.

Poetry is sometimes capable of conducting (like good metal conductors) a quivering of language, communicating to words its fluidity its corrosive and forgetful power. So the word – the image – transforms itself from a simple chemical element participating in the constitution of a composed body (a seme), into an enzyme able to operate the synthesis or the lyse, the unexpected creation of new compounds, which provoke, in what burns them, different flames.

This place of high energy, where words are ordered, that we call poetry is our part of the infinite act in the world, a force field of the laws of our own motion, where our constellations are composed and undone.

Here is a molecule that provokes the saturation necessary for the formation of a crystal, an enzyme that unleashes some construction, or "recognizes" elements that without it had no meaning, at least not the same one.

And here is this breach opened by a sound, a relation of words, a joining of images that permits us to see where formerly we simply looked. To breathe where we only talked.

The person who is able to set alight those gleams that can be born from such articulations or such defeats in the constellations of language, who knows how to forge them, provoke them, that person, how would we not recognize him? In listening to him, perhaps once, we will understand beyond any borders.

Expressing ourselves, integrating, melting, as we hold firmly onto the wire of this singular motion. The full force of the weaving envelops the disturbed dreams of the rocks, the fright of

Europe *magazine celebrates Lorand Gaspar's 80th birthday*

the depths. Capillaries of a forgotten fresh birth; lightness of the soil under the unexpected step of a cure. Vast steppes and their reaches of tall grasses that rock the slithering of beasts, blood and space of a single melody; lovers you who know how to go leaving almost no traces.

Don't look for the absolute. It is in you like a ravine of dryness which will lose you. All language plowing the earth bears its thirst. Love and doubt. Bitter grass and fruit, the pulse tuned and undone.

The poetic text is the text of life, worked by the rhythm of the elements, constructed, eroded by everything that exists; fragmentary, full of gaps, showing more ancient signs in its faults. Web of ardor and of traffic: everyone can read something *else* in it and also *the same thing*.

What we pompously call creative activity is only just a faculty of combining, of constituting new ensembles from existing elements. What really reveals itself at some moments is a quality, a taste, a coherence and a disintegration proper to this new compound. But to staunch this thirst for composing new bodies, can we associate just anything with anything? There is something of everything in nature. Some find what they want (or their "truth") in the strangeness of dream, of imagined chimeras, others are forever fascinated by life which moves, breathes and operates (but life is also that which produces dreams and chimeras), spreads out here, comes apart there. Still others try to name, to show through these so friable words, what has always invented motion.

The central paradox, the absent key of a certain poetry today is that it tries to break into a domain where the logic of language stops short. Modern physics has had to admit a similar failure of ordinary conceptual language when it was a matter of saying, for example, how an atom went about emitting or absorbing light.

It may happen that the clear water of a language between the words of a poem sends us back to the origins of all tongues and of all language, an augural domain which calls upon us like an unexplained disquiet.

There is a vein of energy that is language, making its continuous way from cosmic dispersions and geological folds to the weaves of life, to the most abrupt motions of the imagination and song. When voice is discovered there, inseparable, it's as if it recognized a face, a modulation, a fundamental relation proposed by the world; as if our language bore all our architectures of stones and winds, suddenly plunged from the present to the ages without memory, recognized its unknown act. Recognized itself.

At the threshold of this indecisive day: the poet with his small packet. Naked in this desert. And naked, screaming and deserted, losing all meaning. Who will hear him in the workshop of unusable dust? Even here, in the laudable work, who will perceive

his silent excavation? What place to allow, avid as we are of
brightness outside, for a lamp that simply breathes? This man has
nothing to propose that will transmute excrement into gold,
which will transfigure the misery of outside into the coin of
salvation. Nothing. Some words in a crude foreign tongue that he
understands as native.

But what poet has ever doubted that language was a river in the
river and breath in the breath?
To pursue the poetic process into its last refuges, to hurl it
above the last wall of words halting the stride of the prophet.
There where discourse leans, too timidly, over an abyss of
language.

To write a poem that would not be a resumé of traces, a
translation or formation, a waning of the different levels of the
lived, of its prodigiously entangled tree-growths – the writing of
a reading at another level – but a simple growth and movement,
issuing from no center and no beginning, its branches, leaves,
fruits not being there to refer to anything else, to symbolize, but
to conduct the sap and the vivacity of the air, to be their humming
and their activity, nourishment and seeding. And reading would no
longer be deciphering of a code, receiving a message; it would no
longer be a matter of reading from your observer's station so
prudently exterior, but rather of flowing into the unforeseeable
progress being, with a same gesture, movement and its laws,
difference and identity, the form constructed and undone.
Reading and writing: to welcome, to accompany, to dig, to
breathe, to flash forth.

Selected excerpts, translated from Lorand Gaspar's first book
*Approche de la parole*, which was published by Flammarion in 1966
and awarded the Guillaume Apollinaire Prize in 1967.
In 1978 a new edition was published by Gallimard, and a third,
together with *Apprentisage,* in 2004.

**HERBERT MASON**

# An autumn afternoon with Lorand

I t was in Boston many years ago that I met Lorand Gaspar. He was a visiting physician at one of our city's major hospitals, and a mutual acquaintance put us together based on our connections with French and Arabic. His connections were first hand and deep, those of a French and Arabic speaking long-time resident surgeon of a hospital in Tunis. Mine were at most a traveler's to the Middle East and the Magreb following a PhD in Near Eastern Languages and Literatures at Harvard. Our first extended meeting was on an autumn afternoon walking in the celebrated "Garden in the Woods" preserve west of Boston joined there by a French friend of his living in Cambridge who brought along his two Great Danes. We spoke a mixture of French, English and a little Arabic. As it was autumn we were awed by the glowing burst of New England's radiant foliage amidst the towering evergreens. The dogs were unleashed and we ambled along behind them for two or three hours.

Lorand, by speaking of Tunisian floral beauty, put us lyrically in two worlds at once. He also commented, however, on the invasive and ubiquitous presence of technical advance and usage he was finding in the hospital he was then visiting. He said in his very quiet but forceful voice: "In my practice I can't interject such machinery between myself and my patients. I must be fully with them where they have been and where they are." Not being a physician, I was out of my depth in the discussion about the "onerous dependence on technology in American and European medical institutions". Lorand inhabited a different experiential and philosophical world. He was there in the "Garden in the Woods" but also not merely there. In all the years I have known him since – through correspondence, exchanges of our writings and translations, shared political causes, and chance meetings when we both happened to be in Paris – he has always been wholly present as a friend while sharing of another world. He is by knowledge and calling a physician and surgeon, a poet and philosopher, a multilingual translator, and through the journal *Alif* a facilitator of others' gifts and works.

L orand Gaspar's *Hospital Notes* reveal his foremost calling, I believe. While nagged by metaphysical questions, he has been guided always by compassion for the patient he serves. Reading and translating his *Hospital Notes* has been a rich experience for me and my wife who requested them for the book she was preparing. They are the thoughts drawn from a long career of service with profound reflections on the sufferings of others. They are the direct account of a person who loves what he does and would have chosen no other career. His experiences have called upon all of his gifts as a person who confronts another's suffering and whose singular passion is to fight it. These notes, written by a lyric poet with an ever-questioning mind, embody understandings far beyond the reach of medical textbooks. The following are a few selections:

•  "I return again and again to a point essential to my eyes which I do not want to lose sight of. For the doctor there can be no other immediate meaning for suffering than to mobilize all his strength and knowledge to fight it."

• "I recently heard a child suffering from mucoviscidoses say, with the disconcerting maturity that serious illness gives to children, that he knew that his days were limited; however, even under these conditions, he considered it better to be able to live (and do everything to continue, even if it were very difficult) than to have known nothing of life. What exact reality lay behind these words, this discourse suited to an adult, I do not know, but the emotional maturity of this child in saying this is unforgettable to me. Surrounded by suffering and death, he seemed only to care about life."

• "It has happened that I have the bad feeling that all the 'machinery' of knowledge, the research and means, put to work is destined to please us doctors, to satisfy our ambitions, our thirst for knowing, to publish, and to discuss. The "medical game" becomes a closed field where what bothers us most is excluded: the living human being."

• "There is something diabolical in extreme, overwhelming pain, because it deprives us of our fundamental capacity to step back, reflect, to see ourselves from the outside, and to untangle the confused web of our infliction. It destroys what is properly human in us : the ability at least in part to elucidate what is confused by thought, and the patience to trust the intrinsic truth of our life and that of all others."

• "We need another person, capable of hearing us, to help us see and think in the darkness, who can lend us a hand in order to regain a bit of peace and clarity."

• "Apart from Spinoza, no one has tried to think with much ardor about the rigor of God, a Being absolutely infinite and eternal, existing for itself and simultaneously the source of all conceivable ways to exist by an infinite understanding. No one has really contemplated the idea of a present and living God in full light, of a divine eternity that also includes the duration."

These excerpts of Lorand Gaspar's *Hospital Notes* are from Jeanine Young-Mason's *Critical Moments, Doctor and Nurse Narratives and Reflections*. 1st Books, Bloomington, Indiana, 2003.
Translated by Madia Thompson with Herbert Mason.

# LORAND GASPAR

# Hospital Notes

## EXCERPTS TRANSLATED BY MARILYN HACKER

• That man standing in a hospital corridor. He doesn't know how it happened, but he is there, standing – painfully, but standing, after all. No shadow of rebellion on his face. On the contrary, all is instant adhesion to what is, that is, to all evidence, beyond his comprehension. He is there like a concrete articulation, incarnate, of the unbordered fluidity of worlds. A gift that has always enfolded him. Joys, sorrows. Things that are there, that are no longer there, that dissolve, that crumble away – touch does as well – while elsewhere something else is built. To be there, completely, to miss nothing. To try.

• All these dead bodies no one comes to claim.

• What doctor, what surgeon, even if he has never worked near a battlefield or under fire, has not thought of the extent of inter-human carnage at the moment when his team is working furiously to patch up the life-fragments of someone gravely wounded? And every day, as every night, as we concentrate on relieving pain, on trying to cure just a few – paid by society for that – hundreds of thousands are killed, wounded, tortured by others. A banal thought?!

• Montaigne, Rousseau and Schopenhauer champion compassion (or pity, although there are subtle differences that can be defined between them) as an emotion directly opposed to cruelty. It through compassion that we pass from barbarism to a society where the other seems to be our fellow creature, even if daily experience shows us how close the "barbarian" is (the return to our archaic cerebral structures) under the whitewash of civilisation.

• Torture, that summit of human cruelty, precisely human, has never ceased to be practised. The truly " inhuman" universe in the larger sense of the term: inability to recognise the other as my fellow human.

• Abu al-'Ala al-Ma'arri, Syrian poet and philosopher (973-1057) wrote in his *Luzumiyyat* that if he were a dog he would do everything in his power to ensure that his offspring did not endure what men endure:

*Your temples and your brothels are the same.*
*Stay far from me, O humankind!*

• The essence of the patient's problem of human relationships, es-
pecially the patient in intensive care, practically bound hand and
foot to multiple life supports, is that he or she is delivered over to
the good will of others. In these modern sanctuaries, direct contact
with the outside world, friends and family, is considerably reduced
when it is not completely closed off. The respirator, one of the most
frequently used means of mechanical substitution, of immeasurable
value, increases even more acutely the reality, not even to speak of
the feeling – of dependence and isolation. And yet, the more com-
plex this kind of care and the technology that it implies become,
requiring additional attention, the more we tend to treat these pa-
tients as objects. Our conscience is at ease: the essential thing is to
have a vigilant eye on the data, to make the gestures and adjustments
necessary at the right moment. However, it is exactly in these ob-
jectively difficult situations that we must find a few moments to ad-
dress/make contact with a human being, establish a bridge between
two subjectivities. Stop, express an interest in what the patient is
feeling, wants – explanation, reassurance, touch, are another kind
of oxygen, of which we never think enough. Once more, we must
do everything so that the technical intervention, important as it is,
doesn't prevent attention to the other, our fellow-creature, who is
at the center of our enterprise.
• These small, simple joys, sudden absences or deepenings, I'm
not sure how to say it, of the quotidian – a colour of the sky or of
the mountains in the evening, the pattern of a tree's bark, the smell
of wet grass or of jasmine in the night, a gaze, a hoopoe's call in
pre-dawn grey – where something is made manifest of which we
can say almost nothing, that reminds us from time to time, like a
fact, of a certain music.

In the hospital corridor, a vigorous youth, immobile, his face
completely oblivious to the outside world, consumed by an invisible
flame, holds tightly against his chest a pale old man, exhausted,
breathless.

• The great souqs of the Middle East remain more magical to me
than all the theatres in the world. Those of Sanaa, Jeddah, Damascus,
Jerusalem, Aleppo, Antioch and others, less famous. The poetics of
a living art expressed by daily exchanges. A creativity unceasingly

renewed in the order of objects proposed to view, by the movements of desire. The contrapuntal development of colours, the two melodies that cross paths and rub shoulders, in the opposite direction from the passersby and onlookers, and all that to arrive at the hand-ballet of shoemakers and ropemakers, of tailors, carpenters and barbers. What a feast for the sense of smell, the eyes of the body-brain.

• The splash of two goldfinch-droplets dries and evaporates gently from my vision. Long after the two birds – a couple – disappeared into the bushes, my ears continued to resonate with their rustling wings and their throats' liquid embroidery.

Selected and translated from "Feuilles d'Hôpital" by Lorand Gaspar, published in *EUROPE* magazine, issue #918, October 2005

# Lorand Gaspar

Lorand Gaspar is a traveller, a poet, surgeon, scientist, historian, photographer and translator. He is recognised as one of France's most important contemporary poets and over the years has received many awards for his work, including the Grand prix de poésie de la Ville de Paris (1987), the Prix Mallarmé (1993), the Grand prix national de Poésie (1995), and the Prix Goncourt de la poésie (1998). He has translated poetry from a number of languages, often in collaboration with Sarah Clair, including works of Raine Maria Rilke, János Pilinszky, D. H. Lawrence and Giorgis Seferis, while his own work has been translated into Hungarian, Romanian, German, Arabic, Greek, Spanish, Italian, English and other languages. He has written a study on Spinoza and in recent years has worked and published in the field of neuroscience – brain research and neuro-cognitive vision.

Lorand Gaspar was born in 1925 in the town of Marosvásárhely into a Hungarian Jewish family with Armenian heritage, growing up speaking Hungarian, Romanian and German, and learning French and later Latin, Greek and Arabic. Until the end of World War I the town had been Hungarian, in Transylvania. After the war it became Târgu Mures, in the Romania that it is today, still with half the population being Hungarian speakers. However, in the crucial years of 1940-1945, the town reverted back to Hungary. In 1943 Lorand attended Bucharest Technical School (now the Politehnica University of Bucharest) where he entertained a secret wish to become both a doctor and a poet, but when Hungary was occupied by the Nazis in 1944, his dream came to an end as he was mobilised and deported to a labour camp in South Germany. However, in May 1945 he escaped and joined a French unit in Pfullendorf. At the end of the war he found his way to Paris and began to study medicine. In 1954, married with three children, he moved to Jerusalem, taking the post of surgeon at the Bethlehem French Hospital. During the Six-Day War the hospital was severely damaged and his own house stripped and robbed. In 1968 he published *Histoire de la Palestine* (Maspero), the first of a number of prose and travel works, illustrated with his own photographs.

In 1970 he left Jerusalem and travelled to Tunis, for the next 25 years practising at the Charles Nicolle Hospital and living in the picturesque cliff-top village of Sidi Bou Said, not far from the ruins of ancient Carthage, which had already inspired the artists Paul Klee, Gustave-Henri Jossot and August Macke. In Tunis, with Jacqueline Daoud (who became his wife) and Salah Garmadi, he founded and co-edited *Alif* magazine, publishing 12 issues between 1970 and 1982 with the Tunisian Ceres Editions (founded in 1964).

Medicine and writing have always been inextricably linked in the work and life of Lorand Gaspar. He is as much fascinated by Rimbaud's poetry as by Einstein's theory of relativity. His first book (excerpted above), *Le Quatrième État de la matière*, published in 1966 by Flammarion, established him as a vibrant new creative voice, and in 1967 he was awarded the Guillaume Apollinaire Prize for the work. Lorand Gaspar then published further collections, with Gallimard, *Sol absolu* (1972), *Approche de la parole* (1978) (excerpted above), *Égée suivi de Judée* (1980), *Feuilles d'observation* (1986), *Patmos et autres poèmes* (2001), and *Derrière le dos de Dieu* (2010). One of the few translations into English is *Four Poems*, translated by Peter Riley (Shearsman Books, 1993. ISBN 9780907562184, 43pp.) Peter Riley has translated a few more poems of Lorand Gaspar, accessible only online.

الجائزة العالمية للرواية العربية
INTERNATIONAL PRIZE FOR ARABIC FICTION

# THE 2013 SHORTLIST OF

### Saud Alsanousi for The Bamboo Stalk

The protagonist's mother went to Kuwait from the Philippines to work as a household servant and there she meets Rashid, a spoiled only son. After a brief love affair, they marry but things do not go to plan, and the wife and baby are sent back to the Philippines. This daring work looks objectively at the phenomenon of foreign workers in Arab countries and identity through the life of mixed race son who returns to Kuwait, the 'dream' or 'heaven' his mother had been describing to him since he was a child. It is written as a translation from the son's Filipino text into Arabic.

### Mohammed Hasan Alwan for The Beaver

The hero, Ghalib al-Wajzi, goes from Riyadh in Saudi Arabia to Portland in the USA. He travels back in time, through the story of three generations of his troubled family: separated parents, and brothers with nothing to connect them except the house where they live. He heads to such a distant city to try to restore his memory with fragmented stories, and with the help of a beaver that accompanies him on fishing trips at the local river Willamette. And throughout, he contemplates his relationship with his girlfriend who visits him over many years in different towns when she can get away from her husband.

### Sinan Antoon for Hail Mary

The events of Hail Mary take place in a single day, with two contradictory visions of life from two characters from an Iraqi Christian family, drawn together by the situation in the country and under the same roof in Baghdad. Youssef is an elderly man who is alone. He refuses to emigrate and leave the house he built, where he has lived for half a century. He still clings to hope and memories of a happy past. The novel raises bold and difficult questions about the situation of minorities in Iraq, with one character searching for an Iraq which was, while the other attempts to escape from the Iraq of today.

### Jana Fawaz Hassan for Me, Her and the Other Women

Following her marriage, Sahar feels a sense of loss and loneliness within her family. She had hoped to become a different kind of woman from her mother but after her marriage to Sami finds herself falling into the same trap. By constructing another self in her imagination, she finds an outlet which brings her intellectual and existential fulfilment. The novel has an innovative structure, psychological and philosophical depth and a profound humanity.

### Ibrahim Issa for Our Master

Sheikh Hatim Al-Shanawi, 'our master', is the permanent guest of a television programme. The charming Sheikh answers viewers' questions and by exploiting visual media to the utmost becomes one of the richest people in the country. Using his natural cunning his replies please everyone, including the security services, though they bear no relation to his personal convictions. The Sheikh has a number of adventures and plunges into the depths of Egyptian society, while uncovering its secrets in a witty and satirical style.

### Hussein al-Wad for His Excellency, the Minister

This novel tells the story of a Tunisian teacher who unexpectedly becomes a minister. He witnesses first hand the widespread corruption in the country, eventually becoming embroiled in it himself. It is a richly humorous novel which successfully describes many aspects of human weakness.

*SAUD ALSANOUSI*

# The Bamboo Stalk

AN EXCERPT FROM THE NOVEL,
TRANSLATED BY THOMAS APLIN

My mother came to this place to work, knowing nothing of its culture. The people here were not like the people there: the faces, the features, the language, even the looks they gave had different meanings, which she did not understand. Nature here resembled nothing of nature there, save the rising of the sun each day and the appearance of the moon at night. "Even the sun," my mother would say, "at first I wasn't sure if it was the same sun I knew."

My mother worked in a big house, where a widow in her mid-fifties lived with her son and three daughters. This widow was later to become my grandmother. My grandmother, Ghanima, or the old lady, as my mother used to call her, was stubborn and very nervous most of the time. Despite her seriousness and the strength of her personality, she was highly superstitious. She had absolute belief in what she saw in her dreams. In every dream, no matter how insignificant or unintelligible, she saw a message that could not be ignored. She spent a great deal of time trying to interpret her dreams. If she could not fathom the meaning of a dream by herself, she usually resorted to the dream interpreters. Because of the differing opinions she received from them she sometimes ended up with a total contradiction. Yet despite this, she believed every word those dream interpreters said, and looked for anything that would prove what she saw in her dreams was real. Along with this belief in her dreams, she would consider any occurrence, no matter how innocuous, as a sign that was not be taken lightly.

Once, while my aunt Aida and I were sat with my mother in the small sitting room of our house there, she said: "I don't know how this woman lived, scrutinising every happening and coincidence. One day she and her daughters were invited to a wedding party.

They set off only to return home just half an hour later. I said to her: 'The party was over quickly, Ma'am!' but the old lady ignored me and made her way upstairs.

"Hind, the youngest daughter, answered for her: 'The car broke down halfway along the road.'

"I thought of all the cars parked in front of the house, and asked her: 'What about the other cars?'

'My mother believes that if the car hadn't broken down halfway along the road, then our souls would have been reaped before its end!' she answered, wiping the red off her lips with a handkerchief.

'How come?' I asked her, my face full of surprise.

'She'd foreseen that something terrible was waiting for us!' Hind had replied bending down to take off her shoes."

Compared to the houses there, the house my mother worked in was huge. In fact, a single house here is big enough to fit the house my mother came from ten times over or more. My mother arrived in Kuwait at a critical moment. My grandmother had been very pessimistic about her arrival, which showed in her face whenever she saw my mother. My father would apologise, explaining: "You came to our home, Josephine, at the same time the Emir's convoy was bombed. But for the grace of God, the explosion would have claimed his life. My mother sees your arrival as a bad omen!"

My father was four years older than my mother. My grandmother treated her poorly, and my aunts likewise, except the youngest, who was prone to mood swings. My father alone was always kind to her. He argued many times with my grandmother and my aunts over their treatment of Josephine, my mother, the maid.

I had only just turned ten when my mother began to tell me about the things that happened before I was born; she was preparing the way for my departure [to Kuwait]. While I was there, sat by her side in the sitting room of our little house, she read me some of my father's letters. She told me everything about her relationship with him, before I returned as he'd promised her. Sometimes, she liked to remind me that I belonged to another, better place. After I started to talk, she taught me some Arabic words: "salam 'alaikum . . . peace be upon you . . . *wahid, ithnain, thalatha* . . . one, two, three . . . *ma' salama* . . . goodbye . . . *ana, anta* . . . I, you . . . *habibi* . . . my love . . . *chai, gahwa* . . . tea, coffee." She was adamant that when I grew up I would love my father, the man I hadn't even set eyes on.

In our house there, I sat at my mother's feet, listening to her as she told me about my father, while my aunt sighed, as was her custom whenever my mother spoke of him. My mother said: "I loved him and still do. I don't know why or how. Perhaps because he was kind to me when everyone else treated me badly? Or because he was the only one who spoke to me in the old lady's house, other than to give me orders? Maybe it was because he was handsome? Or because he was a cultured young writer, who dreamed of finishing his first novel, and I was addicted to reading novels?"

How strange. She smiled as she spoke, tears almost spilling from her eyes, as though what she described had happened only yesterday.

"He was happy with me, as he'd say, because like him I loved to read. He'd tell me about his novel. Every time he sat down to begin writing it something would come up, dragging him into the fray of the region's politics. He wrote a weekly article for one of the newspapers, although they were rarely published because of the censorship there at that time. He was one of a few writers opposed to their government's position during the First Persian Gulf War. Imagine how crazy your father was! He would talk to the maid about literature, art and his country's politics, when no one talked to the servants except in the language of 'Bring! Wash! Sweep! Wipe! Prepare! Come!'

Despite aunt Aida's constant sighing and fidgeting, my mother continued:

"I'd wash, sweep and wipe all day long so I could be free for the night's talk with your father in his study, after the ladies of the house had gone to bed. I'd try to keep up with him as he talked about politics, to hold his attention and demonstrate my own scant knowledge of the subject. One day, I told him how thrilled I was by Corazon Aquino's[1] victory in the presidential elections, making her the Philippines' first female leader. She restored democracy after leading the opposition that brought down the dictator, Ferdinand Marcos.[2]

"Your father seemed unusually interested in what I had to say. 'You brought a woman to power then!' he said, and I answered him proudly: 'Five months ago, on 25th February.' He burst out laugh-

---

1 Corazon Aquino: the 11th president of the Philippines (Translator).
2 Ferdinand Marcos: the 10th president of the Philippines. He was brought down by the opposition (Translator).

*Saud Alsanousi*

ing and then, regaining control of himself so as not to wake his mother and sisters, he exclaimed: 'On the same day we celebrated my country's 24th National Day!' Drumming his fingers on his desk, he said as though to himself: 'Who has the right to be the other's master?' I didn't understand then, what he was getting at. He talked to me about women's stolen rights, as he put it, since women in your father's country do not have the right to vote. He seemed suddenly very sad and began to talk at length about their parliament, which was suspended at the time. I continued to follow his voice and his expressions closely, even though what he said didn't interest me."

I interrupted her: "Why did he talk to you about these things, Mum?"

"Perhaps because his surroundings refused his ideas . . ." she replied quickly, but without conviction.

She described my father:

"I thought he was the ideal man; I'm sure that's how everyone saw him. His mother doted on him. He was, as she would say, the man of the house. He was calm and rarely raised his voice. Most of his time was spent between reading and writing in his study. These were his interests, along with fishing and travelling with his friends. Of your father's friends, only Ghasan and Waleed used to visit him, either in the library to discuss some book or to talk about literature, art and politics, or, when Ghasan brought his oud, in the little diwaniyya that adjoined the house. Ghasan was an artist and a poet. He was very sensitive, even though he was a soldier.

"At that time, East Asia, Thailand to be precise, was at the height of its renown among Kuwait's young men. Your father talked a lot about his travels there with his two friends. One day, while he was talking to me about Thailand, he looked me straight in the eye and said: "You look like a young Thai girl!" Did I really or was he getting at something else? I wasn't sure.

"When he was away travelling with his friends, the old lady's house was made miserable by his absence. I'd count the days until his return, for the house or the diwaniyya to be filled again with the racket he and his friends made whenever they got together."

Suddenly my mother paused, and looking at the floor, she said: "I used to watch them from the kitchen window. Their laughter would ring out in the courtyard as they got their fishing equipment ready before heading to the sea. I'd wait hours for your father's return, when I'd take the fish and put them in the freezer and wash their smell from his clothes."

My mother turned her head to look at me: "José, when you return to Kuwait, I want you to have friends like Ghasan and Waleed."

"Tell me more, Mother. What about my grandmother?"

"Because of your father's pastimes the old lady was afraid for him. How often had she said to him: 'I'm scared the books are going to carry away your mind, and that the sea is going to carry away your body.' Many times she had gone into the study and begged him to stop reading and writing, to occupy himself with things that would benefit him. But he was insistent that he was only good for writing. Next to his love for his library was his passion for the sea. He was intoxicated by the scent of fish in the same way him mother was in-toxicated by Arabic perfumes or the scent of incense."

My mother closed her eyes, and drew a deep breath, as though to inhale the scent of her loved ones.

"Your grandmother fretted constantly over your father. Not only was he her only son, he was also the last man in the family. Many of his male ancestors had disappeared at sea along with their boats a long time before, and some in other circumstances. As for those who remained, their offspring were limited to girls. The old lady blamed this situation on the witchcraft of an envious woman from a lowly family, who many years before had cursed the family with the survival of its girls over its boys. Your father didn't believe in such things, but your grandmother was absolutely convinced of it. In those distant days, your grandfather Issa and his brother Shaheen were the last of the family's remaining men. Shaheen died young without marrying, and Issa married Ghanima late in life. She gave birth to your father, Rashid, who after his father's death became the only man in the family."

As she spoke images came to my mind: men perishing at sea, sail boats struggling against fierce waves, a woman casting a spell in a darkened room, the extinction of the males, one after the other, as a result of witchcraft. Through my mother's words, my family took on a mythical aura, capturing my imagination. My mother continued to talk about my father:

"He was the only thing that made being in the old lady's house bearable. He was powerless to do anything except offer a few kind words at night, when everyone was sleeping. He'd reach into his pocket, pull out some cash and hand it to me: one, two or three dinars. Then he'd leave, and I'd have no sense of the value of the money in my hand."

"All men are scoundrels!" interrupted Aida.

My mother and I both looked at her.

"No matter how nice they seem."

My mother replied with two words: "Except Rashid."

She continued:

"One evening, in the kitchen his hand brushed against mine and he whispered in my ear: 'Don't be angry with my mother. She's an old lady and doesn't mean what she says. She's highly strung but has a good heart.' I wished he'd never take his hand away. I forgot all the old lady's insults. After that I would, from time to time, deliberately set out to make the old lady mad: dropping a glass so it smashed on the kitchen floor, and leaving the fragments scattered here and there until the morning; turning on a tap so that water gushed loudly all night; or leaving a window open on a day when the air was full of dust, allowing it to settle on the floors and furniture. By morning the old lady would be furious. She'd wake everyone in the house, screaming 'Josa!' – the name she had given me, as according to her Josephine was too hard to pronounce. She'd swear and curse, and I'd sweep up the glass from the kitchen floor and spend an entire day cleaning up the dust, waiting for the night to come, bringing with it your father's gentle hand to brush against mine."

My mother took a handkerchief and dabbed at her eyelashes, which had become heavy with tears, and continued:

"One day, in the study, he was writing his weekly article, resting his left elbow on a large file that contained the notes for his first novel. I placed a cup of coffee in front of him and said: 'Sir, I love to see you write!'

'Can't you call me anything other than "sir"?'

"I said nothing. Not for a moment did I imagine calling him by his name, Rashid, as his mother and sisters did.

" 'And don't you love anything other than to see me write?' he said.

'Is there something else?' I answered. He put his pen down on the desk, laced his fingers together and rested his chin on them. 'Something, or perhaps someone . . .' he said.

"After that, I knew I loved him, or almost did," my mother continued, "even though for him I was nothing more than a listener who he could express his ideas and beliefs to without encountering any opposition. Because I was certain he had not and would not fall in love with me, I made do with my love for him in exchange for his attention and his kindness."

## MOHAMMED HASAN ALWAN

# The Beaver

### AN EXCERPT FROM THE NOVEL,
### TRANSLATED BY PAUL STARKEY

Badriyya was not just a long-standing educational supervisor in the Girls' College, but also a sister who had appropriated most of the beaver's physical build genes, so that every year her backside got fatter and fatter. Every time I met her, I sensed it was even bigger than it had been before. She would blame cortisone, hormones and big bones, but never say more than that. Even though she was my only full sister, and we should have told each other more than we told half-brothers and sisters, we never did.

She was just a year older than me. Someone said, though, that on the first day of marriage a person ages several years all at once, and on that basis, because she had married twice, and I had never married, she would be several years older than me. And she really did behave like it.

If she hadn't married a second time, she would have kept on and on blaming me for her first divorce despite the fact it was an unconsummated marriage. The wedding was arranged while I was still only seventeen. When I went back to our house in the Murabba' Quarter I found his red car standing in front of the door – the sort of brash Cadillac they used to make in the eighties, long as a fishing boat and broad as a wrestler's shoulders. I straightaway rushed for the small stick I used to hide for no particular reason under the seat of my car and resolved to take a stand that would expedite my passage from adolescence to manhood. I smashed the car windscreen to smithereens.

My father spat expertly in my face several times, shouting "She's engaged to him, you idiot!" I pushed Badriyya in front of her husband-to-be, screaming "Go upstairs, girl!" in a sham hysterical way. When she walked past me in the direction of the staircase, I thought she'd gone upstairs, though in fact she hadn't. Meanwhile, I stared sternly into the eyes of her future husband, who returned my stare with a look of contempt. Suddenly Badriyya came up behind me, gave me a blow on the top of my back, then slapped me twice on the back of the head before I started an ill-matched fight with her in front of the husband-to-be.

The red Cadillac came back and was parked outside the door for several more nights with a new windscreen without my being able to get rid of it. Badriyya deliberately shut herself away with him in the sitting room with the door locked, as if to mock my confused manhood. My father forced me to kiss the head of her husband twice and to take a horned ram to his house by way of apology. But even so, the marriage was still not consummated.

Even now, I still don't know the precise details, but it seems that the spectacle of our little quarrel in front of him had made Badriyya look neither as beautiful as he wanted his wife to be, nor as composed as he expected. Instead, she was the sister of an impetuous young man not at all fit to be an uncle to his children when they came. Something like fate, certainly something with my features, made Badriyya separate from her husband while still a half-crazed virgin, though I don't really know why everyone pinned the responsibility on me. If I had been really impetuous I would have done things properly and smashed his head in instead of his car windscreen, but in fact I was just a young man playing the same part I had found the local boys playing and bragging about. The part disguised a spirit that had lacked confidence ever since I was born, but I had finally found some use for my coward's stick, which I covered every night with black tape like a professional fighter. It cost me a lot of pride.

Mohammed Hasan Alwan

Sometimes I think Badriyya has perhaps been the most important woman in my life, despite the fact that she is a long way from me in spirit these days. I have shared with her a cup and a salty loaf — as we say — an important period of our lives, and memories I could not share with anyone else. I am amazed both at how little we have had in common and at how powerful and influential our relationship has been. I don't think I would have chosen her as a sister, if we could choose things like that, and I don't think she would have done either. We were ensnared in a single womb that bore us in quick succession, with an unwanted father, and we grew up in a constricted atmosphere that only reluctantly embraced our sterile childhood.

My mother didn't want my father and he didn't want her. Immediately after my birth, she flew off to another man, with whom she had a better son. Badriyya insists that it was the whisper of a devil that after a time made her take fright at being married to her husband and them being turning into what our own parents had been. When the conversation reached that point she would roll her empty eyes and repeat her imprecations, as if to put an end to the discussion before a page was turned containing something she didn't want to read.

A couple of days ago, I phoned her from my apartment in Portland and listened to her begging God, in the same tone, for protection from all sorts of dangers and slanderous accusations. But this time her imprecations were longer and more eloquent, as if she had stolen them from the mouth of a preacher. After a few more minutes of the telephone conversation I became convinced that she had become a sort of "woman with a beard" and begun to dress like one of the devout. She told me that she had been able to join a religious *dhikr* circle, that she regularly went to schools for memorising the Qur'an and that she participated in voluntary classes for washing the dead.

I smiled as I looked at the Portland street before me through a window dulled by drops of rain, and imagined Badriyya in her new guise. I don't know why I imagined her crossing that street dressed like a nun, her usually unkempt hair having finally succumbed to piety, having found in God something with which to complete her unfulfilled life. She would certainly have to follow the rules, stop listening to singing and give up her tapes of 'Abd al-Karim 'Abd al-Qadir, whose patient, suffering voice had given her so much pleasure in the past.

Thirty years had gone by since I had struggled with her for one of his tapes – so passionately that we had ended up writhing on the floor, as though we were fighting for the elixir of life. We had started in her room and finished up in the rear courtyard of the Murabba' house, by way of the corridors, staircase, lounge, sitting room and kitchen. My wrists and the backs of my hands were covered in scratches from her hard nails, and her shoulders and back were bruised from my savage blows. The struggle continued for more than a quarter of an hour, as she became bluer and I became redder. Eventually, the case broke in our hands and the little spool unwound as she dragged behind her the shiny brown tape, which quickly became entangled in itself and turned into a stray ball of songs that the wind carried off to hang on the gas pipe near the rear kitchen door. Badriyya went off to her room, her mouth full of burning threats and insults, while I went straight out to the street, not turning to look at anything.

"Well then, shall I come to get all 'Abd al-Karim's tapes?" I asked her on the phone.

Badriyya gave a fake laugh as if she were not happy at the memory.

"No, I won't give you anything! Do you want me to be saddled with your sins as well?"

Her piety seemed to me like a last attempt to carve her name on a wall somewhere in the world. When I look at her life I feel as if I am looking at a documentary about a potential murderer, but luckily life hadn't given her enough anger. Divine providence rolled her onwards towards a quiet and acceptable destiny, though she was still a stranger to everything, with hardly any relationships, no preferences, no attachments, no particular appetite for anything. Not that she spoke of, anyway. Inside her, there had piled up some obscure and half-formed dreams and ambitions which she herself was unable to articulate in any meaningful way. She only knew that she was in need. So when she could, she would race ahead, and when unable to, she would simply retreat.

Our half-brother Salman had also been religious for some years. The difference was that he had done so at the beginning of his twenties while she was in her late forties. The two of them had hastened to the same lamp at most stages of their development because they needed light as they passed through a dark tunnel where no one could see them. A young man in his twenties with no voice or respect, and a woman in her forties with no history and no future.

As soon as I found that Ghada was online that evening I wrote to her: "Would you believe it? Badriyya has joined the religious police!" When she asked me why, I told her it was the custom for Riyadh to demand one sacrifice from each family but in our case it had overwhelmed us with kindness and chosen two.

"Thank God it wasn't you that was the victim, or I couldn't stand it . . ."

"Everything is still possible. Riyadh isn't full yet . . ."

"Ha! God protect us! Thank God I'm from Jeddah!"

"Don't you have sacrifices in Jeddah?"

"God, I've no idea. I've been away a long time. Let me see how things stand when I go back!"

Salman had escaped while still young from the mould he had almost become stuck in, though he continued to bear traces of a picture it is hard to erase. But would Badriyya manage that? She was on her final lap, and there was no scope for further adventures. If I gave her my advice, she would give me a sermon, and if I made fun of her she would cut me off for several months. She only phoned me at all because she believed it was unacceptable for siblings to desert each other in this life. Otherwise . . . Anyway, nothing would convince Badriyya that she was doing exactly the right thing more than if I opposed it. In her eyes, I was the measure of life reversed.

# SINAN ANTOON

# Hail Mary

## AN EXCERPT FROM THE NOVEL,
## TRANSLATED BY MAIA TABET

"You're living in the past, Uncle!" Maha exclaimed angrily as she ran out of the living-room after our argument. Her husband, Lu'ayy, was upset and his face was flushed. "Hey Maha, where are you going? Come here! Maha!" he called out after her but she was already hurtling up the stairs that led to the second floor.

His eyes were sad as he apologized. "Forgive her, Uncle. You know how much she loves and respects you. She can't help it, she's a nervous wreck," he said, his voice tinged with shame.

Before I could think of anything to say, the sound of her fitful sobbing reached us from the second floor.

"It's all right. It's not a big deal. Go calm her down, and comfort her," I mumbled.

Sinan Antoon

Maha's husband got up from the grey sofa where they had both been seated and came towards the chair set smack in front of the television. Placing his hand on my shoulder, he leaned down and kissed the top of my head.

"I'm so sorry," he said, adding, "I owe you one." He turned away and slowly climbed the stairs.

The voices of a host and his guest in heated discussion boomed from the TV. Although I was seated right in front of it, their faces seemed hazy, as if they were fading away, and I really couldn't make out what they were saying. All I could hear were the words ringing in my ears. "You're just living in the past, Uncle!"

## 2

I didn't sleep well that night. I tossed in the dark as Maha's stinging pronouncement played over and over in my head. I kept asking myself whether I really did live in the past, but all I could come up with were further questions. How could someone my age, to some degree or another, not live in the past? Being eighty years old, most of my life was behind me and very little of it still lay ahead. She was in her early twenties and, however gloomy the present may be, she had her whole future before her. She was kindhearted and well-intentioned, but she was only half-formed. Just like her past. She too would begin to revisit the past once it had grown a little, and she would also dwell on it for hours – were it to be made up of nothing but misery. Her wounds would heal and she would only retain the good things. In any case, for me to stop living in it, the past would have to be dead – and it wasn't. The past was alive and well, in one form or another, and it not only co-habited with the present but continued to wrestle with it. Or was it merely being held captive inside the framed photographs hanging on the wall and in our albums? Hadn't she stood before them often enough and asked me to point out members of the family and asked what had happened to them, where they were now, how they had died? And when? How often had she asked me to tell her the stories contained within those picture frames? I had always responded to her questions readily, coloring in the details and following threads that sometimes led to other photos or to other stories that had not been captured by the camera – stories intertwined with sighs of pleasure or laughter that were lodged in my memory, and others preserved in an archive guarded by the heart.

Did I really escape the present and seek refuge in the past, as she alleged? And even if it were true, what shame was there in it? What else was there in the times we lived besides ambushes and explosive devices, killing and horror? Perhaps the past was like the garden which I so loved and which I tended as if it were my own daughter just to escape the noise and ugliness of the world. My own paradise in the heart of hell, my own "autonomous region" as I liked to call it at times. I would do anything to defend that garden, and the house that went with it, because that was all I had left.

I really had to forgive her. My youth was not her youth, her time and my time were worlds apart. War and sanctions were what her green eyes beheld when they had fluttered open, and her earliest tastes of life were deprivation, violence and displacement. I, on the other hand, had lived in prosperous times which I still remembered and continued to believe were real.

## 3

I woke at six thirty, as I had done for many years without using an alarm clock. My bladder, which woke me up several times a night, was all the alarm clock I needed. I washed my face and shaved in front of the mirror in the bathroom next to my bedroom, without intoning a favorite song – which is what I would normally do – as I wanted to recapture the details of my dream. I took my dentures out of their glass of water, opened my mouth and secured them in place. I had lost all my teeth years ago and eventually grew used to the dentures after being bothered by them for a good while. I was proud to still have a full head of thick, though white, hair. Anything was better than being bald.

In the dream, I had gone bald and that alone made me feel as if the dream had been more of a nightmare. The house was the same in every particular, except that it was a museum. Each room had become a hall, with the chairs and beds cordoned off and signs everywhere warning visitors not to touch or get too close. I was the docent, and as I recounted the history of each room, I explained who had lived there and where they had gone. Although I heard people whispering and giggling, no-one was around. I went from hall to hall looking for visitors but they were all empty. Then, I heard the voice of another man and I saw him leading a group of visitors down the hallway and giving them faulty information about the house. I went up to them and shouted: "This is my house, and I am the docent here." But no-one heard me or took any notice of me. I looked in the mirror and saw I was bald.

I combed my hair and thanked my lucky stars I still had all my hair. I opened my eyes wide and peered into my face in the mirror, raising my thick grey eyebrows slowly and crunching the wrinkles that time had painted on my forehead. I stepped back from the mirror and dried my face and forehead once again.

On my way from the bathroom to the kitchen to make tea, I stopped in front of the hallway calendar just as I had done for years. I never gave up the habit, even after I had retired and there was no business to attend to or any appointments to keep. I would stop in the hallway every day and use the pencil hanging by a thread from the nail holding up the calendar; I would cross out the previous day to signal the beginning of a new one. I looked at the photograph for that month: there was an empty bench with a few yellowed leaves lying on the paving stones in front of it; a fall wind had blown the leaves down from a nearby tree, whose only visible part was the trunk. Below the photograph, only one day remained, the last day of the month of October 2010, which was a Sunday. "Hinnah's passing" I had written into the small square. Truth be told, I needed no reminder of the day my sister had left us, on a morning like this one seven years ago. I had been to the church earlier in the month and asked the priest to offer a prayer for the repose of her soul on the anniversary of her death, and I had also agreed to pay an extra tithe. The special service would not take place at the sanctuary of the convent where my sister went for decades and which had become her second home. The convent had closed its doors to worshippers for security reasons, and so the special service would be held at what was popularly known as Umm al-Taq, the Cathedral of Our Lady of Deliverance. It was the church Maha and her husband attended on Sundays because he was a Syriac Catholic. Hinnah would not mind the service being held there rather than at "our" Chaldean church, as she called it. The differences between the two were insignificant: both were Eastern Catholic denominations and the liturgy was almost identical, except for a few words here and there. And in the final analysis, the prayers were all addressed to the same God, regardless of language or denomination, and that's what counted.

Hinnah always got up before I did and made tea for the two of us. Her breakfast was very simple: a piece of bread with a little white or yellow cheese, a spoonful of the apricot or fig jam that she loved and made herself, and two glassfuls of tea. She would leave the teapot sitting on the kettle on the burner, with the flame turned all the way down so that the tea would still be hot when I woke up and was ready to drink it. Then, she would walk to church. Her walking had worsened in recent years, she moved slowly and only with the help of a cane. She wouldn't hear of waking me up so I could give her a ride to the church and she wouldn't listen when I suggested that she should go just on Sundays instead of every day. She could be quite hard-headed, especially when it came to her religious observances.

When I went into the kitchen that morning, I saw that Hinnah had not made the tea. The teapot lay upturned on the dish drainer by the sink, just as it had been the previous night after we'd had our evening tea. I assumed she was feeling out of sorts, and so I filled the kettle, placed it on the right-hand burner and lit a match under it. I put two generous tablespoons of tea leaves in the teapot, moistened them with a few drops of water, covered the pot and placed it on top of the kettle, and waited for the water to boil before pouring it over the leaves. I walked away from the kitchen and went to her room at the end of the hallway, just by the door to the back garden. Her door was shut. I rapped three times, calling her name. "Hinnah, Hinnah, Hinnah, dear . . ." There was no answer. I gently turned the doorknob and opened the door as quietly as I could. She was still in bed. The curtains were drawn to, but the morning sun filtered through the gaps in the middle and at the sides. I stepped inside the room, which I rarely entered, and pressed on the light switch to the right of the door. Nothing. I remembered her telling me the day before that the bulb had burned out and needed replacing, and although I said I would take care of it, I hadn't; I blamed myself for having put off fetching the ladder from the storeroom, but my knee hurt whenever I had to climb up and change the bulbs. What with all the power outages and trying to save on using the electric generator, I had rationalized that we would just use candles at night. Putting off this sort of thing was clearly never a good idea. I called out once more. "Hinnah, what's wrong? Get up! Come on, Hinnah!" I went to the window on the right and pushed open the curtains. The sun flooded into the open space at the center of the room. I covered my eyes from the glare, turned around and went towards the bed. She was lying on her left side, with the quilt drawn up over her shoulders. Approaching the edge of the bed, I looked at her intently. Her eyes were closed and a few strands of her silvery hair lay matted by her face on the pillow. Her hands were clasped together at the bottom edge of the pillow on the right of her face, with the rosary wrapped around them; this rosary never left her and was made of tiny red beads whose rhythmical clicking sound accompanied all her prayers and invocations. She must have kissed it before falling asleep because the small silver cross at its tip was resting on her lips. I leant over and shook her shoulder, gently repeating her name: "Hinnah, Hinnah." She didn't stir. Her shoulder felt rigid and there was a waxy pallor to the criss-cross of wrinkles that mapped her face. "Hinnah, Hinnah dear," I repeated quietly. I tried to take her pulse but her right hand was all tangled up in her left and in the rosary. My heart sank. She felt cold to the touch and I knew in that instant she would not wake up. I circled my hand around her wrist with the tip of my finger against her vein, but my index finger could not pick up a pulse.

That night life had gathered its last vestiges and vacated Hinnah's body, leaving it now to death's undivided attention. The good Lord had granted the wish she had often repeated over the years, especially at odious and painful moments. "Dear God," she would exclaim, "take me to you, and relieve me!" She always wished others a long life but for herself only sought its curtailment. "No more, Lord. Let me be done!" she would say.

I sat on the edge of the bed. I wanted to embrace her one last time, but only stroked her silvery hair with my left hand. I hardly ever touched or kissed her, maybe once or twice a year on the occasion of a holiday. The last time I remembered stroking her hair was when I was still a child. We had lost our mother, and despite Hinnah's tender age, it was to her that fell the task of caring for my younger brothers and me. She was only fifteen when she had to give up her dream of entering the convent, and she devoted the rest of her life to ensuring we were comfortable and had enough to eat. Her duties discharged, whatever time was left she spent in religious devotion, either at home or at church. I released her rigid hand to wipe away the tears that had begun to run down my cheeks. I kissed her cold forehead and said out loud, as if she could hear me: "Rest in peace, Hinnah."

A picture of the Virgin Mary hung above Hinnah's bed in which the mother of Jesus appeared, full of grace, holding the fruit of her womb against her robes of blue. A shaft of celestial light pierced the sky above and angels circled around her, wings aflutter. Despite the beatitude of her features, there was a sad cast to the eyes looking down towards my sister and me.

The tears flowed as I prayed for Hinnah's soul. I intoned "Our Father who art in heaven" just as she had done for me over the course of an entire lifetime. And I followed the prayer with "Hail Mary, full of grace. Our Lord is with thee. Blessed art thou among women, and blessed is the fruit of thy womb, Jesus. Holy Mary, Mother of God, pray for us sinners, now and at the hour of our death. Amen."

## JANA FAWAZ ELHASSAN

# Me, Her and the Other Women

AN EXCERPT FROM THE NOVEL,
TRANSLATED BY GHENWA HAYEK

## 8

Whenever I try to clutch at a tangible memory of my relationship with my husband, I seem to be standing before a room that is locked, chained off and difficult to access. I don't know the reason for this. Perhaps it is because his entrance into my life was so confounding for me. Perhaps I only grew attached to him in order to obtain a visible presence for myself, one which was grounded in reality and in my thirst for life, and would be far far removed from the tangible world I lived in alone. He was the physical manifestation of a sexual desire I could recognize, but was never, not once, the desire I was trying to achieve. He would lay me on the bed and kiss me hungrily, and I would imagine him trying to consume as much of my body as he could. He took me rapidly, before I had time to even gain awareness of my state. Often, I would be on the verge of tears as he lay over me. How I wished he would pause for a moment, and prepare me with just a sliver of tenderness. But he was always in a hurry to take control. He was incapable of making love slowly, as if the extra time might reveal how far apart we in fact were. As if it might allow the truth that our intimacy was not real to seep out.

*Jana Fawaz Elhassan*

In the span of a few moments, I would become a tiny kitten waiting for the giant lorry barreling down a narrow road to crush it. It was as if I could hear the roar of the engine and as if I were surrendering to death by terror in the face of an impending onslaught.

Such was the reality of my relationship with him. Compared with my impressions, which were gorged in images that seemed closer to fantasy, it had become a huge disappointment. However, I buried all my feelings of anger alongside the sorrows of my childhood. I told myself real life was completely different from the world of dreams, that reality must be endured, not changed. Bit by bit I became my mother, the one woman I had refused to become.

Several times, I would look in the mirror and feel I had become hideous. It wasn't that I was becoming featureless, that I was losing my form, as I had felt in the years of despair I had lived through. No, I was becoming something dark and rotting. I had swelled up in myself till I had exploded, and become a bundle of ugliness drowning in a wave of disdain. I wanted to leave my self, extinguish her in some way so that I could match my life, so that I wouldn't resemble her. Now, I no longer know if I was seeing myself, or that Other. Why did my features change depending on the circumstances and faces I encountered? Does a woman need a man's affirmation for her beauty to become whole?

I knew Sami was pursuing me, and I wanted to hide in any way possible what his fear of me provoked. It was as if he knew that I masturbated in secret, and so with him I could stop being that blank slate, to be coloured any way he wanted, and become my own, multi-coloured creation. Now I know that I grabbed onto him because I sought in him the affirmation I had not received from my parents. That affirmation was so much more important than its consequences – the annihilation of that self whose depths I had never known.

I was prepared to endure anything for that permanent piece of paper, the contract, the feeling of being tied down and on the safe side of existence. I pretended before him, giving him that absolute power which he needed, to feel as if he possessed me. And he snatched away from me any identity separate from his. He gained the power to form me and mould me however he wanted.

While my husband seemed to grow calmer as his control over everything tightened, he became increasingly anxious when he felt any danger or threat, he felt I could escape him even for a moment or that he wasn't my one priority or center. He fretted that some of my thoughts did not come directly from him, or that I could have an idea which undermined his absolute dominance, since it could mean that some of what he said could be wrong.

My attachment to Sami became more pronounced in my mother's presence. I cannot forget the day she came to visit and revealed her loathing of a painting in the dining room. Suddenly, it seemed as if she were mounting a revolution, and she began to fume against the painting hanging in our dining room. She hated it because it made reality more beautiful. When I told her that that painting turned life into a slice of Swiss roll, she snapped back that paintings tried to make us believe the the world is devoid of disaster, destruction, and despair, and this angered her. During the outburst, she seemed more miserable than anything I could imagine. I wept that day, imagining her being consumed by scorpions.

My husband pounced when she had gone, delighted to see me suffering on account of my family. He spoke badly about my mother, and I was powerless to respond or argue because at that moment, I felt like an orphaned child, bereft of any family. Puffed up and pompous he would follow every movement I made and come towards me with a lecherous look in his eyes, as if my body had no refuge but him. Stripped bare of any pleasure, I submitted. During those times I would be that body, that nothingness that he could transform whichever way he wanted – into an image, perhaps, or perhaps just a shell.

After that, he would deliberately bring up the fact that my father was not religious, telling me about the men of his family who wrote out Qur'anic manuscripts until their fingers bled, and who had built one of the finest mosques in the city with their own hands. Sami had an old, faded picture of his family patriarchs, most of them puffy-cheeked, shaved-head effendis who wore red fezzes with black tassels and heavy baggy sherwals wrapped around their bellies. He made fun of my father who was somewhat short, had nostrils as hairy and dark as caves, and thick eyebrows, one of which was always raised higher than the other, as if in interrogation or mockery. I stayed silent, refusing to take the bait, since if I showed any sign of emotion, I would enter the labyrinth of terse conversation he was trying to drag me into.

For an instant, I would be overtaken by the desire to curse him or mock his family but I remained silent, letting my other self go about the business of cursing him in silence, out of earshot. And so Sami slowly changed from the liberator I had drowned myself in into a man I despised. I wished I could liberate myself from the part of my self that was trapped inside him, that creation of his that I had become.

When I lost him from inside myself, my own self sprang out from somewhere I did not know. I became more intimate with myself, seeking out the details of other modes of existence. Sami's other face began to reveal itself, and I began to see clearly what I had been unable to understand when I was seeking refuge. I married him as a woman only half aware, a woman with no self, and I had allowed him to seep into me, enduring his madness and anger without understanding them.

I spent hours on the balcony watching the labourers feverishly working, their bodies sweating, moving as if dancing over stones. I watched them, shirtless, wild-haired, in constant motion. I envied them; they had no time to sink into their thoughts for hours like I did. They were moulded from life and sunshine, and there I was, dreaming. I would wait warily for Sami's return home, overcome by fear when I heard his steps on the landing. I would rush from the balcony and run inside, pretending to be busy with housework.

During the long hours he spent at home, I would leave the house to throw out the trash, taking each step down as slowly as possible. Before climbing back up, I would spend a few minutes with my back against the wall, staring at my Russian neighbour who swept her balcony day and night. I wondered why this woman who – as my mother put it, had come from the land of freedom and prostitutes – had got married. I watched all my neighbours, the older ladies and their modern young daughters, and I questioned why we had been raised with the idea that a woman could not take part in public life, and why they kept us women away from the world, even after our sons were born.

From my first pregnancy onwards, I was committed to living for my sons. That was what was expected of me, and I did not dare to defy expectations. I became another copy of my mother, but even harsher. My father's dismissal from his job had resulted in his wife being diminished, and fading, while Sami's utter possession of me, his absolute power over me, and his constant beatings had transformed me into nothing more than a source of sustenance and nourishment to others. My mother was consumed by her desires, which embalmed her like a mute mummy buried in the depths of the earth, but I was ruled by an inner hunger and before I even knew of desire, I become an instrument with which to please Sami and annihilate myself. With him, I could only reach the stench of death. What else could I have been since he had transformed me into a grey body, consumed hurriedly and inured to abuse?

I often wondered whether it was every woman's fate to weep into her pillow once her husband was asleep because she wasn't sure whether she existed or not. Do the fates of women only depend on their husbands' characters? I compared the tears of my mother to those I shed today and could not believe my life had become so miserable.

## 9

I met the man who became my husband late. During the beginning of the relationship, I was nothing but cautious. Had he known I harboured all these fears, had he discovered the shortcoming in my personality, I would not have been able to marry him. However, I did nothing but be receptive towards him, cautiously and calmly. In truth, I didn't really give him a single glance before tying myself to him. He swept me away from the tide of nothingness I was drowning in. In those first nights of our early encounters, I would fall asleep on a cloud, dreaming of everything I would gain from my upcoming marriage – including liberty and existence.

My husband's true character first revealed itself through his utter rejection of my father's communist beliefs, and his insistence on reminding me that my father was a worthless piece of trash for giving me an atheist upbringing. He spoke of him as if he were a speck of dust or mould, as if his actions would never – could never – be forgiven. He asked me questions with the single-mindedness of an inquisitor, reducing me to tears, forcing me to tell him that he was right, that his ancestors, who were like pieces of antique furniture, were treasures the like of which would never be found again, that he, like his elders, was an inimitable man, and that I knew I should thank my lucky stars every day that I had found him. He had to compare my father to a parasite that had infected my childhood and youth, so he could ensure I shared nothing of my father's 'different' ideas.

Sami always asked about my father's Christian friends and how they practised their religion, and whether we had ever eaten in their homes. I told him of the visits we had made a few times to the mountain village of Bsharre in winter. I described watching snowflakes quietly filling the sky and how at peace they made me. He listened to my story with a child's hunger, then his mood would suddenly change as if he had remembered he shouldn't admire anything related to my past.

"Did he just sit in his office all day long?"

"Yes."

"Did you sit with him?"

"No, but I sometimes snuck in."

"Why?"

"To see what he was reading."

"Do you think there's any point in reading?"

"Sort of."

"He never once tried to pray?"

"No."

"He never went to the mosque on Friday?"

"No, never."

"And your mother?"

"I think she was more religious than he was."

"Did he forbid her from praying?"

"No, but she never told him she enjoyed praying."

"Did he have visitors?"

"No, hardly anyone, ever."

"And you, did you see his friends?"

"No. Why do you keep insisting on talking about my father's life?"

"Because the neighbors say things about him."

"But you know they're lying."

"Sheikhs don't lie, and they don't like him."

Before I could express my discomfort at his questions, he would ask me to come closer and make love to him. After questioning like this, he knew he had stripped me bare of everything – of excuses to defend my family, of my faith, of my lack of faith, of my body, of my being. That made his mission of absolute domination over me easier, because I was far too weak to resist.

Every time he entered me in moments following such conversations, I felt he was snatching me from my father's lap and making me into his own obedient doll. Eventually, the only feeling I had when our bodies connected was that I was a huge black void in life, a woman without a smell, a branch snapped off a tree and thrown to the ground, to be trampled on by passers-by.

## IBRAHIM ISSA

# Our Master

AN EXCERPT FROM THE NOVEL,
TRANSLATED BY RUTH AHMEDZAI

She was dabbing powder on his forehead with the deft fingers of a professional, hoping he would be pleased, as she said: "There we are, Sheikh."

Hatem laughed.

"God bless you, sister Georgette," he replied.

Anwar Osman repeated the same tiresome question that he had

been asking over and over since Hatem became his main guest on the programme a year ago.

"How do you think the faithful feel when they come and stand in prayer behind you and study your words, and they see that our Sheikh Hatem puts on make-up before filming?"

"Brother," replied Hatem firmly, "the Prophet, peace be upon him, used to dye his hair with henna and line his eyes with kohl. Shut up, Anwar, and stop those pesky questions of yours!"

Sheikh Hatem couldn't stand Anwar. It had been that way since he first saw him, when Al-Dunya TV station had invited him to be a regular guest on their new programme. They had pitched him the line that, as popular as his lectures and classes were, with his dedicated disciples filling halls up to the rafters to hear him teach and preach, his impact was limited to his congregation and to young people. This daily programme, on the other hand, took questions from viewers of all ages, from every generation and social class, and would bring him a much wider audience. He wasn't quite convinced by this argument, as he himself could see the crowds, the cross-section of society who attended his sermon every Friday at the Sultan Hassan Mosque. They crammed noisily into every corner of the huge space which could hold thousands of worshippers, not to mention those gathering outside the mosque and in the surrounding area. And then there were the hundreds of men and women who flocked to his father's house in the citadel district every Tuesday seeking blessings, advice and alms. The TV channel executives had managed to persuade him to take the job, with the lure of a tempting salary, but right from the start Anwar seemed to him to have something insect-like about him and he told them so.

"He's like a pesky fly that gets into the car when you put the air conditioning on and forces you to open the window to get it out. It sits on the glass buzzing away, so you assume it wants to get out, but as soon as you open the window it comes flying right back at you or falls asleep on the back of your neck."

They laughed at the way he said this so solemnly, in the same voice he used for reciting the Qur'an and with the enthusiasm normally reserved for the Prophet's hadith. His actual words came as a bit of a surprise. They seemed to enjoy his observations and were probably glad to realise that, though he was a preacher and a mufti, he was not averse to the occasional cheeky comment and had physical needs like anyone else. It was as if they could relax in the knowledge that these sheikhs were not in fact close to God, but close to them. Hatem was well aware of the image people had of Sheikhs, and every witty remark he made was like graffiti defacing the stereotype, as though he were casting off his dignity as a mufti. The strange thing was that he enjoyed it; he liked doing it and he liked the reaction. Somewhere deep down inside, he longed to disfigure the image of the Sheikh as it was perceived in people's minds, and through the lens of a camera. That very day, he had already found himself chafing against the role fate had determined for him. He had been sitting on the second floor of his house in the citadel which had been turned into a large, open seating area. It was regularly teeming with visitors, all eager to see him for advice, fatwas, charity, mediation with officials or a reference for a job.

In the quiet of the early hours, he was just about to set off for the dawn prayer along with the small group that still remained, when his father came for him and led him to the only private room at the end of the hall. He sat him down in front of him, both of them exhausted. He saw in his father's features the same ambiguous expression that he had long struggled to decipher. Between them stood the pain of when his father had taken a second wife – a divorcée twenty-five years his junior. Then, Hatem had still been in the early days of his media appearances and was only a preacher at a state mosque, although he was already impressing worshippers with his eloquence: the mosque was starting to fill up and people were recording his sermons on tape. Throughout those years, he had buried the pain of his father's actions deep within and neither of them had uttered a word about the marriage. Neither of them confronted it nor could even consider confronting it, not even when his mother came to him, broken and dejected, and told him that his father's new wife was pregnant and that her daughters, his four sisters, had decided to boycott the house. None of them would ever again bring her family to visit. He had remained silent and embraced his mother that day, immersing himself in the primordial intensity of the relationship between a mother and son, something untamed in his carefully structured life. Later, his father's second wife gave birth to a stillborn child. Hatem found out when he was in the studio recording a programme, and in front of the lighting technicians, camera men and studio audience, he had said out loud: "All this medicine and science . . . and still we have children dying as they come out of their mother's bellies. Our Lord does like to remind us that we're nothing!"

He treated the matter lightly at the time, but it always came back to haunt him. Even now he felt a crushing pain on seeing his father. Drained by sadness and grief, his father seemed physically healthy but psychologically broken. He was entering his eighties and had left behind any desire to engage with the

Ibrahim Issa

world. There in that room, shortly before the dawn prayer and after a long night receiving visitors, Hatem had a rare moment of sitting together with his father, at his request. He felt like the door of destiny had been pushed ajar and there was something new, or renewed, asking permission to enter.

"What's wrong, Hatem?" his father asked.

"What do you mean, Dad?" he replied.

"What's the matter with you? Why can't you believe that you're a Sheikh?"

He was taken aback by the observation. It wasn't because it was so out of the blue or because it had struck a nerve, but, rather, because it had come from someone he had presumed for the last five years was content merely to observe from afar.

"What makes me a Sheikh, Dad?" he countered.

"Well, if you're not a Sheikh, then what are you? You've memorised the Qur'an, you're always reciting it, leading prayers and giving sermons, you memorise fatwas and deliver your own, you're full of stories from the Prophet's life . . . all of that definitely qualifies you to be a Sheikh, no doubt about it. And your success with people puts you at the forefront of them all."

Hatem sighed and then revealed something that he'd never truly admitted even to himself: "Does all of that make me a Sheikh? I suppose it does sound like a Sheikh's job description. But I'm not sure. I'm just trading in what I know." He put his arm around his father, murmuring: "All right, Dad. Shall we say the dawn salat together? I can recite Sura Yasin if you like?"

"No, no need," his father replied, earnestly. "But I'd love you to finish the salat with the dawn prayer. You do that so nicely."

"OK," he laughed, touched by his father's opinion of him. "I should have a show called 'The Prayers Request Show'!"

The lighting suddenly came on more brightly and the make-up lady finished powdering Anwar's forehead and cheeks. Anwar straightened his tie and checked his fly before turning to the director.

"Medhat, does my tie look OK? Is it straight?"

Sheikh Hatem no longer felt the shiver of nerves creeping up his throat or the contractions wrapping around his stomach just before they were about to go live on air. He shouted to the control room, where the director sat with his assistants grunting commands and prompts, or soothing words, into Anwar's ears through the tiny headset buried in his ear and attached to a wire coiled around his back.

"Guys, can someone put a picture of me on the monitor so I can check. Quickly, otherwise I'll ask God to curse you!"

They all burst out laughing. Then, after seeing his picture on the screen and being quite reassured, he heard the director's voice. "OK, we're ready to go, Mr Anwar, Sheikh Hatem. Ready in three – two –, one – , roll."

Anwar smiled and, somehow looking better than he normally did, began.

"Good evening, ladies and gentlemen. Peace and God's mercy and blessings be upon you and welcome to another episode of our programme. Today we have with us the preacher and Islamic scholar Sheikh Hatem Shinawi." As he turned to his guest, the camera zoomed in and showed Hatem smiling and nodding.

"And peace be upon you, too, my brother Anwar. I look forward to your questions, sir. Let's see if you've set any traps for us tonight!" They both laughed.

Contemplating the red light that illuminated a rectangle above the camera, Hatem had the sense of being in an enhanced state of readiness, like troops lined up for review. It was this light that, the instant it was turned on, unleashed the latent potential of its colour. Washed with this blood-red tinge, everything was tainted: human beings were reduced to mere objects to be inspected on television. It forced an introvert out of his shell, lent solemnity to the depraved and dignity to the farcical, added a veneer of respect to those fallen from grace. Hatem had never suffered from the awkwardness most feel when facing this light for the first time. Many people needed time before they adapted to the red light, before they were transformed and could move about comfortably in its glow. They waited like inanimate objects for the light above the camera to bring them to life the second the live broadcast began; they needed this command before they adopted their new persona, wearing another's clothes or assuming the voice or soul of another, which enabled them to sit there in a captive pose of homage to this entrancing light.

But this was Sheikh Hatem. From the first instance, he was fully at ease with it, as though already trained to perform or as though every step he took in his daily life were bathed in this red light. Whether he was at the pulpit or delivering a lecture, on Facebook or on his website, in the company of friends or those who came to study and pray with him, in a restaurant or relaxing at home – he was always in the red spotlight. Even in his car, people would gather round wanting to greet him and shake his hand, praising him, asking him for a blessing or firing questions at him. Like a famous storyteller performing on a street corner, being coaxed into telling another joke, he would find himself surrounded by crowds lurking out of curiosity, hankering after his informed opinion on one thing or another. He even basked in this red light when he went to the bathroom in a restaurant or when he parked his car at his apartment block and had to fight his way through the swarms of security guards and doormen. They would try to push their way into the lift with him, desperate to experience his presence first hand and be able to go home and tell their friends and family they had been blessed with his close proximity, reporting back every detail of the way he whispered or laughed or scowled or walked. For Hatem, this red light seemed to occupy the space between his soul and his body – and Hatem was confused about whether there was an imaginary gap between the two or whether they somehow touched – and it compelled him to obey. As he could never be sure if someone might be looking on, watching and witnessing his life, he tended to his appearance constantly, glancing up every now and then at the ceiling of his bedroom, as though waiting for the crimson light to flash on, turning him into the self that was open for display. The result was that his real self seemed to have gone astray, and he was no longer sure he would recognise it or its distinguishing features, making him resort permanently to this other self, the reassuring, well-trained performing self. This was why his relatives – who longed to cling to the bond they once had with his rarely seen original self – found him strangely silent. They found the silence of a talkative man strange, just as he too found his own silence strange, though it helped save his energy for facing the moments in the real red spotlight. After all, he needed to be in good shape and fully alert to obey orders to do this and that and go here and there. One day he discovered it was no longer him but rather the well-trained beast of the red light who appeared in the company of his father and his sisters. It had reached the point where the question of his self filled him with such doubts that he no longer knew if Hatem Shinawi had become an entirely new person, replacing the old one altogether, or if he had just become so well-versed and proficient at performing to the red light that he barely seemed the same man he once was.

## HUSSEIN AL-WAD

# His Excellency, the Minister

AN EXCERPT FROM THE NOVEL,
TRANSLATED BY JOHN PEATE

M y wife had become royal mistress to a housemaid, cook and gardener, with a car and driver to take care of her own needs, and the children's too. The children had shunned going to school by car to begin with, but then soon got so used to it that they never left the house till a few minutes before lessons. Riding in a car was better than walking every time. The gardener would make tea and sit himself down in the shade and the

sun, my little garden stretched
out in front of him, not a veg-
etable, tree or flower to be
seen. The maid had presented
my wife with a list of necessities
for her work: a washer, a drier
and a vacuum cleaner. The cook
had nothing to do but spin my
wife tales and gossip – amusing
to her; silly, trivial and boring
to me. I meant to tell my wife
to keep a certain distance be-
tween herself and the maid –
since a minister's wife is a dig-
nitary herself, of course – but I
didn't want to hurt her feelings inadvertently.

Hussein al-Wad

My wife, immersed in her schemes for the house, said: "Let's add
another bedroom and extend the lounge." I took no notice, wrapped
up in ministerial affairs. "Did you hear me?" she said. I looked
around in surprise, only for my eyes to land on her huge, sagging
chest. My secretary's rather firm, fulsome one flitted through my
mind. I had noticed, after my initial display of reserve towards her,
that although she began to come to the office dressed modestly, no
sooner had she sat down at her desk than she would loosen the trans-
parent silk scarf she wore over her usually demure clothing to reveal
the large expanse of her chest. When she caught my gaze lingering
on the wellspring of those breasts of hers she began to come to my
office more frequently. She would loosen her blouse even more and
contrive, when handing me files, to lean over in such a way as to
reveal the full glory of their full, supple roundness. My eyes were
totally transfixed sometimes by their fulsomeness, firecrackers pop-
ping away in my head. I contemplated my wife's sagging chest and
felt disgust. Is this the same chest which was once so beautifully
adorned with those two firm pomegranates, whose stalks I used to
amuse myself with? I used to sing hymns to them – snatches of that
lewd popular tune my wife and I loved so much; a song recounting
every inch of a woman's body with tremendous relish. She wanted
me to sing it to her, but would always ask: "Where on earth did you
learn it? I'd never heard anything like it before . . . ever!" And I

would say: "It comes from the secret coffers of the people's genius."

When I heard His Excellency the President wanted to see me, anxiety took hold, started gnawing away at me, instantly, intensely. I had barely been sworn in before him in the blink of an eye just a few days before, so what would he want from me now? Word was relayed to me from the presidential office: "Tomorrow you are to be afforded an interview with His Excellency the President at 10 am. Arrive around nine."

I have not even acquainted myself with the remit of my ministry. What would I say to the President? I spent most of the night in the office with my head of civil service, thinking, mulling it over, writing texts, comparing texts to texts, numbers to numbers. I found out my assistant was highly skilled which, despite his repellent appearance, made him seem to me extremely pleasant. I rang my cousin, who said: "It would be normal to acquaint his excellency with any suggestions you might have."

In the morning, I ran off to the palace. The advisory minister and official presidential spokesman welcomed me. A scheming and a shrewd man, he was the type of man whose words and expression on his face always told you nothing of what he was thinking. He could pinch you while smiling, and twist the knife deeper without appearing to even twitch. After a long and mechanical speech on the importance to the President of the trust he placed in his aides, he asked: "What will you say to him if he asks after your ministry?" I started to reel off the information I had memorised the evening before. "What if he questions you about matters unrelated to your ministry?" he asked. I said: "I'll reply with what I know and what I believe to be true." He fired back a blunt: "No!" Then explained: "I would advise you not to. We must not tell His Excellency anything other than His Excellency would love to hear. Never spoil the joy of his days with troubles. That would also harm the national interest." I didn't understand him and asked: "What will I say to His Excellency, then?" He replied: "You tell him everything is going well. That things could not be better thanks to his conviviality, sophistication, great wisdom and good fortune." I remained silent, imploring God not to let the President ask me about anything beyond my ministry.

I was ushered in to see him, knees trembling in panic. He simply said: "Welcome." He was looking at a computer screen I couldn't see, reading away to himself. Then he turned to me and said: "You used to be a teacher, didn't you?" I said: "Yes, Mr President, may favour be upon you." He said: "How have you found the ministry?" I replied: "Your confidence in me and my association with your prestige and pleasure is beyond everything I could have hoped for." He almost smiled and then said: "Clever, these wordmongers." I couldn't make out approval from disapproval in this phrase. Then he said: "Slowness and steadiness is the key. I don't like either impetuosity or complacency." He then returned to his screen.

I don't know if there was some secret buzzer or if it had been pre-arranged, but his advisory minister and spokesman entered and showed me out. He sat me down in front of him and quizzed me as to what the President had said to me and what I told him. I then headed back, still understanding nothing. My blood pressure was up. I was almost back at my ministry, when my cousin came up to me. He asked me about the meeting so I said: "Good as could be expected." He straightaway wanted more details, so I replayed it all, second by second, step by step. He didn't comment. I found it too difficult to tell him how anxious this interview had made me. I was about to go to my office when he said: "Speed up on your work. The President wants results." I almost said: "What work? Which results? I still don't understand anything. Give me the medicine even if it tastes bad." Then I fell silent.

I sat in my office thinking it over, this meeting, trying to work out what it meant to no avail. Anxiety gnawed away at me. My nerves were shot. I gave up on it all. What did they want from me? What were the right words for a minister – any minister – to say to the President so as not to trouble his days or upset his wise equanimity? Was that normally how he met with his ministers? I was at a loss, deep in thought, when my civil servant came in with his files. I tried to disguise what I felt, but couldn't. I listened to him without understanding a single word. Then I said: "I need you tonight from ten. Go home early and come back quickly."

Time was drawing on heavily towards evening and my anxiety was mounting. I had to put together some clear ideas about my ministry to shock them all with something no one expected.

My temples were almost boiling.

My secretary must have noticed my inner turmoil. She instantly sent the driver off to fetch me a cool drink to revive me. I really appreciated that from her. She came in with assorted files to show me and phone messages to pass on. She would put the files in front of me on the desk and remain standing to my right, her perfume wafting over me as she bent to turn over the pages. My hand touched the back of her leg and rested there, brushing it gently. She smiled and leant further forward, a lock of her hair brushing my face. I was suddenly overtaken by her proximity. I ran my palm higher up to her thigh. Then higher, like my heartbeat. I got up. She signalled with her finger for me to keep quiet. She went to the main door and locked it. She went to her office to make sure it was empty and locked that as well. She came back in, locking the connecting door between her office and mine. She turned out all the lights but rushed lightly over and lit up every everything within my troubled self.

Is it my fault, Your Honour, if my interview with His Excellency made anxiety triumph over self-control like this? Is it my fault if my secretary has such a wonderful, bounteous pair of breasts, always on display whenever she comes into my office? Is it my fault, Your Worship, if the waft of the perfume she wore that day raised my restless spirits? Are you sure it's really a sin to extend an affectionate hand to her when she did not push me away? Do you yourself have a secretary like the one my cousin gifted me? Is it my fault if I've got a private secretary? My fault if so many fathers, mothers, brothers, husbands are happy enough to let their daughters, sisters, wives become private secretaries, knowing full well what might happen? Is it anyone's fault if thirst recognises neither good nor evil, if our workplace relations often seem ones of master and slave? I just felt so much affection, compassion and gratitude towards my secretary. She had lifted a great weight off my chest.

I stayed in my office late into the night. I savoured the joyful memories of that evening that had taken away the anxiety of a morning spent searching exhaustedly for something I needed desperately. Our country is poor in resources. Nothing above the earth or below it might have made something of a starting point. I had searched high above the earth and deep into its hollow core, combed its shorelines and dived into its deepest oceans. I found nothing but more sorrow. The little that we possess is wasted, destroyed and shipped abroad. Most of the little we have built for ourselves hangs over us miserably, like crows hovering over a tattered corpse.

I returned to the facts with a more optimistic eye. I grasped the fact that the present was more than enough if we made wise choices and actions in a measured way. I ended up thinking that the problem lay not in natural resources, but in the way we manage them. Our country has fed its people, and numerous oppressors, corrupters and robbers, for more centuries than anyone could count. This, at least, I had learned in two unsuccessful years at university. A red glare flickered harshly in my head. Management is not covered by my ministry's portfolio. It was where slippery slopes were everywhere to be found.

I noticed that my civil servant had fallen asleep, face propped on his palm, eyelids clamped together. It had been his snoring that had made me notice him and I thanked God sleep had taken him off before those wicked ideas had made themselves felt to me. I feared he would have read my thoughts. I woke him gently and we left.

A longing swept me towards "The Dish of Lablabi"* in a working-class district I frequented. The desire grew and grew within me. But what might others say if I was seen there and word spread where word always does? Is my driver's tongue to be relied on not to wag if I ask him to bring me the dish? What pleasure it would be eating it on the seat of my ministerial car? I crushed my craving in an iron fist and went home instead.

Everyone was asleep. I tried to find something to quell my hunger, but nothing could suppress my desire for of the devil "Lablabi". I went into the bedroom and slipped in next to my fast-asleep wife. She sensed me there, made as if to notice, but was overcome by drowsiness again. I gave thanks and toyed in my mind, as I tried to sleep, with comparing those attractions of my wife which had withstood the test of time and the attractions of my alluring secretary. I was brimful of both affection and disgust for my wife.

I was attracted to her, despite her own foul and caustic tongue. Yes, I played around from time to time, like all men do, with women thrown in my way by chance or by boredom or by that longing for variety which sends us off on their trail. Once I see a woman I want, I want her in bed. It was my own woman, my own wife who showed me the path – after marriage, naturally – that led to my endless chasing after others.

The first time was with one of her friends whom she had had a special affection for. She would visit her often and they would chat away together for hours. She would then tell me titbits of her friend's news.

I, My Lord, Your Honour, respect friendship. I put it above all else. I had never cast a lustful eye on my wife's friend. I hadn't even recognised her beauty. I was home alone one day when she knocked on the door. I said hello and told her her friend was at the hairdresser's. I waited for her to go, but she said, unhesitatingly: "I'll wait." How can someone leave his wife's friend in the hall all alone? I told her: "I think she might be back a little late. She took the children with her." She sighed hotly and said again: "I'll wait." I asked how she was. She replied curtly before suddenly bursting into tears. I intended leaving her to cry all she liked, but the heaviness of her tears made it awkward. I was forced to be charitable. I offered her a handkerchief to wipe away her tears and she raised her face to me. She rushed suddenly into my arms and there I was, ready to receive her.

We only had a few opportunities after that to renew our joy, but the future was mapped out for me. I found something different there, or so I believed at the time. I'm still chasing after that something else. Is there any other playing field for me and my kind to compete on than chasing after women?

* Lablabi is a cheap Tunisian dish based on chick peas in a thin garlic and cumin-flavoured soup, served over small pieces of stale crusty bread.

> **When we crossed the road separating Palestine from Lebanon it was the first day of November 1948, if I remember well.**

MOHAMMAD KHASHAN

# The Day the Olive Harvest was stopped

A CHAPTER FROM A MEMOIR
TRANSLATED BY ISSA J. BOULLATA

*Mohammad Khashan, Beirut, 2012.*
*Photo by Samuel Shimon*

About two months before the Nakba,[1] a dirt road was opened, approximately one kilometre away from the village and parallel to the main highway that passed through the lands of the villages of Suhmata and Deir al-Qasi. Working on it was by forced labour imposed by the Liberation Army, I think. I heard someone say "When we finish opening the road, we will be kicked out". And this was what happened.

In October, the season of olive harvesting began. I always joined in the harvest with my family and I enjoyed it. The climate was moderate and my work was no more than collecting olives in a container, then loading them into a large sack. When the sack was full, my father loaded it onto a donkey, which I then led to our home where the olives were emptied and piled on a flat platform in front of the house. Finally, the olives were taken to the old-fashioned press (before the engine-driven one was built in the year before the Nakba) and were ground and pressed. This was one of the most beautiful occasions: a large millstone was turned by a mule or other animal; the olives were ground and made into fine pulp and put in hair-baskets, which were then heaped one on top of the other in a metallic press operated by men who increased the pressure on the baskets. The olive oil then ran from the baskets into a channel that led to a cistern. The oil was scooped from the cistern and put into vessels brought in by the owner of the olives. At the bottom of the cistern, dregs of the oil remained and these were to repair house platforms and in making black soap. White soap was made from the pure oil by adding a chemical ingredient the peasants called *qatruna* and boiled with the oil to make it fluid. This was then poured into flat receptacles and, before the fluid solidified, was cut into cubes.

As soon as I entered the oil press chamber with my father, I found myself in a world of traditions that has been passed down, especially when our turn to have our olives pressed was at night. The press chamber was lit by an oil lamp that was just a small bowl with a wick in one end. My mother made food for the workers, who, if it was lentil soup or *mjaddarat-burghul*,[2] added fresh oil, making it a delicious and nutritious meal. In a similar lovely group atmosphere, many other tasks were completed, such as winnowing – which is removing the chaff from the grain; such kind of work could not be done by the owner of the threshing floor alone but only with the help of his neighbours, with whom he would take turns to share the

work. The owner of the threshing floor prepared lunch for the win-
nowers. Those who passed by the winnowing group did not say,
"May God give you health", rather "May it be blessed!". I waited ea-
gerly for such occasions year after year.

We harvested half or, sometimes most of the olives, but did not
grind them. They remained in a heap on the platform in front of the
house. That was in October 1948 and [political] conditions were be-
coming worse; yet people continued to act as though nothing had
happened. Some simple precautions were taken by us, such as hiding
our provisions in the hayloft, and perhaps other and better safe-
guards. We saw people who had been forced to leave for exile from
the district of Tiberias and other places; they passed by our village
in May and June on their way to Lebanon, our village being not
more than a few miles away from the border. My father knew a lot
about the villages there, and had acquaintances too. We therefore
took another precautionary step, and moved provisions of wheat,
bulgur, lentils and oil to the Lebanese village of Rmeish.

A few days before the fall of my village, when people forced into
exile were increasing in number, I heard about a battle between the
Jews and the Liberation Army. I attended the funeral of one of the
army's soldiers in our village cemetery, and a group of soldiers fired
five shots in the air in his honour. In those last days, I saw the Lib-
eration Army withdraw their field hospital and set it up in an olive
grove in front of our village; two days later they withdrew again and
took away sacks of provisions with them. I felt that bad things were
about to happen. Some of those forced into exile entered our village
thinking it was safe, although they had fled from villages not more
than twenty kilometres from our village. One of the scenes that af-
fected me greatly was that of a young woman driving several animals
carrying various loads, and one of the animals carried two earthen-
ware jars. As she and others were entering our village, the animal
carrying the jars bumped into a wall; the jars broke and the oil in
them flowed over the ground. I heard the woman say "There is no
power and no strength save in God". I admired this woman's forti-
tude and was sorry for her.

At the entrance of our village, on the curve of the road where our
house was, my father helped those forced into exile as they came in
sight. My mother from inside the house shouted to him: "Kamel,
come in here and let us see what we ourselves should do." The next

day, I was in a fig tree grove of ours near the village cemetery – it was the threshing floor's fig tree grove or the Abbas fig tree grove. There was a man grazing a few goats in the cemetery. All of a sudden, two aeroplanes flew from the west: they were as large as passenger planes and moving slowly. The man said to me: "Mohammad, do you think those aeroplanes are Arab or Jewish ones?" The man seemed to have confidence in my knowledge as a schoolboy, maybe because he was illiterate and I was well known in the village – and this made him think I perhaps knew about the aeroplanes. I immediately said to him: "They're Arab planes." He asked: "What makes you think so?" I said: "Don't you see that they're flying low? If they were Jewish planes, they wouldn't do that." I had forgotten that our village had only rifles. I had hardly finished my words when we saw smoke enveloping the village of Deir al-Qasi, four kilometres to the north of our village. I hastened home. About an hour after Deir al-Qasi was bombed, a jeep belonging to the Liberation Army arrived; they had also seen the smoke and thought the bombing had happened in Suhmata. Despite my young age, I was surprised the Army did not know the exact spot that was bombed. My family went to the metal box containing money and our land documents, and took everything out. I had an earthenware savings jar and we broke it; it was as if we were sure we had been defeated. In the jar was the sum of seven pounds and about thirty piastres. The pounds were added to the family money, and the thirty piastres went into my pocket – and this was what the Israeli soldier stole from me.

My mother had advised me to take the family Qur'an with me as, should the Jews come, she said, they would tear it up and trample on it. But the next day, when the aeroplanes attacked our village, I forgot my mother's advice. The people being forced into exile were arriving in droves and were increasingly at a loss what to do. The day following the bombing of Deir al-Qasi, which I think was the 27th or the 28th of October, 1948, my mother was at home in the afternoon baking bread on the round iron fire-dome. All of a sudden, Jewish aeroplanes appeared from behind the western hills. I had thought of a hiding place if there should be bombing – it was a room-sized cave in the middle of the village, which dozens of others like me, considered a good shelter, too. I ran to the cave, which was west of our home, but my mother saw me and shouted at the top of her voice: "Go back! Get out of the village!" I rushed back and ran eastward. Directly outside the village houses, there were enclosures for goats, some of which were old, unused, and in ruins; they were called Caesar's Enclosures. When I reached them, I heard the sound of the first bomb from an aeroplane which we called "Kazan". I hid closely behind a wall. On the other side of the road, I saw the two mukhtars[3], Ali Saleh and Jiryes Kaisar. Like me, they too had left the village for fear of the bombing. When they heard the sound of the bomb, they lay flat on the ground which was a very stony dirt road. When I saw them do that, I laughed and, instead of lying on my belly too, I stretched out on my back and looked up at the aeroplanes above, with the two letters UN. They released the second bomb and I saw it coming down through the air; it was big, long and black and it appeared to be coming down on me vertically. I recited the Muslim creed of faith[4] and did not move. Then I heard the sound of the second bomb exploding in the south of our village, while I was at the north. I got up and walked to the threshing floor of the upper neighbourhood, where I saw almost all of its inhabitants assembled: babies crying, women screaming and looking for their children, brothers, fathers, and mothers. I was alarmed at this scene and I ran home. We left our home with two beasts carrying mattresses and things we could gather up, and we went up to a plot of land on the mountain. My father went back to our home to bring what he could; but when he returned, he had brought nothing. My mother asked him the reason and he told her: "The bombing damaged the lock and I did not want to break down the door to get in", as though he would go back later and repair the lock. It was with such naïve thinking that people treated matters! This time, the situation was not like the times when, as danger loomed, we had gone up to the mountain and later returned home. The bombing from the air was a prelude to the advance of the Jewish army as an occupier. We slept that night, and the next day my father began to move what we had brought from home and take it to the village of Bqei'ah, no more than four kilometres away.

As a result of the Israeli bombing, there were martyrs and wounded. The names of the dead were: Hassan Mousa and Khalil Salloum (he was sick and they killed him at his home), the blood of Christians and Muslims thus mixing in the defence of their village; Khalil 'Abboud, who was from the village of Bqei'ah but happened to be in Suhmata during the bombing; Sumayya 'Amer, wife of Tawfiq al-'Abed Qaddoura; 'Atallah Mousa; Mustafa 'Ali Qaddoura; Mohammad 'Abd al-Rahman Qaddoura; and Mozeh, wife of As'ad Nimer Mousa. Among the wounded were Hammoudi and Mohammad al-Hajj Ibrahim.

My brother carried the rifle we had bought. During battles, the Army positioned the young fighting men of the villages mostly on the nearby hills and in the rear. This raised suspicions among the young men because, before the Arab armies entered the fray, they used to confront the enemy and win victories, and their morale was high. But after the 15th of May [1948] and the entry of the Arab armies, the situation changed.[5] My brother and the other young men found themselves in a bad position with the Liberation Army arriving late so they advanced to the front lines. However, before the Jews began the attack, the Liberation Army was ordered to withdraw, and abandoned the peasants, leaving them with old weapons that were dangerous. I myself saw many a rifle explode and injure the person firing it. Someone went to the fighters and asked: "What are you doing here? The Liberation Army has withdrawn!" So the fighters abandoned their positions and went back to their villages. Meanwhile, my father had moved us to the Bqei'ah, a mountain plot, and had then gone back to fetch some things. He found my grandfather there, for he used to live with us, sitting on a straw mat. He told my father my brother As'ad had come, hidden the rifle under the mat and made him sit on it, and told him: "I'm going to Lebanon."

Of the memorable scenes of those two days when we were on the mountain plot is the break-up of the Liberation Army, with each soldier left to his own devices. Groups of two or three soldiers, as well as men on their own, came to us and asked my mother for directions to the road leading to Lebanon. Slapping her cheeks in lamentation, my mother had pointed north, saying: "I don't know what will happen to these people as the Jewish army will have reached the Palestinian–Lebanese border before them."

My mother, my sister, and I spent the night in Bqei'ah and my father remained on the mountain plot. In the early morning, almost at sunrise, my father arrived with my grandfather and the rifle. Divine providence may have saved them for no sooner had they arrived than we heard the sound of bullets, to which there was no response. There was a group of Jewish commandos, perhaps less than a hundred strong, who had arrived at the square in the middle of the village, where there was a fountain. I saw them, after a brief pause for a muster, washing their faces in front of the house we were sleeping in. I went out to the square to look at them. Their weapons were ordinary and not all of them wear in uniform; some of them were clean-shaven and others had beards. They walked along the village road and I walked behind a tall, slender soldier carrying a small machinegun of the kind we used to call Sten-gun or Tommy-gun. Walking behind him, I wondered to myself, "This is the man who will expel us from our country!" I did not have any fear of this soldier, and I walked behind him for a few steps, then returned home.

I remember we were not the only guests in this home, there was another family. The host had a good cow, for which he was offered thirty-five pounds; but he did not sell it. It was a very good price in those circumstances. The morning after the commando group had entered the village, a company from the regular Jewish army entered wearing uniforms and helmets with nets. A Jeep driven by a tawny female soldier led them. The soldiers climbed on to the roofs of the houses, some of them were on the roof of the house opposite ours, with machineguns of the type we used to call Bren-guns. Unlike the previous day, I was afraid of these soldiers although they did not harm anyone. The people of our village and other nearby villages knew how to hold out and remain in their country; they were our brothers, our neighbours, and our friends from the sect believing in one God called Bani Ma'rouf, and known as Druzes. The house in which we spent two days was close to the road leading to the village of al-Rameh. I went up the road and saw women with their children in tow; they were barefoot but their outward appearance suggested they were city dwellers; I did not know the reason for their distress. In the evening, we heard a voice shouting: "Everyone who is not of the people of Bqei'ah must come outdoors at seven o'clock in the morning, and walk in the main road. Whoever does not walk in the main road will be fired on by the army." A humiliating and sad silence reigned, but we did not forget that we were guests. So we packed all our things – I saw some people throw away the wool stuffing of mattresses and keep only the cloth covers. I do not know how we spent that night! Following the orders of the occupying forces, in the morning we went outdoors not knowing what would happen. We were about to leave the village. We were at its entrance, where there is another fountain, not the one in the middle of the Square (Bqei'ah has a third fountain called Tiriyyeh that irrigates a group of gardens, while the one in the village irrigates the gardens that surround it as well as the houses). At the entrance of the village, we remembered we had forgotten to take with us two containers of *labneh*[6] (called *labnet ambris* in Lebanon[7]). One was large and could hold six rotls[8]; we used to sell one rotl for one Palestinian pound; the other container was small and held about two rotls. My father had hung the two containers on two pegs at the entrance of the house where we stayed, the larger container on a somewhat high peg and the smaller on a lower one. My father had said to me: "Go back, Mohammad, and fetch the containers of labneh". I went back quickly and tried to lift down the large container, but I could only touch the bottom of it so I took the smaller one, carried it on my back, and hastened back to my family. The container was dry, for we were at the end of October, which was usually the time we sold the labneh in the large container, keeping that in the smaller one for our own home consumption: it would be cut into small balls or cylindrical pieces and placed in glass or earthenware jars and steeped in olive oil, making a nutritious and delicious food. When I returned to my family, my father asked me: "Why didn't you bring the large container?" I said: "I couldn't." In fact, I was afraid, as a Jewish soldier had placed his machinegun on the terrace in front of the house and I did not want to ask for any help from the house's inhabitants; I did not even notice if they saw us or not. As soon as we left the village and took the main road, I saw thousands of people walking just like us. I had not seen these people in Bqei'ah, and, I realised they had been forced into exile, like us, from neighbouring villages and had spent their nights in the open air around Bqei'ah. We walked for a while, then we saw a man going the other way, perhaps having forgotten to take something, like us – as confusion and bewilderment had taken hold of everyone! Among those walking beside me was a young man whose name was Hussein Hassan Mousa; he was driving some cows and goats. A man from our village asked him: "Where are you taking these cattle, Hussein?" Hussein replied: "These are our cows and goats, man." The man said: "The Jews have put up a checkpoint at the intersection of Tarsheeha-Bqei'ah, and they seize cattle." Hussein drove his cattle away off the road and abandoned them on the plain of Suhmata. I looked back at the abandoned cattle – this, too, is one of the scenes I find difficult to forget.

The farther we went forward, the larger the number of people on the road until we arrived at the checkpoint manned by some soldiers who spoke Arabic like us. One of them stood in the middle, he alone granted permission to pass. Others stood by and watched; they asked the women to put down the loads they carried on their heads and wait for their turn to be inspected. Let me pause here, and say that my father was fortunate to reach the village before the Jews had entered it, and brought with him the rifle my brother had left and made my grandfather sit on. That night my father took it and gave it away to a man he knew. He, my uncle, and my grandfather had given that man forty of their goats to graze that, after some years, would be divided according to a designated system; this is a matter that required knowledge and trust. After some hesitation the man agreed to take the rifle as his part, as my father later told us, for these were no times to carry weapons. My father kept the rifle's leather strap for possible later use.

The distance between Bqei'ah and the checkpoint near the village to the west was no more than four kilometres. The position of the checkpoint was strategic; to the right was a slope and to the left a wide, open plain. I heard the sound of a bullet and someone say they fired at a man they had seen at a distance. I saw some young men disguise themselves by covering their faces with soil and, in the middle of this crowd and in the midst of fear, I saw the man who did not sell his cow or abandon it the way Hussein had earlier. Like us, he reached the checkpoint. One of the soldiers said to him: "Tie this cow to that rock." He handed the soldier its halter and said: "Take it, Sir." The soldier screamed at him: "I told you: tie it there!" So he tied it up. I saw a soldier frisk people, seizing any money or jewellery they had. I was overcome by fear, for our money was with my mother and she had wrapped it in soft muslin tied to her waist. She usually wore a large dress with a broad belt [to tighten it at the midriff] but under these circumstances she had undone the belt so the dress appeared larger than her slender frame. She approached the soldier and said to him: "Come now, ya 'ammi,[9] search me and let me go." He looked at her and said: "Go!"

The soldier at the checkpoint spoke Arabic and stood in the middle of the road, helped by other soldiers. After my mother went through, she said to him: "Brother, let my children pass." He said: "Where are your children?" My sister and I were beside him, so she said: "These are my children." He said: "Follow your mother." We followed our mother but she said to me: "Go back to the Jewish man and beg him to let your father pass." I returned and said to him: "*Ya 'ammi*, let my father pass." He searched me and found on me the change that had remained of the savings jar that amounted to about thirty piastres, He seized the money and said: "You're all pimps . . .You smuggle money on animals." I went back disappointed, without my father or my money. This is an act I can never forget, how a single soldier can harm the reputation of his army with his behaviour. Till now, I hold no respect for this army in spite of all the heroic deeds and capabilities attributed to it. A little later, I saw my father at a distance. A soldier was slapping his face hard, then he let him go. This soldier was not the one who robbed me of my money. In Lebanon, we asked my father: "Why did the soldier hit you?" He said: "He asked me what town I came from, and I named a village other than our own, so he slapped me. I took a good look and recognized him, but said nothing." This soldier used to be a government employee who counted cattle for tax purposes. They dropped in on shepherds when their cattle came to drink, asking them about their herds and their owners.

This checkpoint was a short distance from the other main road that came from Acre in the west and then turned at the entrance of Suhmata toward the north. The farther north we walked, the denser became the crowd – families c of adults and children, with animals carrying belongings. Exhaustion and fear took hold of all. I saw more than one woman discard the load on her head and carry on walking. No one was sure of safety at the intersection of Suhmata–Bqei'ah. We were at the western entrance of our village and, although the road was good, it had a difficult ascent called al-Dabash. On both sides of the road, I saw abandoned mattresses, sacks of grain and boxes of ammunition. I saw similar scenes all along the way from the checkpoint almost to the borders of Lebanon. There were also smouldering armoured cars. As we were making the climb, we saw a fat woman coming back and we asked her: "What's the matter? Why are you coming back in a hurry?" She said: "They're firing on the young men at the entrance of Suhmata." I was never as frightened as at that moment. I was afraid for my father. He said to my mother: "Zahra, take the children, and I'll escape from here through the olive trees, and we'll meet in Lebanon." She said to him: "Do you think the Jews are not paying attention? They are on the roofs of the houses – as you saw in Bqei'ah. As soon as you leave the road, they'll fire at you! It's better for you to stay with us. We either live together or die together." My father accepted my mother's advice and soon afterwards we reached the entrance of the village without running into any soldiers. The woman, who said she had seen a young man from our village being fired at, might have come to know about the incident later on. Driving the two animals with a short stick, I could barely keep up with them as they were going fast without being prodded. When they reached the entrance of the village, they instinctively turned as if to go in. I had to beat them hard, especially when I saw Jews sitting on the hayloft of our home. My mother used to say to me: "If the Jews come, they will sit nowhere but in this house." And I used to respond jokingly: "Yes, of course. It is Yaldez Palace!" I used to hear this name mentioned in my village and came to know that it referred to one of the Ottoman palaces in Istanbul. I was able to direct the two animals north; when they sensed that they were not heading home, they slowed down and I had to urge them to keep going. This too is one of the things difficult to forget: it is as though an animal knows when it is going too far from its homeland and decides it does not want to go farther.

On the way from the checkpoint on the Lebanese borders, Jewish lorries and jeeps passed by, each driven by only one soldier. Each jeep had something covered as though it were a cannon. On the road there were cars, people and animals, not to mention the terror and rumours about people getting bombed and killed! It was the day of "gathering"! This was my feeling on the road. It was the Day of Resurrection! We were less than one kilometre from our village when, suddenly I saw my beautiful blond cat running, frightened and meowing, among the cars, the young men and the animals. It was looking for us and it ran passed us, meowing like a crazy animal. I tried to shoo it away from the danger of being run over by cars. I saw it running toward the olive tree groves. My heart was torn to pieces! How often did this cat lie beside me or sit on my lap allowing me to play with it and stroke its back as it arched its tail! I was very sad, a silent sorrow – for who knows whether one will stay alive?

My father carried a metal can that he had filled with water at Bqei'ah. There was thirst and fear! People asked my father for water. He lifted the lid only to find the water almost boiling because of the heat. He emptied it and walked away. These were unforgettable moments of great terror! A nation being driven away from their land by the force of weapons; evicted from the land of their fathers and forefathers!

Deir al-Qasi lies between Suhmata and Lebanon, a distance of about four kilometres. We crossed the centre of Deir and, not far from it, was the road that separated Lebanon from Palestine; it was on a line extending from Ra's al-Naqura on the Mediterranean in the west to the Syrian village of Banyas in the east. We crossed the road – and I did not know that this was to be my last personal moment of Palestine!

The day we crossed the road separating Palestine from Lebanon was the first day of November, 1948, if I remember well.

Excerpted from the author's memoir *al-Khat al-Shamali* (*The Northern Line*), published by Manshurat al-Jamal, Beirut–Baghdad, 2012

Translator's Notes:

1 "Nakba" in Arabic means catastrophe, calamity, or disaster. "The Nakba" refers to the loss by Palestinians of their ancestral homeland by the establishment of Israel on the land on May 15, 1948. See The Palestine Nakba: *Decolonising History, Narrating the Subaltern, Reclaiming Memory* by Nur Masalha (London & New York: Zed Books, 2012).

2 *Mjaddara* consists of lentils and rice usually, but *burghul* (parched cracked wheat, called "bulgur" in English) replaces the rice sometimes.

3 A *muktar* is a village chief.

4 "I testify that there is no god but God and that Muhammad is the Messenger of God."

5 Army units from the Arab states entered Palestine on May 15, 1948, to support the Palestinians by a decision of the Arab League, and the Arab Liberation Army was ordered to withdraw.

6 A sort of cream-cheese, made by straining yoghurt.

7 So named after Ambris (Qambris), the Lebanese family who makes it and markets it. Information provided by Lily Farhoud Boullata.

8 A rotl is a unit of weight in the Near East, equivalent to about 3 kg in Palestine.

9 *Ya 'ammi* literally means: O my uncle. But it is used in common speech in Palestinian Arabic when addressing another who is not really an uncle, and it is said as a means to urge, to cajole, and sometimes to tease or even to oppose.

# Sawiris Literary Awards

*Ibrahim Farghali receives the award for his novel (Sons of Gebelawy) from Samih Sawiris*

In their eighth year the Sawiris Cultural Awards are becoming the most important literary awards in Egypt. They were established in 2005 by the Sawiris Foundation for Social Development, with top prizes of LE100,000. There are separate awards for both established and emerging authors of both novels and of short stories, as well as awards for established and emerging film scriptwriters and playwrights, with awards for first, second and third places.

The top novel award went to Ibrahim Farghali for (*Sons of Gebelawy*), published by Dar al-Ain, which takes Naguib Mahfouz's iconic *Children of the Alley* as its starting point and imagines a world without literature. Author and critic Youssef Rakha has described Farghali as "among the most prolific novelists of his generation. In his devotion to the genre and his formal conservatism, he is perhaps the worthiest heir to Mahfouz."

The Award of Best Short Story Collection for Established Writers went to Ibrahim Dawoud for (*The Atmosphere*), published by Dar Merit, with his 38 short stories portraying Cairo's cultural workers. Farghali and Dawoud each received LE100,000. Both writers are journalists with *Al-Ahram* newspaper.

The emerging authors' prize for the novel was awarded to Yasser Ahmed, with Mahmoud El-Ghitany and Mohamed Salem joint seconds, while the winner of the emerging writers' short story award was Mohammed Rafee', with Amira Hassn Dessoki coming joint second with Mohamed Farouk Shamseddin.

*Susannah Tarbush reviews*

## The Silence and the Roar
by Nihad Sirees
translated by Max Weiss
Pushkin Press, London, 2013, pbk, 164pp.
ISBN 9781908968296

## In Praise of Hatred
by Khaled Khalifa
translated by Leri Price
Transworld/Doubleday, London, 2012,
hbk, 301pp, ISBN 978 0385617635

# Syria's literary roars

These two powerful novels appear in English translation at a time when the great city of Aleppo, where their authors were born, is being torn apart in Syria's savage civil war. The novels first appeared in Arabic in the mid-2000s; in their different ways they highlight why it was that Syrians half a decade later found the courage to break through their silence and take to the streets in protest at the brutal and corrupt dictatorship.

Khaled Khalifa's *In Praise of Hatred* is set in Aleppo during a previous uprising in the early 1980s. Sirees's *The Silence and the Roar* is set on one day in an unnamed city and country but is clearly inspired by life under dictatorship in Syria.

## The Silence and the Roar

Nihid Sirees is the author of seven novels, and also a screenwriter and playwright. His work has been banned since 1998 after the screening of his popular TV serial "The Silk Market", set in the political turbulence of 1950s Syria. It was not a Syrian publisher but Dar Al Adab in Beirut that published *The Silence and the Roar* in 2004, as *Al-Samt wal-Sakhab*.

Sirees left Syria in January 2012 moving first to Cairo and then to Brown University, Rhode Island, USA, where he had an International Writers Project Fellowship from October to the end of Feb-

*NIhad Sirees, Manhattan, December 2012.    Photo: Samuel Shimon*

ruary. He has written a moving afterword for the English translation of *The Silence and the Roar*.

Max Weiss, Assistant Professor of History and Near Eastern Studies at Princeton University, gives us a lively, commendably clear translation of the novel. The informal, conversational tone suits the first-person narrator's laconic humour.

The first-person protagonist of the novel, Fathi Sheen, is a well-known 31-year-old journalist and broadcaster who has been black-listed and silenced by the regime. The novel is set over the course of one sweltering day on which the regime has organised noisy mass marches to celebrate the Leader's 20th anniversary in power. "The roar produced by the chants and the megaphones eliminates thought," Fathi observes. "Thought is retribution, a crime, treason against the Leader."

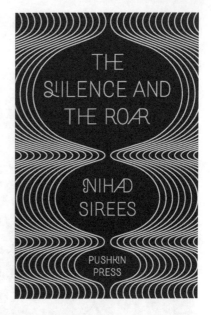

Fathi says he has grown to love silence ever since the revolutionaries starting making their addresses and leading their marches. "The most beautiful thing in the entire universe is the silence that allows us to hear soft and distant sounds." But the authorities are not content for Fathi to remain silent; they want him to use his writing and media skills in the service of the regime, as other writers and intellectuals have done.

Fathi has suffered unhappiness and self-loathing since being barred from all outlets for his writing and broadcasting. But his humour and his sensual relationship with his girlfriend and confidante Lama have saved him from total despair. "Laughter and sex were our two weapons of survival" he says. He uninhibitedly depicts the couple's nudity and lovemaking in Lama's flat.

During the marches Fathi embarks on an odyssey through the city streets, and his accounts of his various encounters lay bare the machinery of dictatorship. He lampoons the behaviour of the Leader, with his childish whims and attempts to manipulate the masses.

Fathi has several run-ins with regime thugs, three of whom take his ID card after he intervenes to stop them assaulting a young man. His journey becomes in part a quest to recover his ID from the maze of Party and security institutions. When he comes across a young woman trampled under the feet of marchers, he carries her to hospital in a vain attempt to save her life, injuring his hand in the process. At the hospital a distraught doctor tells him that so far more than 45 people have been killed in the march and hundreds injured by trampling, suffocation, or stray celebratory gunfire. "Human beings have no value whatsoever," the doctor says. He begs Fathi, as a writer, to give a name to what is going on. "Surrealism," Fathi replies.

Another man tells Fathi how he had been in charge of photocopying documents at a government department and had been told to make ten thousand copies of a picture of the Leader. The copies were pasted on walls. But the photocopier was faulty, and each copy had black splotches on one eye of the Leader ,making him look like a pirate. The man was detained, beaten and tortured for six months.

During his passage through the city Fathi visits his fifty-something widowed mother Ratiba, and is appalled when she announced that Mr Ha'el Ali Hassan, head of the Leader's personal security, has proposed marriage and is just waiting for Fathi to give his permission. She is set on the marriage, saying: "I'm still a young woman. I deserve this". Lama warns Fathi that the proposed marriage may be part of a trap to lure him into working for the regime.

Fathi's efforts to retrieve his ID card take him to the Party building and there, in one of the novel's most remarkable scenes, he comes across a basement centre where the regime's propaganda is designed and manufactured. Psychologists, educationalists, intellectuals and poets work on slogans and poems which are tested on focus groups for effectiveness.

Continuing his search for his ID card Fathi is directed to military security. After he is subjected to a beating he finds himself in a one-to-one battle of wills, presented with a seemingly impossible choice.

# In Praise of Hatred

Khaled Khalifa's novel was shortlisted for the International Prize for Arabic Fiction (IPAF – often known as the Arabic Booker) in 2008, the prize's inaugural year. The novel was first published by Amisa in Damascus in 2006 as *Madih al-Karahiya* but was banned soon after publication. Dar Al Adab republished it in Beirut in 2008.

Leri Price's highly accomplished translation of the novel has received the honour of being longlisted for this year's Independent Foreign Fiction Prize. Price writes in her Translator's Note at the end of the novel that in consultation with Khalifa some editorial changes to the novel in translation were made and "the result is a novel that ends differently from the original".

Like Nihad Sirees, Khalifa is a screenwriter as well as a novelist. His gift for storytelling is shown in this rich, multi-layered novel with its many interlocking tales and its wide-ranging geographical and time frames. The novel alludes to various events from the 1980s uprising which the regime has attempted to airbrush out of history including the massacres in Hama and at Palmyra prison.

The nameless female first-person narrator and protagonist is part of a well-off Sunni family. She lives with her three maternal aunts and the blind old family retainer Radwan in the house of her late grandfather, a carpet dealer.

Sectarianism is rife. In the discourse of the narrator's circle the ruling Alawis are "the other sect" and have "descended from the mountains". The Baath Party is "the atheist party". At secondary school the narrator is one of a group of veiled girls scorned as "the Penguin Club" by their secular non-veiled classmates.

The narrator is tormented by her developing sexuality. She is both repelled and fascinated by her changing body and by the bodies of other females. Some of her desires are projected onto her school friend Ghada. She is dismayed when Ghada throws off her veil and starts a disastrous affair with a 50-year-old regime official who waits at the school gate for her in a Mercedes.

Some other girls are having relationships with officers from the regime's death squad. The school is a microcosm of the corrupt political system: girls with strong regime connections intimidate the teachers and are allowed to fiddle academic results.

Khalifa's characters are complex flesh-and-blood creations. The narrator's uncle Bakr, an Islamist militant who frequently travels outside Syria, is a key figure in the Aleppo rebellion. He has got to know a Yemeni activist Abdullah through their mutual friend, a Saudi prince. Abdullah had been a Marxist and spent 10 years in Moscow before becoming disillusioned and then seeing God in Mecca. Bakr arranges for his sister Safaa to become Abdullah's second wife. Abdullah gets intimately involved in the anti-Soviet mujahidin movement in Afghanistan and the rise of "Arab-Afghan" fighters. The narrator is much influenced by Bakr and Abdullah. She joins a cell of militant Islamist women whose leader urges the hatred of all other Islamic sects. "By the end of that summer hatred had taken possession of me. I was enthused by it; I felt that it was saving me."

*Khalid Khalifa, The Hague, The Netherlands, November 2007.   Photo Samuel Shimon*

On her seventeenth birthday she thinks: "We need hatred to give our lives meaning". She goes as far as declaring that she wants martyrdom.

Not all members of the family are hard-line Islamists. Bakr's brother Omar has a reputation as a dissolute womaniser who colludes in smuggling operations with Syrian officers who are controlling Lebanon.

In the second section of the novel, entitled Embalmed Butterflies, the youngest aunt Marwa – who has split up from a violent husband

– collects butterflies and starts running wild. She falls in love with an officer who comes to search the house and leaves the house to pursue an affair with him. To try and control her Bakr sends men to the house who chain her by her ankles to the bed.

The narrator changes profoundly after she is captured by the regime and sent to prison where she is at first tortured and spends 100 days in solitary confinement. As she nears death she realises that she wants to live: "It occurred to me for a moment that I loved life more than the title of 'exemplary martyr'."

When she is released into a cell with women from her organisation and from other factions she finds herself, to her astonishment, becoming close to a member of an underground Marxist party. "We hadn't expected that religious opponents and ideological enemies could ever share the same space, but we were forced to share that air and pain, and break dry bread together."

They relationships between the imprisoned women are convincingly portrayed. When one of them gives birth her fellow prisoners regard the boy as "our child" with 22 mothers. The narrator finds that "the hatred which I had defended as the only truth was shattered entirely". After four years in mukhabarat cells the women are transferred to the women's prison in Damascus. Soon after her 26th birthday she is released.

Both novels end on a relatively hopeful note, and suggest a need for qualities including tolerance and courage to help Syria overcome dictatorship and its legacy. In his afterword to his *The Silence and The Roar* Nihad Sirees writes: "I believe that love and peace are the right way to confront tyranny."

# Naguib Mahfouz Medal for Literature 2012

Egyptian author Ezzat El Kamhawi was awarded 2012 Naguib Mahfouz Medal for Literature for his novel *Bayt al-Dib* (*The House of El Deeb*), published by Dar al-Adab in 2010.

The judges described the novel as "a tour de force of fiction that interweaves a fictional village with strands of Egyptian history from Ottoman rule to fin-de-siècle Egypt", and stated: "The personal and political are intertwined subtly, and thus the formative years of the place and its inhabitants are inseparable . . . Despite its breadth of vision, the novel manages to balance both sides of the equation to create an intricate dynamic that captures much of the essence of the country's recent experience . . . El Kamhawi weaves with exceptional skill the interaction between man, time, and place . . . This unique novel affirms the necessity of separating fiction from the logic of history through the imagination, which brings together history and reality without distinguishing between them."

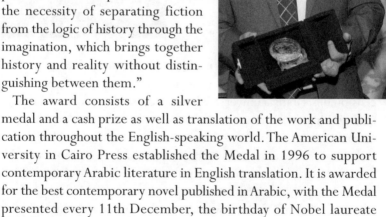

The award consists of a silver medal and a cash prize as well as translation of the work and publication throughout the English-speaking world. The American University in Cairo Press established the Medal in 1996 to support contemporary Arabic literature in English translation. It is awarded for the best contemporary novel published in Arabic, with the Medal presented every 11th December, the birthday of Nobel laureate Naguib Mahfouz.

Ezzat El Kamhawi is the author of ten books, including four novels and two collections of short stories. In 1993 he helped to found the literary newspaper *Akhbar al-Adab* in 1993, and was editor-in-chief until 2011 when he moved to Qatar to become editor-in-chief of *Doha* magazine.

*Mona Zaki reviews*

**The Book of Epiphanies** by Gamal al-Ghitani
translated by Farouk Abdel Wahab
AUC Press, Cairo, 2012, ISBN: 978 977 416 546 7, pbk, 288pp.

# A time travel technique

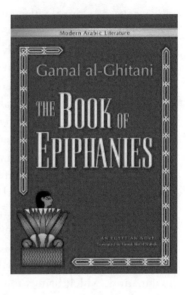

Originally published in 1983, *The Book of Epiphanies* is ambitious, following closely Ibn 'Arabi's Sufi masterpiece *The Meccan Illuminations*. Guided by the Prophet's grandson, al-Husayn, and by Ibn 'Arabi himself, the narrator moves across stations and levels as he sheds layers of his worldly ego to ascend the ladder of spiritual knowledge. Not being with his father at the moment of his death, the seeker sets out to know more of his father's life as well as his own.

The ingenuity here lies in using the ascension (*mi'raj*) as a time travel technique. Many Sufis reported emulating the Prophet's ascension describing a universe where trees, birds, stones or dust disclose information. Historical events ground the reader: Nasser's nationalization of the Suez canal, the 1967 defeat, the 1973 war, and the normalization of relations with Israel. It is clear from the narrative that the four *awtad* or poles (if one were to stick to Sufi hierarchy) are: Ibn 'Arabi, al-Husayn, Gamal Abdel Nasser and the narrator's father. The ascension allows the narrator to "see" and describe events as they happen. We learn of the poverty that drove peasants to the city and the special relationship some developed to al-Husayn's mosque. Large sections of the book relate the history and fate of the Prophet's grandsons. We learn that the universe is in constant motion, no event is lost, and vignettes describe images of regret, abandonment, sorrow and betrayal. On visiting the family of a friend killed in the 1973 war, for example, the narrator learns that they have moved on with their lives succumbing the dead to more oblivion.

No one can disagree that the works of Ibn 'Arabi are opaque at best. Volumes of commentaries, not to mention societies, exist to discuss their obscurities. Sufis proudly claim that their works are not for everyone – only the elect few can fully discern these jewels of insight. Using Ibn

*Gamal al-Ghitani*

'Arabi as the literary model makes this book a difficult read. With no linear narrative, the novel becomes one long "bumpy ride" – a string of images, of moments, a mix of historical events, poetry lines, clarifications, and "lessons" for surrealistic flair. The length of the book adds to the frustration (and exhaustion) of any reader. There is a point in the book, on page 178, when Ghitani apologizes: "Please forgive me, sagacious reader, if I tend to be long-winded and verbose, for these are symptoms of our condition in our twisted times." The novel ends at page 239!

Ghitani's *al-Zayni Barakat*, published thirty years ago (and also translated by Farouk Abdel Wahab), emulates the style of the sixteenth-century chronicle by Ibn Iyas. Literary critics explained the "miracle" of al-Zayni Barakat as the "lucid objectification of the self" – a prophetic element that allows the narrator to stand outside the text, to explain past trajectory and the future with exactitude. One should then ask if the miracle can work twice this time with a different appropriation – a seminal Sufi text laden with complexity? Parsing this novel's subtleties and insights will, no doubt, be left to academics, the elect few who study and teach al-Ghitani's works.

*The Book of Epiphanies* left me grappling for facts, hoping that sticking to the straight and narrow was the safest way of navigating the text. The questions one is left with are pertinent: Should the appropriation of any medieval text be hailed as literature? Why should we expect the reader to settle for an approximation of Ibn 'Arabi when one can go to the Master himself, download his books from the internet or join any of the Ibn 'Arabi societies? To keep things in perspective, *The Book of Epiphanies* was written five years after *al-Zayni Barakat* and belongs to an earlier part of the author's oeuvre. The Ghitani that I am more familiar with is one who wrote *Hikayat al-Mu'assasah* (1996) a novel that examines the intricacies of power with much literary merit and social commentary. Ghitani is a recipient of many awards, notably the Sheikh Zayed Book Award in 2009. The one hero to emerge from this odyssey is the translator, Farouk Abdel Wahab, who patiently dedicated and worked his way through a very difficult text.

## Mona Zaki reviews

### Tales of Encounter: Three Egyptian Novellas
by Yusuf Idris
translated by Rasheed El-Enany
AUC Press, Cairo-New York, 2012,
ISBN 978-9774165627, pbk, 240pp.

# Narrative voices

This collection, *Tales of Encounter*, is a wonderful addition to the translated works of Yusuf Idris. The first two novellas, *Madam Vienna* (1959) and *New York 80* (1980) are encounters with women while the third *The Secret of His Power* is an encounter with a saint. The first, serialized in the Egyptian newspaper *Al-Masa'*, describes the pursuit by an Egyptian civil servant, Darsh, of a sexual adventure in Europe. Darsh is a man driven by needs and consumed by how he would fulfil them. "What he wanted defined was what was legitimate, what was right." In Vienna, Darsh is a male predator on foreign soil, hanging around the central square, waiting for his catch. He is well dressed having invested in a suit and his main tactic is limited to asking for directions. He carefully assesses the gaze, or the hesitancy, of the women he talks to. As the night progresses and getting desperate he follows a woman he had asked directions from earlier, takes the last tram, chats her up and invites himself in! Her husband is on a business trip and for both their encounter is a first in their marital lives.

The second novella picks up the theme of an Egyptian abroad, this time with a call-girl, who does look nothing like what the narrator imagines a prostitute to be. The exchange is between two nameless characters and here Idris argues against the commoditization of the body as akin to white slavery and dehumanizing the soul. It is clear from her response that the prostitute believes in the free market economy, arguing that her skills and expertise are not unlike those of a psychotherapist, in fact she has a PhD, and can name her price!

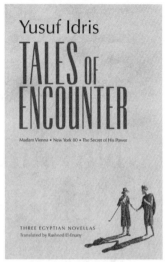

Twenty years separate these two encounters with women who remain anonymous except for the names of their cities. *Madam Vienna* would have landed Darsh in this day and age in trouble! Stalking and harassment is a serious offence and what Idris does best is show the tenacity and stamina of the predator. *New York 80* was written with Egypt's economic changes amid Sadat's Open Door policy. The issues Idris raises through the call-girl are similar to those raised at the same time back home in Egypt as luxury goods flooded the market amid stagnant wages. Privatization and free market economy was all the rage.

The third novella, *The Secret of His Power* is one of the most enjoyable pieces Idris has ever written. Those of us who enjoy Idris will realize how much they miss him. Here a young boy in a Delta village questions the sanctity of the village's decrepit mausoleum of Sultan Hamid. He learns how most villages have similar mausoleums dedicated to Sultan Hamid as well. Over the years he learns about the "myth" of the saint and the "reality".

*Tales of Encounter* reminds us of Idris's eye for detail, the brevity of his style is captured in the excellent translation by Rasheed El-Enany, an authority on Idris' writing and the genre of "foreign encounters". These three stories capture three distinct narrative voices: the predator, the indignant moralist, and the inquisitive little boy. It is hard to imagine any writing of Idris that hasn't been translated. This edition is a reminder of just how good a writer Yusuf Idris really was.

*Margaret Obank reviews*

**Horses of God**

by **Mahi Binebine**

translated by **Lulu Norman**
Granta Books, 2013, UK, 2013.
12pp, pbk, £12.99. ISBN: 9781847085139

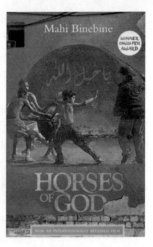

# The ghost of Yachine

M ahi Binebine is a well known Moroccan painter and since 1992 has authored nine novels, all dealing with the difficult, painful and often seemingly inexplicable issues that face people today as parents, families, politicians and human beings. The novel under review, *Horses of God*, has been adapted for the big screen as *Les Chevaux du Dieu*. Mahi Binebine studied and worked for a number of years in Paris, where until the late 1980s he taught mathematics, before devoting himself full time to painting and writing, and also living in New York and Madrid. Since 2002 he has settled in his home city of Marrakech.

The original novel, written in French, *Les Etoiles de Sidi Moumen* (Flammarion, 2010) won the Prix du Roman Arabe, the annual prize awarded by the Council of Arab Ambassadors in France in partnership with the Institut du Monde Arabe in Paris for works by Arab authors writing in French. It was also awarded the inaugural Mamounia Literary Prize of Marrakech. Translator of the English edition, Lulu Norman, who was awarded the 2013 English PEN Award for outstanding writing in translation for this translation, also translated Binebine's *Welcome to Paradise* (Granta, 2003, original title *Cannibales*, translated by Lulu Norman, with an excerpt first published in *Banipal 9* in 2000) which was shortlisted for the Independent Foreign Fiction Prize. Mahi Binebine's novels have been translated into German, Portuguese, Spanish, English and Korean.

The painter's eye of Mahi Binebine is transformed into a powerful voice with a resonating vision that echoes long after the book is put down. But in *Horses of God* it is not the vision of the destruction caused by the real life suicide-bombing of the Casablanca hotel 10 years ago that one might expect from reading the back cover blurb. Rather it is the fateful "game of life and death" played inexorably by the shanty-dwelling poor and deprived kids of Sidi Moumen, where the "grim reaper was a part of everyday life" and where Yachine and his eight brothers live with their mother Yemma and unemployed father (2 siblings died before the sons

*Mahi Binebine in his studio in Marrakech*

could count as a football team). Yachine would play with the other kids, who gathered together by the town dump, and scavenged for stuff to sell, or sniff. But more than that, they would play football – they were the stars of Sidi Moumen.

In a clever device the narrator is the ghost of the dead Yachine, one of the suicide bombers, and through this the author slips into Yachine as he looks down on the scene below, remembering his passion for football that led him to change his name to that of his idol the footballer Yachine. The burials of Yachine and his older brother Hamid, and the terrible distress and grief of his mother are described poignantly and touchingly. The pain of the community is physical, "not a single kid's shout". As for Yemma, her "eyes had almost disappeared", they were "dead, just like Hamid and me . . . ".

They were young, the lads, when they first met Abu Zoubeir – fifteen, maybe sixteen. Hamid was first, and the others followed, drawn in, at first imperceptibly, beginning their "slippery descent into a world that would suck us in deeper and deeper and finally swallow us for good". Yachine recounted how Abu Zoubeir had "given us back our pride with simple words", and then he too was drawn in until he recited that "Jihad was our only salvation. God demanded it of us. It was written in black and white, in the book of books."

Mahi Binebine, in Lulu Norman's brilliant translation, is poetic, edgy, tragic-comic, and at times too painful to read. "We were dead, just dead", says Yachine, but "still waiting for the angels". Powerful food for reflection and thought. At Banipal we are pleased to have published a painting by Mahi Binebine on this issue's front cover, and as well, earlier, on that of *Banipal 9*.

*Norbert Hirschhorn reviews*

**A Land Without Jasmine**
by Wajdi Al-Ahdal

translated by William Maynard Hutchins.
Garnet, London, 2012.
ISBN 9781859643105, 82pp.

# Violation and murder in the world beyond

A beautiful, twenty-year-old Sanaa University student named Jasmine has gone missing; possibly raped and murdered. In what begins as a crime story, Al-Ahdal continues an extreme of erotic writing that forced his temporary exile from Yemen for previous fiction, notably *Qawarib Jabaliyyah* (*Mountain Boats*), reviewed in *Banipal 19* (Spring 2004, pp. 152-154).

The book comprises six chapters, each with a different narrator, Rashomon-like, the titles revealing his or her character. The first is voiced by Jasmine ('The Queen') who keeps a detailed diary. Although fully veiled, she feels under constant siege by men who ogle and touch her: a grocer, a bus driver, and a pederast professor. Her diary reveals both revulsion about sex, as well as highly charged dreams of sexual gratification ('I sensed that the phalluses of billions of men were ejaculating into my vagina simultaneously as I climaxed along with all of them'). A police inspector tells the second chapter in pulp fiction parlance, but he is unnerved by the spooky turns his investigation uncovers; and a well-connected suspect cannot be touched. Next comes the proprietor of the University café, who after twenty years of observing students and faculty knows all the dark and dirty secrets within. He is a realist whose eyewitness testimony uncannily matches Jasmine's dreams. The fourth narrative is from the adolescent, Ali ('The Sacrificial Lamb'). From age twelve to sixteen he was Jasmine's playmate whose games included 'playing doctor'. In puberty his hormones are roiling. He is a 'sexual volcano', infatuated with and stalking the now veiled Jasmine. It is he who discovers her school notebook and underclothes in a hollow at

Wajdi al-Ahdal in Detroit,
Summer 2012, during his
residency in Ann Arbor, Michigan,
as a Beirut39 author, with the US
Alliance for Artists Communities

Photo by Samuel Shimon

the root of a pomegranate tree on campus. Although he denies ever touching Jasmine, her brothers kidnap, torture, and dismember him in revenge. The police inspector's deputy ('The Sceptic whose Scepticism Disappears Like a Scattering Cloud') is so haunted by the spectre at the core of the story that he must seek Qur'anic exorcism.

The spectre has been seen or sensed or dreamed of by all the main characters. Jasmine's mother, who reads and relates Jasmine's diary in the final chapter one year after the disappearance, finally understands its identity. It is an *ifreet*, a malevolent spirit oft-told in Arab and Islamic tradition, including the Qur'an. This *ifreet* manifests as a handsome, well-built, middle-age man with glistening white hair, who carries a white book with entirely blank pages. He comes as a bridegroom ready to woo Jasmine in her dreams, and perhaps also in reality. He comes to claim her. She is never found. As William Blake wrote, 'And his dark secret love/ Does thy life destroy' (*The Sick Rose*).

The author makes abundant use of symbolism. In the Qur'an the pomegranate tree is considered to bear the forbidden fruit of Eden. A colourful, crested bird, the hoopoe, hovering near the tree stands as a guide to the invisible world. The jasmine flower symbolizes modesty and grace, but also sensuality. Thus the author's message is that sexual frustration, affecting men and women alike, can only lead to violation and murder, whether in this or the world beyond, political and sexual repression being cut from the same cloth. Unfortunately, here is where the novella fails. In part this is due to the chopped-up narrative; but more that the author makes his characters into mannequins to exhibit his point. For western readers, the story and caricatures may, inadvertently or not, reinforce orientalist fantasies about Arabs.

# 30 years of Palestinian poetry

*Stephen Watts reviews*

**The Palestinian Wedding** *A bilingual anthology of contemporary Palestinian Resistance Poetry*
Collected and translated by A M Elmessiri
Lynne Rienner Publishers, 2011 (A Three Continents Book)
pbk, 250pp, ISBN: 978-0-89410-096-3.

**Like a Straw Bird It Follows Me**, *and Other Poems*
by Ghassan Zaqtan, translated by Fady Joudah
Yale University Press, Margolis poetry series, 2012, hbk, 144pp,
ISBN: 978-0-300-17316-1, £18.99. E-book ISBN: 978-0-300-18363-4

**Rain Inside**, *Selected Poems* by Ibrahim Nasrallah
translated by Omnia Amin and Rick London
Curbstone Press, USA, pbk, 120pp, ISBN: 978-1-93189652-8. USD14.95

T he subtitle given to *The Palestinian Wedding* by its editor, A. M. Elmessiri, who died in 2008, defines its scope very precisely – "A Bilingual Anthology of Contemporary Palestinian Resistance Poetry". A reprint of a volume first published by

Three Continents Press in 1982, it both was, and is, a substantial book, not just in its 250 page length but also for its bringing together of work by such poets as Mahmoud Darwish, Samih al-Qasim, Rashid Hussein, Tawfiq Zayyad, Jabra Ibrahim Jabra, Fadwa Tuqan and Salma Khadra al-Jayyusi. Altogether 21 poets are included and it is salutary to be reminded of the poetry of Mu'in Bsisu, Fawzi al-Asmar, Tawfiq Sayigh and others, whose work has almost 'disappeared' in English translation in the years since 1982. It is, quite simply, very important to see all these poems together still: seminal poems such as Darwish's 'A Lover From Palestine' and 'Blessed Be That Which Has Not Come', 'Abd al-Latif 'Aql's 'Love Palestinian Style' and 'On One Single Face', Walid al-Halis's astonishing 'Mayy And Other Primitive Things' and Mu'in Bsisu's 'God Was A Soldier Behind The Barricades Of Damascus' among them.

It is a book of its time. It followed on from such anthologies as the 1974 *Anthology of Modern Arabic Poetry* (University Of California Press), *Modern Arab Poets* (Three Continents, 1976), *Women Of The Fertile Crescent* (Three Continents Press, 1978) and *Victims Of A Map* (Saqi Books, 1984 and 2005) and it both defined a state of Palestinian poetry in the early 1980s and helped allow modern Arabic poetry to gradually become more widely known in English over subsequent years. As such its current reprint acts as a way of both looking back and defining. But it is more than this. As Elmessiri says in his long and strongly helpful introduction: "When I first read his poem, I learned a great deal about Palestine and about myself as an Arab." He was writing of Darwish's 'A Lover From Palestine' but his sentence rings true for us as readers of the whole anthology now: reading it we learn a great deal about Palestine and about ourselves as human beings. As he lucidly reminds us, the premise of the anthology is that "Palestinian resistance poetry should be placed in a pan-Arab context".

Ibrahim Nasrallah and Ghassan Zaqtan had hardly published their own first books when the first edition of *The Palestinian Wedding* ap-

peared in 1982 and, not surprisingly, neither poet is included in the anthology. However both poets have risen to prominence in the thirty years since, and have given new direction and energy to Palestinian poetry, as to Arabic poetries in the wider sense. It is therefore to be much celebrated that both now have books in recent English translation. Nasrallah's *Rain Inside* was published in 2009 by Curbstone Press, Zaqtan's *Like a Straw Bird It Follows Me* in 2012 by Yale University Press.

Ibrahim Nasrallah writes (in the translation by Omnia Amin and Rick London): "Whenever I catch a poem / I've caught a wing that takes me to the steady radiance / at the heart of the world . . . " and then, in a later poem, he tempers this with complexity: "He leaned toward my heart/and sang a lot. / I asked: Singing helps?/He said: A little. // And he sang a lot." The tone, the experienced language, of these poems has already moved from much of the atmosphere of Palestinian Wedding deeper into layers of ordinary speech and human

*Ibrahim Nasrallah with Banipal publisher Margaret Obank during his UK visit to launch his novel* Time of White Horses

compromise, embracing vision with everyday breath. In a very recent discussion of his work in London (January 2013) Nasrallah admonished "if we don't have dreams and internal contradictions . . ." and in the same discussion related the process of integrating oral histories into the weave of his language and spoke of being "an engineer, or architect" reacting to the request that he construct houses, as a writer, where each home will be itself but be felt differently by those who inhabit the buildings – to keep hold of homeland while widening out the whole idea of home.

The introduction to *Rain Inside* makes much of the poet's avant-garde import, but I'm not sure that this is very useful. His poetry doesn't echo with the linguistic radicalism of contemporary UK and American poets and doesn't need to. His considerable significance, surely, has more to do with a simultaneous deepening down and widening out of the layers of contemporary Palestinian and Arabic poetry, both harking back to and pulling forward from the substance of *The Palestinian Wedding*.

Nasrallah is also, of course, a very fine novelist. In a way it's a pity to talk about his poetry aside from his prose work: partly because his fictions are densely poetic and because they are by nature extended (*Time of White Horses* runs to 400 pages), it is tempting to say that his novels are almost more poetic than his poetry). But his prose also often has a particular relationship to his poetry. He initially conceived his first novel – *Prairies of Fever* – as a book of poems, but in the writing found its scope impelled him towards an extended prose and all the time we can sense a back and forth between the inner discourse of his writings and wider arts. After all, he's a painter and photographer too. But whether we consider Nasrallah as novelist, poet, or visual artist, his work is always somehow hallucinatory. And this is the quality that most shines through *Rain Inside*. "Their sun has been guillotined / and their smiles are muddy with blood", "Life surges right before his eyes / and deserts creep toward him", "he waved back with his wooden arm / and a tremendous joy flooded us / in a homeland of friendship", "Is there a difference to tell / between a soul and a wound to the body?", "As the sun goes down like / a fallen foal or a slain crescent", "Rest a little on my body. / I am the ruins that flow with your love", "And the wind that has knifed its horses." Just as the introduction tries to encompass a 'definition' of Palestinian poetry as well a compressed outline of Nasrallah's life and work, and the trauma of emotional and physical exile, so also the translations seem to pass across the surface of the words. The book is in four sections, but we are not given a sense of how these sections, or individual poems, fit within the poet's wider oeuvre. This doesn't diminish the quality of the poems, but may diminish our abilities to take them in whole, or to fully see through their beauty into the hallucinatory life of the language.

Ghassan Zaqtan, like Nasrallah, was born in 1954 to a Palestinian family that had been forced to flee their homeland and would live as refugees in Jordan. His poetry reflects such experience as surely as does Nasrallah's. But Zaqtan – who would later return to live in Ramallah – has a quaver of doubt, an astonishing self-doubt that richly defies his certainties: to hear his poetry read aloud – as it was both in Arabic and English by the poet and his translator Fady Joudah on a recent tour of America and more briefly Britain – is to feel the frisson of exacted intensity, the sharp flake of experience, the vectored pathways of his words. I saw someone buy the book and then sit down immediately to read what she had just heard read aloud. This is quite rare in London and indicates a rare reader, a rare poet.

Fady Joudah shows great understanding, both in his translation and in his introduction. Thus he says, with beautiful exactness, of Zaqtan's lyricism, that it is "as intense as he is slack and disarming" and he talks of the poems' "private and collective enunciation" as the poet enters the vital possibility of "unwriting himself". This 'unwriting 'is an essential aspect of Zaqtan's art. Palestinian poetry (prose also) makes much reference to horses, black or white (think of Darwish's 'Why Did You Leave The Horse Alone?' or Nasrallah's *Time of White Horses*). In 'Black Horses' Zaqtan says: "Whenever I fall asleep/ a horse comes to graze my dreams." His poems, if anything, put me in mind of the wonderful paintings of horses and hills done by Zoran Mušič between Venice and the Croatian islands in the years after terrible experience of war and prison camp, paintings that un-write the pastel air.

From this it might be expected that Nasrallah be seen as closer than Zaqtan to Palestinian traditions as evinced so effectively in *The Palestinian Wedding*. But I don't think this is so: for both poets pick up on different strands and ply them their own way. Yet it is notable that Mahmoud Darwish – who perhaps more than any poet exemplified the Palestinian thread and is still seen as the Palestinian poet par excellence, that it was he who as editor of *Al-Karmel* first and enthusiastically published Zaqtan's superb long poem 'Alone And The River Before Me' and the sequence 'Pretexts', even as they pull at and away from the tradition that Darwish is most seen to have created. Surely this is because poetry – and Palestinian poetry as much as any – is always more complex and richly structured than political analysis, or indeed political need, might want to allow. Whatever, Zaqtan's quiet, subtle and almost constricted, but wholly unconstricting, voice is astonishing to hear or read. It is also not by chance that Fady Joudah, translator of two of Darwish's volumes, should have managed to translate in so supple and effective a way Zaqtan's seemingly very different voice.

*Ghassan Zaqtan and Fady Joudah in London at the book launch*

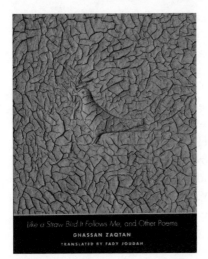

Like a Straw Bird It Follows Me, and Other Poems
GHASSAN ZAQTAN
TRANSLATED BY FADY JOUDAH

Zaqtan 'approaches' the epic dimension by observing, by paying attention to detail. But we have to be careful in our use of verbs here: approaching and observing do not do justice to what the poet gives us. He homes in on the precise, on ordinary specifics, on living detail and, just exactly as he does this, so also he pulls away, retaining all the detail, to supply an overview, a vision even, to our reading. It is a marvellous achievement. Pierre Joris puts it very well: "Zaqtan's work is exemplary in that its lyrical intensity simultaneously hides and foregrounds" the poet's trade of exile. He can tell us that: "Noon gathers/like a stabbed horse", and later that "beneath the mud/the drowned prepared fish of nets" leaving unsaid (because it does not need to be said as such) that the living above the waters prepare nets for fish. Of the "talk that remained in the house" when everyone had gone he tells us "I used to see it searching/like the mad/ for a gap in the silence." Such gaps in the silence are rare in poetry – but also precisely are poetry. "Don't wake him/he's dead/by a bend in the story." A bend in the story! Doesn't that say it all.

The detail, the naming of places and sometimes people, the loose exactness of the titles, keep us on the edge of violent simplicities. In a beautiful, but heart-rending, poem late on in the third section of the title collection, as the poet refrains for us the "thought of going back there", he says not 'I' but 'he'. "He thought long of going back." And then it is a generic he, some one person but also everyone: "There was a man crossing the street without looking/whereas his infidelities were behind him like a heap of loose women": beautifully warm description, no whiff of moral approbation, and the man "careful not to bump into the pampered flower pot":

"He thought long of going back/where he had left her
listening/with honey eyes and a cloven heart"

And then suddenly a bell rings and Zaqtan, or Fady Joudah, compresses all gradients for us, the bell ringing, the ancient bell on the hill, the hill which the pampered bougainvillea had since covered, the man, memory, all 'he's' and 'I's' into the hill where that night "the eleven brothers killed/their only sister".

Ilya Kaminsky likens Zaqtan's poetry to that of the great Serbian poet Vasko Popa for its "approach to violence and the nation's dream time" and it is an appropriate thought. Apt also that the poet has found as empathetic and sensitive a translator as Fady Joudah to bring him into English. And Joudah himself, to key-ring the open circle, talks of echoes in Ibrahim Nasrallah's poetry of Zbigniew Herbert.

So, circling back on *The Palestinian Wedding* – in its new edition of 2011 and thirty years on from the first – what are we to think and where do we feel that we are? Without a doubt it's excellent to still have the book in print and it bears very well the passage of years: it is not only a document, among others, of how Palestinian poetry was in 1980, it also has clear resonance with poetry readers today. Maybe it's a pity that it is simply a reprint: the bibliography and notes, excellent for the time, have not been updated and no mention is made of the editor's recent death. But the book itself still stands beautifully for "Palestine . . . in a pan-Arab context".

Perhaps the pity is that there hasn't been another translated anthology of Palestinian poetry contemporary to our present now. The poetries of Ghassan Zaqtan and Ibrahim Nasrallah, as with other poets from Mourid Barghouti to Najwan Darwish or Marwan Makhoul, show us that complex layers of human experience pervade a poetry that remains Palestinian while pulsing outwards into other world poetries. Their detail is precisely what gives human value to their objective stance, widely global but never 'globalised' or 'globalising'.

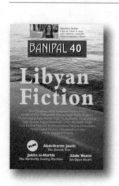

# Poetry from *Two Lines*

### Norbert Hirschhorn reviews

**Wherever I Lie is Your Bed**
Two Lines World Writing in Translation, No. 16
Edited by Margaret Jull Costa (prose), Marilyn Hacker (poetry)
Center for the Art of Translation, San Francisco. pbk, 275pp.
ISBN 9781931883160.

The Center for the Art of Translation, a non-profit organization, seeks to "broaden cultural understanding through international literature and translation". *Two Lines* is a series of the Center's anthologies that feature prose and poetry from around the world, translated into English with the original on the facing page. No. 16 provides work from many European writers, and special sections of poetry: one of Adonis's works – five poems translated by Khaled Mattawa, and one a focus on a new generation of Palestinian poets. Marilyn Hacker writes that the Palestinians, looking to Mahmoud Darwish for their inspiration, "go beyond a mythology of exile, of recreating a formerly promised land frozen in idealism and despair, to the expression of an internalized exile . . . an imagination of *al-watan* [homeland] as also something internal, intimate, the apotheosis of daily life". Much credit goes to the editor for presenting the arc of Palestinian poetry as written today.

Nine poets, the majority born in the 1970s, are presented in sequence: Mahmoud Darwish, Ghassan Zaqtan, Ayman Ghbarieh, Nasser Rabah, Ghada al-Shafi'i, Samir Abu Hawwash, Najwan Darwish, Hala al-Shrouf and, in an end paper, Ibrahim Nasrallah.

The section leads with Mahmoud Darwish's "Rita's Winter", translated by Fady Joudah. This work demonstrates the poet's signature prosody, much emulated by younger poets, of mixed, often clashing imagery; one that is surely enriched by the sounds and rhythms of Arabic. The love affair with Rita, of "Rita and the Rifle", will end, an early casualty of the strife between Arabs and Jews:

"Rita will depart in a few hours and leave her shadow / as a white prison cell . . . And she broke the ceramic of the day against the iron windowpane / she place her handgun on the poem's draft . . . Prison, broke, ceramic, iron, handgun." To read Darwish, much attention must be paid to nouns.

Zaqtan's language is less lush than Darwish's, generally with shorter lines and more abrupt stanza breaks. The two poems represented here, "Like One Who Waits for Me" and "He Thought Long of Going Back There", also translated by Fady Joudah, are more accessible yet still highly lyrical. The other poets represented show that the elliptical lyric isn't the only style. Ayman Ghbarieh, also translated by Fady Joudah, pulls no punches in his sardonic send-up of Israelis in "Why Should We Teach Our Enemy How to Raise Pigeons?", while existential despair that transcends metaphor for the local to the universal is found in Nasser Rabah's 'Absence', Ghadah al-Shafi'i's 'Fenced Solitude', and Samir Abu Hawwash's 'The Very Handsome Man' and Hala al-Shrouf poignantly tells of the emotional clash of gender in 'She and He'.

## Cafés by Abdulkareem Kasid
Translated by the poet with Sara Halub
The Many Press, London, 2012. ISBN
9780907326390. 31pp.

This pamphlet is the Iraqi poet's first publication in English translation. He writes from exile (Kuwait, Yemen, Syria, now London) where the café becomes a form of social and intellectual "homeland". The pamphlet's two sections, 'Cafés' and 'Windows' – are epigrammatic contemplations, with the title section numbered, the other separated by ellipses. Cafés and Windows stand in for exile, isolation, and poetic observation. The various cafés with their customers find themselves bombed, swept away by flood, visited by ghosts or the dead, or totally isolated. Magritte-like imagery abounds – "In a far away station / There was a chair / And a cup of tea, / No sign of a train / No travellers either / Just the café, all by itself". Harold Bloom says a poem should surprise and delight. Kasid's poetry does both.

*Margaret Obank reviews*

## Art Home Lands

by **Oded Halahmy**

Poetry in English, Arabic and Hebrew Pomegranate Gallery Press, NYC, September 2012, pbk, 162pp ISBN: 978-0985759612

# Homelands: Baghdad, Jerusalem, New York

Art Home Lands is the first book of poetry by internationally renowned sculptor Oded Halahmy and contains images of his artworks created over the last fifty years as well as the story of his journey from Iraq to Israel and New York. In reflecting on his three languages, English, Arabic and Hebrew, and his three homelands, Baghdad, Jerusalem and New York, in this extraordinary work, Oded Halahmy said:

"I have been creating paintings and sculptures for over five decades, and now for the first time I am combining the artistry of poetry with the visual expression of paintings and sculpture. The poems appear in the three languages that I grew up with in Iraq before we emigrated to Israel: classical Biblical Hebrew, which we only used for praying in Iraq, but now has become more widely used; Arabic, which we used in everyday life, and English, which is not my native tongue but one that I speak most often."

Oded started painting and sculpting in Baghdad, studied in London at St Martin's School of Art under Anthony Caro, then moved to New York in 1971, where his talent was soon recognised.

He was inspired to create *Art Home Lands* by the "Al Mutanabbi Street Book Project" founded by poet and bookseller Beau Beausoleil after the Baghdad street was bombed in 2007. When asked to participate, he explained: "I was excited to participate in this project as it brought me back to my childhood in Baghdad. When Iraqis want to read, the

Photo by Samuel Shimon

*Oded Halahmy in the Pomegranate Gallery in New York, which he established in 2006*

first place they turn to is Al-Mutanabbi Street, a Mecca for all writers, poets, novelists, students and anyone who is thirsty for knowledge. I remember at the end of my school year, my mother and I would walk from our home to Al Mutanabbi Street so we could sell my old schoolbooks and purchase new ones . . . I loved to learn, so these trips became food for the mind, for the body and for the soul."

Oded Halahmy has dedicated his book to "the living spirit of Al Mutanabbi Street, to those who lost their lives in its destruction, and to those who aim to keep its memory alive", as well as to the memory of his parents and many scattered relatives.

*– A poem from the book*

### I LOVE YOU

The Land of Milk and Honey
We sat by the rivers
Ate *geymer* and *dibis* (clotted
  cream and date syrup)
With flat round bread
Of wheat and barley (*hintah* and
  *shear*)
Ate *kibbeh* (dumplings) stuffed
  with almonds, raisins and spices
Grilled fish by the river (*masgouf*)
Ate figs and pomegranates
Dates with *tahina*
Sweet black tea with cardamom
Lady apples, grapes, apricots
Sweet watermelon and feta
  cheese
White berries (*tickey*) and
  cherries (*nabeg*)
Baklawa and "Manna from Heaven"
We sang holy songs
So that in exile
We do not forget the love

## POETRY

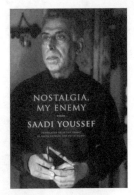

**Nostalgia, My Enemy** presents the English translations of 50 poems by great Iraqi poet Saadi Youssef. In their introduction, translators Sinan Antoon and Peter Money describe the huge influence Youssef has had on the trajectory of modern Arabic poetry, both through his original work and through his translations into Arabic of poets such as Whitman, Cavafy and Ritsos. As they observe, his poetry is inseparable from Iraq's recent turbulent history but it also captures the eternal and ephemeral moments of existence. In exile in London, Youssef's response to the atrocities suffered by his country has ranged from angry political invectives in essay form to tender poems, recuperating his fractured memories of Iraq. In his "Prologue: On Poetry", Youssef writes that, "If science and politics struggle, promise and prepare for another time, poetry is current, direct and immediate ... Poetry is transformative. Poetry transforms in that intimate moment combining the current and the eternal in a wondrous embrace."

The poems in this collection do indeed capture both the fleeting and the eternal, many are devoted to scenes from nature in which every word is, in Youssef's words, "delicate like a taut string": "On the door/ the spider weaves/ what has disappeared:/ it weaves the meaning of the garment ..." Antoon and Money's translations capture the tender, ephemeral quality of the original, receptive to every nuance of the Arabic. The book's frontispiece displays the original Arabic of the poem "Fulfilment" in Youssef's own handwriting. Several poems, including "Nature", "The Evening the Game was Over" and "Andes Butterflies" were previously published in *Banipal 43 – Celebrating Denys Johnson-Davies* (2012). Translated by Sinan Antoon and Peter Money. Graywolf Press, Minneapolis, 2012, pbk, 82pp. ISBN: 9781555976293. CB

**The Parley Tree: Poets from French-speaking Africa and the Arab World**, edited, translated and introduced by Patrick Williamson, presents a rich array of poetry which, in Williamson's words, aims to "bring together writers ... from both Africa and the Arab world, in order to explore what they have in common and what sets them apart". Among the 18 poets featured are Mohammed Dib (Algeria), Amina Saïd (Tunisia), Vénus Khoury-Ghata (Lebanon) and Abdellatif Laâbi (Morocco). Arc Publications, Todmorden, 2012, pbk, 220pp. ISBN: 9781906570613. CB

**Homage to Etel Adnan**, edited by Lindsey Boldt, resulted from Etel Adnan receiving the Small Press Traffic Literary Arts Center's Lifetime Achievement Award, dedicated to "those who push the limits of how we speak and think about the world". Twenty-two writers have contributed texts to celebrate Adnan's lifetime of artistic creation as poet, essayist and visual artist. The book features poems dedicated to Adnan, anecdotes about her life, studies of her work and reflections on teaching her poetry. The Post-Apollo Press, 2012, pbk, 102pp. ISBN: 9780942996791. CB

**Transfer** by Naomi Shihab Nye, is a collection dedicated to the poet's father Aziz Shihab, and very much about him. He "wanted us write a book together" are almost the first words in her introduction that brims with snap-shot memories of a much-loved and missed man. Arranged in five sections, some with titles as enticing as the poems themselves, as in II – "Just Call me Aziz" 11 poems – Titles by Aziz Shihab – from his notebooks. These verses are sabre-sharp, sparse and sensitive, and deserve worldwide readings. Boa Editions, Rochester, NY. ISBN 9781934414521, pbk, 128pp. (ISBN 9781934414644, hbk.) MO

**my name on his tongue** is a first collection by Arab American novelist, Laila Halaby, which she describes as "a memoir in poems". Hers is a poetry that manages to be open and simple, but rich and dense at the same time. She writes the experience of the closely personal as a direct part of the struggle between (two) cultures, the body politic of her identity and of perceived otherness. There is naturally some paradox here: her language is very much in an American grain, and yet the experience of the poems is pulled and stretched against that grain. The poems however are not jagged or barbed as a result, nor does Halaby engage with radical language issues (beyond use of the lower case throughout), as say Khaled Mattawa and others do. Rather

these poems carry our breath through the pain, wit and candour of disorienting memoir: as she says of the books her grandfather could not read: "I devour them in his honor/spit them back in English/in his memory." She does so in a clear flow-force of language: this is a paradoxical, richly achieved first collection. Syracuse University Press, NY, 129pp, 2012. SW

**The Square Root of Beirut** by Lebanese British poet Omar Sabbagh is his second collection with Cinnamon Press in two years. The poems, written in English, concern family, love (personal, erotic, political), memory, rites of passage. But in another way they are about language: its richness, its paradox, its closeness to and distance from experience. Its alchemies, conceits (Sabbagh at times seems steeped in English poetic traditions), its imageries. Beirut is a constant presence, or absence, as also both of his parents, his loves. The poems seem so well settled into English, yet have the added quality of being unsettling to the language. Cinnamon Press, Wales, 64pp, 2011. SW

**Salwa** by Yasmeen Makarem comprises 41 compelling poems by a young Lebanese poet writing in English who has lived through the destruction brought upon her country by war and the paralysis of sectarian strife. The poems tread the flickering boundary between the personal and political realms, each interrogating the turmoil of simultaneous existence within both. "If only someone would have told her what to expect/ That shiny marbles have two sides, both are fake." Salwa means solace, and the reader is persuaded by the elegance of the poetic voice in its search. RoseDog Books, Pittsburgh, USA, 2012. ISBN 9781434930668. 41pp. NH

## FICTION

**A Muslim Suicide,** which won the 2012 Saif Ghobash Banipal Prize for Arabic Literary Translation, is the third historical novel by the award-winning novelist Bensalem Himmich to be translated into English and all three by Roger Allen. Himmich is a Moroccan novelist, poet and philosopher, and recent Minister of Culture who has published 26 books in Arabic and French, including 11 novels, with *My Torturess* being shortlisted for the 2011 International Prize for Arabic Fiction.

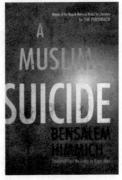

The protagonist of *A Muslim Suicide* is Ibn Sab'in, a radical Sufi philosopher from the thirteenth century whose unorthodox opinions regarding separation of religion and state, not to mention his controversial lifestyle, lead him to flee his native Spain for what is now Morocco, and in later years to settle in Mecca, where he is reported to have killed himself at the Ka'ba. In depicting Ibn Sab'in's physical and spiritual journey Himmich re-creates the political tensions together with the intellectual and religious antagonisms of the time. The judges described it as "is a highly ambitious and erudite work that opens up remarkable historical, cultural and religious perspectives on the Islamic heritage" and were inpressed "with its remarkable sophistication and ambition, its rich philosophical and literary tapestry, and the seamless way in which it has been translated". Translated by Roger Allen. Syracuse University Press, New York, 2011, pbk, 414pp, ISBN 9780815609667. AR.

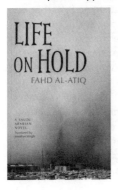

**Life on Hold** by Fahd al-Atiq depicts the radical changes in Riyadh in the wake of the oil boom, focussing on the changing nature of everyday life as people move from bustling old city neighbourhoods to new, suburban villas. Protagonist Khaled is caught in a rut, unable to escape the tedious rhythm of his days. The novel follows his innermost thoughts as he struggles to come to terms with his disappointments and disillusionment. "The days are all much the same here," is a constant refrain throughout the book as the novel shifts between third and first person narrative. *Life on Hold* is written in simple, stark prose, capturing the essence of everyday existence in the suburban landscape and its monotony. Questions pepper the book, revealing the angst at the heart of the new society, embodied by Khaled: "Do I love this Riyadh or hate it? Am I lucky here or unlucky?"

As with many novels from the Gulf, *Life on Hold* attempts to come to terms with the total transformation of society and the disillusionment brought about by it. Silence is a recurring theme throughout, portraying alienation at the heart of society. Fahd al-Atiq is undoubtedly an interesting new voice to emerge from Saudi Arabia and his work has been fluently translated by Jonathan Wright. The book was earlier excerpted in *Banipal 34 – The World of Arab Fiction* (2009), translated by Kathryn Stapely. AUC Press, Cairo, 2012, pbk, 117pp. ISBN: 9789774165665. CB

**The Barbary Figs** by Rashid Boudjedra hones in on the relationship of two cousins, Rashid and Omar, on their hour-long flight from Algiers to Constantine. The cousins, once close, have been driven apart by their past and Rashid thus resolves to delve into this past, forcing Omar to face the many ghosts which continue to haunt his present: "That day at the airport in Algiers, as I was boarding the plane to Constantine, I decided to have it out with him ..."

The complexity of the cousins' relationship, teased out on their short flight, reflects the complex history of modern Algeria from the beginning of colonisation to the aftermath of Independence, moving from horrific accounts of French brutalities in the 1830s to harrowing tales of the regime which succeeded the colonial presence. During the plane journey to Constantine the novel shifts between the present and the cousins' differing versions of the past and of their experiences fighting side by side in the Algerian War of Independence.

As the cousins face challenging and inescapable realities, so too does the reader. In his Afterword, translator André Naffis-Sahely writes that "Boudjedra's may be an uncomfortable voice, but it is inescapable, and haunting". *The Barbary Figs* represents a major contribution to Algerian fiction and won the 2010 Prix du Roman Arabe. A pre-publication excerpt was published in *Banipal 45 – Writers from Palestine* (2012).. Translated from the French by André Naffis-Sahely. Arabia Books, London, 2012, pbk, 191pp. ISBN: 9781906697426. CB

**Le Ravin du chamelier** by Ahmad Aboukhnegar is a desert novel in the tradition of Ibrahim al-Koni, combining Biblical legend, Egyptian mythology and popular folklore in a modern form of fantastic realism. The wild desert setting creates a drama of troubled relationships between man and animal, man and woman, and a struggle to survive amidst arid landscape, jealousy and treachery. The novel begins as a Bedouin caravan wanders over the sandy expanses, retelling legends of the wilderness in a new form. Aboukhnegar lives in a village near his native Aswan and has published numerous works of theatre, short stories and novels. Translated from the Arabic to the French by Khaled Osman. Sindbad/Actes Sud, Paris, 2012, pbk, 208pp, ISBN: 9782330005900. CB.

**As Though She Were Sleeping** by Elias Khoury, the well-known Lebanese novelist who often brings political realities into his works, has an experimental style — juxtaposition of past, present and future, elevation of dreams to a status above reality and treatment of time — that lends it an authenticity which immediately draws the reader. With the background of the political upheavals of 1947, the novel treats the history of the Palestine–Israel conflict by ignoring it, by delving instead into the minds of the people living in those tumultuous times; Milia and Mansour — the newly-married couple unaware of what is in store for them — are vivid characters one can sympathise with without much effort. The novel conveys the

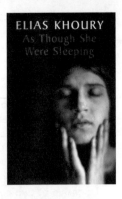

weight of history on individual lives in a manner reminiscent of Tolstoy. The UK edition is translated by award-winning translator Humphrey Davies, published by Maclehose Press, UK, 2012, pbk, 368pp, ISBN: 978-0857050533. The US edition of this novel is translated by Marilyn Booth and published by Archipelago Books, NY, 2012, hbk, 372pp, ISBN 9781935 744023. MK.

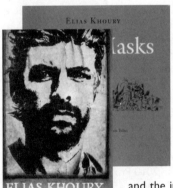

**White Masks** by Elias Khoury was first published in Arabic in 1981 and was "one of the first novels that dared to address the civil war in Lebanon, the terrible atrocities, and the war's reflection in the daily lives of the people". Translated by Maia Tabet, it was commended by the 2011 Saif Ghobash Banipal Prize for Arabic Literary Translation. The judges stated that it was "a fascinating investigation into investigation itself, telling the story of the murder of one man during the Lebanese Civil War, and showing the chaos and incoherence of history as it emerges, and the importance of personal stories to counteract and contain the messiness of history". US edition by Archipelago Press, NY. ISBN: 9780981987323 303pp, hbk, was reviewed in *Banipal 40*, (http://www.banipal.co.uk/book_reviews/85/white-masks-by-elias-khoury/). The UK edition is published by Maclehose Press, London, 2013, pbk, 271pp. ISBN: 9780857052124. CB

**The Bottom of the Jar** by Abdellatif Laâbi is an autobiographical novel depicting the childhood of a young boy in Fez in the 1950s, as Morocco begins to free itself of the French colonial occupation. The novel offers a glimpse into Laâbi's youthful experiences, narrated in the casual style of a friendly, night-time gathering. An excerpt from the novel, translated by Victor Reinking, was published in *Banipal 23* (2005). Translated from the French by André Naffis-Sahely. Archipelago Books, NY, 2012, pbk, 226pp. ISBN: 9781935744603. MO

**The Corsair** by Abdulaziz Al-Mahmoud relates the adventures of Erhama bin Jaber, a pirate living in the Gulf at the beginning of the nineteenth century. Set amidst British attempts to maintain control of the region, fighting pirates and trying to curtail the spread of Wahhabism, the novel is based on historical events, demonstrating that, before the discovery of oil, the Gulf was no quiet, isolated area but one full of intrigue, spies and adventure. Translated by Amira Nowaira. BQFP, Doha, 2012, pbk, 311pp. ISBN: 9789992194720. AR

**Writing Love: A Syrian Novel** by Khalil Sweileh is a meditation on writing, reading, and love. The first-person narrator is "seduced by the notion of writing a novel that can drag a reader by the ears into its private hell". He roams Damascus and books for inspiration. Packed with references to the Arabic and international literary canons, this experimental work is witty and diverting but its loose structure may test the patience of some readers. First published in Arabic in 2008 as *Warraq al-hubb* (Dar el-Shorouk), *Writing Love* won the 2009 Naguib Mahfouz Medal for Literature. Translated by Alexa Firat, AUC Press, Cairo and New York, 2012, ISBN: 9789774165351, pbk, 192pp. ST

**The Palm House**, by Sudanese author Tarek Eltayeb, is set in Vienna (the author has lived in Austria for many years), and chronicles the life of Hamza, a young Sudanese man who cannot help but reminisce about his homeland. Dealing with a foreign culture and way of life, he finds himself constantly looking back to the warm memories of his childhood. An easy read, the story is a fresh take on themes of loneliness, poverty and an individual's attempt to find solitude and peace in a chaotic world. Translated from the Arabic by Kareem Abu-Zeid. AUC Press, Cairo, 2012, hbk, 291pp, ISBN 97877416428. MK.

**Brooklyn Heights** by Miral al-Tahawy. Heroine and narrator Hend moves to New York as a divorced mother with her son. Her story, which tends to mirror that of the author, captures the vibrant immigrant communities of Brooklyn Heights interspersed with flashbacks of her Egyptian childhood, her schooling and her husband's marital infidelities. The Arabic original won the 2010 Naguib Mahfouz award and was shortlisted for the 2011 IPAF. Translated by Samah Selim. AUC Press, US/ME. Faber & Faber, UK, 2012, pbk, 272pp, ISBN 9780571280025. MO

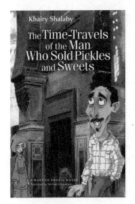

**The Time-Travels of the Man Who Sold Pickles and Sweets** by Khairy Shalaby relates the time-travelling adventures of sweet-seller Ibn Shalaby as he bumbles his way through the Fatimid, Ayyubid and Mamluk periods, briefly returning every now and then to the 1990s. During his travels, he becomes entangled in the court life of different periods and the intrigues rife within them, meeting various historical figures and witnessing the construction of celebrated Cairene monuments. Translated by Michael Cooperson. AUC Press, Cairo, 2010, hbk, 264pp. ISBN: 978-077-416-391-3. CB

**Love in the Rain** and **Midaq Alley** are two new contributions to the wealth of work by Nobel laureate Naguib Mahfouz translated into English. *Midaq Alley* is set during the Second World War and gives a rich account of life in the poor quarter of medieval Cairo. The aftermath of the 1967 Six Day War is the backdrop for *Love in the Rain*, whose characters experience the effects of this calamitous event. Translated, respectively, by Humphrey Davies and Nancy Roberts. AUC Press, Cairo, 2011, hbk, 282pp and 134pp. ISBN: 9789774164835. AR.

**Cairo Paris Melbourne** by Maher Abou Elsaoud tells the story of Zoheir, a young Egyptian boy born in the 'City of Dead,' the infamous Cairo cemetery populated by the living. Amid turbulent events of the Middle East from 1967 to 2003, Zoheir relates his experiences of living in the three cities of the book's title. Zoheir escapes Cairo only to plunge into the dark underworld of Paris from where he eventually travels to Melbourne and, after a lengthy period of depression, eventually finds meaning and a chance for redemption. Black Pepper, Melbourne, 2012, pbk, 333pp. ISBN: 978-1-876044-75-6. CB

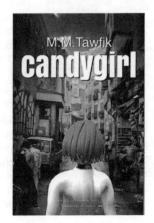

**Candygirl** by M. M. Tawfik follows the Cerebellum, an Egyptian scientist with unfortunate past connections to Saddam Hussein's nuclear programme, seeking to evade American secret service agents in the Cairo underworld. The novel alternates between real and virtual worlds as the relentless chase continues and the Cerebellum struggles to be reunited with Candygirl, a beautiful avatar from the virtual world. *Candygirl* is the third of a trilogy. The second novel was published in English as *Murder in the Tower of Happiness* (AUC, 2008). Translated by the author. AUC Press, Egypt, 2012, pbk, 220pp. ISBN: 978-977-416-559-7.

**Of Noble Origins** by Saher Khalifeh concerns the Qahtan family, a prominent Palestinian family whose claimed descent from the Arabian Peninsula and the family of the Prophet Muhammad has traditionally granted them a degree of influence within society. Following the First World War, however, the family's status is challenged both by the British Mandate and the Zionist movement. *Of Noble Origins* is the fourth novel by Khalifeh to be published in English translation by the AUC, following *The Inheritance* (2005), *The Image, the Icon and the Covenant* (2007) and *The End of Spring* (2008). Translated by Aida Bamia. AUC Press, Egypt, 2012, pbk, 276pp. ISBN: 9789774165429. CB

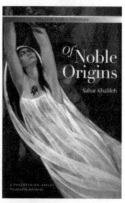

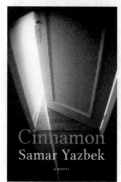

**Cinnamon** by Samar Yazbek explores power relations and sexuality. Aliyah, a young girl from the Damascus slums, is in effect sold by her brutal father as a servant to a wealthy couple, Hanan and Anwar. Hanan is unhappy in her marriage to a sterile cousin and begins to seduce Aliyah when the girl is only 11. One night she discovers Aliyah in bed with Anwar, and orders the girl to leave. Syrian author Samar Yazbek is best known for her non-fiction *A Woman in the Crossfire: Diaries of the Syrian Revolution* (Haus Publishing, 2012) for which she won the PEN Pinter Prize. Translated by Emily Danby, Arabia Books, UK, 2012, pbk, 160pp, ISBN: 9781906697433. ST

**Days in the Diaspora** by Kamal Ruhayyim is set in Paris and portrays the daily struggles of Galal, a young Jewish man who has left Egypt along with his family as part of the great Jewish Exodus of the 1970s. Alongside his colourful and vibrant friends and family, Galal

attempts to come to terms with his new home and identity, searching for a sense of belonging after the radical uprooting of his day-to-day existence. Translated by Sarah Enany. AUC Press, Egypt, 2012, pbk, 299pp. ISBN: 9789774165375. CB

**Light Piercing Water: Guest Boy** by Djelloul Marbrook is the first of the *Light Piercing Water* trilogy. The trilogy echoes both *The Odyssey* and *The Adventures of Sindbad*, and follows the travels of American seaman Bo Cavalieri from Hamburg to Morocco and on to Oman and Manhattan. The product of years of investigation and research into marine archaeology, alchemy and the Persian Gulf, the trilogy is fast-paced and action-packed and offers a glimpse of how the Arab world has historically shaped the contemporary world we know today. Mira Publishing, Leeds, 2012, pbk, 238pp. ISBN: 9781908509062.

**The Sheikh's Detective** by A. Alwan depicts the unlikely relationship of Sheikh Ibrahim and Jeffrey, a postman whom the sheikh employs to track down his long-lost son. Set in Brighton, the novel raises numerous philosophical and ethical issues as Ibrahim and Jeffrey challenge one another's fundamental beliefs and outlooks on life. Translated by Timothy Reece, edited by Gavin Bradbury. Mira Publishing, Leeds, 2012, pbk, 181pp. ISBN: 9781908509000.

**Metro: A Story of Cairo** by Magdy El Shafee is a graphic novel, published in Egypt in 2008 and subsequently banned. The novel details the exploits of two young software designers, Shehab and Mustafa who, after running foul of a loan shark, decide to rob a bank. The fast-paced narrative moves from one desperate situation to another as all characters fall victim to the corruption rife within Cairo and to the general repression of society. Translated by Chip Rossetti. Metropolitan Books, New York, 2012, pbk, 97pp. ISBN: 978-0-8050-9488-6. AR

**The Battle of Poitiers**, translated by William Granara, **The Caliph's Sister,** translated by Issa J. Boullata, and **The Caliph's Heirs,** translated by Michael Cooperson, are three of Jurji Zaidan's five historical novels whose English translations have been commissioned by the Zaidan Foundation. The first is set during the Arab invasion of France at the beginning of the eighth century while the latter two take place during the reign of the 'Abbasid Caliph Harun al-Rashid. Published by the Zaidan Foundation Inc, Bethesda, USA, 2010 & 2011, pbk, *Battle of Poitiers* 239pp, ISBN: 9780984843503, *The Caliph's Sister,* 229pp ISBN: 9780984843510 and *The Caliph's Heirs,* 329pp, ISBN: 9780984843527. AR

**Three Kings of Warka – Enmerkar, Lugalbanda, Gilgamesh**, retold by Fran Hazelton, presents three tales of heroism and adventure from ancient Mesopotamia. As Hazelton, who last year celebrated 15 years of Mesopotamian storytelling, remarks in her acknowledgments, the collection arose from the activities of the "Discover Mesopotamia through Storytelling" project, organised by the Enheduanna Society. Using translations of original Sumerian and Akkadian manuscripts, the group told and retold the stories and, as Hazelton writes, "the project participants provided ears and imaginations to receive the stories as they travelled from the storytellers' mouths". The Enheduanna Society, London, 2012, pbk, 150pp. ISBN: 9780955433023. AR

## ANTHOLOGIES

**Al-Mutanabbi Street Starts Here**, edited by Beau Beausoleil and Deema Shehabi, is a packed anthology of poems and essays, dedicated to Baghdad's main bookselling street. On March 5, 2007, a car bomb exploded on al-Mutanabbi Street in Baghdad, killing more than 30 people and destroying the historic centre of Baghdad bookselling, which had been a meeting point for the Iraqi literary community for centuries.

For Californian poet and bookseller Beau Beausoleil it was imperative that this event should remain in people's consciousness, representing as it did, in his own words, "an attack on all of us," that is to say, everyone who cherishes freedom of thought and expression.

Having resolved to resurrect al-Mutanabbi Street, Beausoleil sent out a call for contributions and was overwhelmed by the rich and dynamic response which followed. What resulted is this beautiful testimony to al-Mutanabbi Street as a place of free exchange and creativity, combining poetry with essays and anecdotes. Contributions to this inspirational volume come from over 140 authors, including Saadi Youssef, Etel Adnan and Ibrahim Nasrallah, and number both authors from the Arab world with a personal connection to the street and others for whom the street symbolizes both the power of literature and the need to protect it. In his Preface, Beausoleil writes: "Al-Mutanabbi Street starts in many places around the globe. Everywhere it starts it seeks to include the free exchange of ideas. We must safeguard that." PM Press, Oakland, 2012, pbk, 306pp. ISBN: 9781604865905.

The exhibition of artists' books, **An Inventory of Al-Mutanabbi Street**, is being held at the John Rylands Library, Manchester, until 29 July 2013, part of "re-assembling" the "inventory" of reading material lost in the car bombing of al-Mutanabbi Street. "The project is both a lament and a commemoration of the singular power of words. We hope that these books will make visible the literary bridge that connects us, made of words and images that move back and forth between the readers in Iraq and ourselves" – The al-Mutanabbi Street Coalition. AR

**New Voices of Arabia: The Poetry**, edited by Saad Al-Bazei, and **New Voices of Arabia: The Short Stories**, edited by Abdulaziz Al-Seball and Anthony Calderbank, present the works of new writers emerging from Saudi Arabia, offering a broad view of the current literary scene, with 40 short story writers and 41 poets. Short biographies are provided for all writers with introductions to each volume by the editors. This is essential reading for anyone interested in new literature from the Gulf. I. B. Tauris, London, 2012, ISBNs: 9781780760988 and 9781780760995.

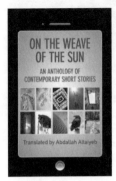

**On the Weave of the Sun** presents 18 short stories by 14 writers hailing from Saudi Arabia (Awadh Shaher, Jubair Al-Melaihan, Wafa Altayeb and Leila Al-Ehaideb), Syria (Ibtesam Trisy, Faysal Abu Saad and Nabil Hatem), the United Arab Emirates (Fatima Al-Nahidh), Morocco (Hasan El-Biqali), Egypt (Hoida Saleh and Samir El-Feel) and Palestine (Khaled Al-Jobour). Editor and translator of all the works, Abdallah Altaiyeb is himself a short story writer. Strategic Book Publishing and Rights Co., Houston, 2012, pbk, 126pp. ISBN: 9781612047102.

## MEMOIR

**Life After Baghdad** by Sasson Somekh chronicles his life after his forced emigration from Iraq to Israel. Somekh, a scholar of Arabic literature, devotes many chapters of his books to people who were 'dear to him'. Somekh's experiences as an Arab Jew in Israel offer an insight into the reality of Israel in its early years. Abstaining from sweeping generalizations, Somekh devotes his time narrating the details of things that he, as a young man interested in literature, found to be important. A large chapter is devoted to Somekh's friendship with Nobel Laureate Naguib Mahfouz and in fact,

the memoir ends with Somekh's reflections on the life of Mahfouz. Somekh has written a memoir that reflects the academic rigor of his personality in its politically disengaged tone; it is, in short, the story of a scholar's life. Translated from the Hebrew by Tamar Cohen. Sussex Academic Press, 2012, pbk, 168pp, ISBN: 9781845195021. MK.

## NON FICTION

**The Philosophy of Desert Metaphors in Ibrahim al-Koni** by Meinrad Calleja focuses on al-Koni's 1989 novel, *The*

*Bleeding of the Stone*, examining philosophical reflections concealed within the text. With a short first chapter devoted to al-Koni's life in Libya, Russia, Poland and Switzerland, Calleja moves on to consider linguistic and thematic aspects of the novel, concluding that, "Al-Koni uses his metaphors to unmask instabilities of truths, to destabilise certainty, and to depersonalise the self". Faraxa, Malta, 2012, pbk, 247pp. ISBN: 9789995702724.

**Classical Arabic Literature: A Library of Arabic Literature Anthology** launches the newly established Library of Arabic Literature (LAL) established by NYU Abu Dhabi. This first volume is a comprehensive anthology by renowned Arabist Geert Jan Van Gelder, presenting an comprehensive line-up of texts from the pre-Islamic era until the 18th century, including brief introductions to every text and extensive endnotes. The texts selected include both poetry and prose, with poetry ranging from love to satire and prose ranging from erotic tales to moral parables. New York University Press, Library of Arabic Literature, New York, 2013, pbk, 468pp. ISBN: 9780814738269. See page 14 above for pre-publication excerpts from *Leg over Leg* by Faris al-Shidyaq, the next volumes in LAL's list, translated by Humphrey Davies. AR

**Conflicting Narratives: War, Trauma and Memory in Iraqi Culture,** edited by Stephan Milich, Friederike Pannewick and Leslie Tramontini, deals with Iraqi cultural production under and after Baathist rule, examining literature, poetry and the role of the artist, torn between a repressive regime and exile. Particular contributions include studies of Iraqi-German Literature, Iraqi novels of exile in Sweden, and an analysis of Sinan Antoon's novel *I'jaam*. The final section, 'Shahadat', presents translations of five essays on 'al-makan al-'iraqi' ('the Iraqi space'). Reichert Verlag, Wiesbaden, 2012, hbk, 268pp. ISBN: 9783895008061. CB

**Gender, Nation and the Arabic Novel: Egypt, 1892-2008** by Hoda Elsadda examines and radically reconsiders over a century of Egyptian Arabic novels and the literary discourse surrounding them, unearthing works that have traditionally been excluded from the dominant cultural canon. In her final chapter, "Liminal Spaces/Liminal Identities", Elsadda discusses contemporary authors Hamdi Abu Golayyel, Ahmed Alaidy and Muhammad 'Ala' al-Din, giving an in-depth analysis of their work. Syracuse University Press and Edinburgh University Press, New York, 2012, hbk, 261pp. ISBN: 9780815632962.

**Once Upon the Orient Wave: Milton and the Arab Muslim World** by Eid Abdallah Dahiyat argues that, although Milton himself neither spoke Arabic nor visited the Middle East, many aspects of his work strongly suggest that Islam and Arab culture considerably influenced his thought. Having spent his first chapter discussing this theory, Dahiyat moves on to discuss critical responses by Arab authors to Milton, and to review various translations of Milton into Arabic. Hesperus Press, London, 2012, hbk, 160pp. ISBN: 9781843913610.

**Cultural Encounters in Translation from Arabic**, edited by Said Faiq. Professor of Translation and Intercultural Studies at the American University of Sharjah, Faiq has brought together a number of articles, that give a new perspective on translation from Arabic, ranging from Ibrahim Muhawi's "On Translating Oral Style in Palestinian Folktales" to Mike Holt's "Translating Islamist Discourse". Tetz Rooke, meanwhile, discusses the groundbreaking literary translation project Mémoires de la Méditerranée. Topics cover modern literature, with contributions on Arabic-Hebrew translation and Arabic autobiography among others, as well as pre-modern topics, with Hussein Abdul-Raof's 'The Qur'an: Limits of Translatability'. This collection represents an intriguing addition to translation and Arabic literary studies and opens multiple avenues for future research. Multilingual Matters, Clevedon, 2004, pbk, 138pp, ISBN: 9781853597435. CB.

### OTHER BOOKS RECEIVED

**Poems for the Millennium, Volume 4**: *The University of California Book of North African Literature*. Edited with commentaries by Pierre Joris and Habib Tengour. University of California Press, Los Angeles, 2012, pbk, 760pp. ISBN: 9780520273856.

**The Art of Party-Crashing in Medieval Iraq**, by al-Khatib al-Baghdadi, translated and illustrated by Emily Selove. Syracuse University Press, Syracuse, 2012, hbk, 177pp. ISBN: 9780815632986.

**The Shipwrecked Sailor in Arabic and Western Literature: Ibn Tufayl and his influence on European Writers**, by Mahmoud Baroud. I. B. Tauris, London, 2012, hbk, 280pp. ISBN: 9781848855526.

# Roger Allen awarded the Saif Ghobash Banipal Prize for Arabic Literary Translation at London ceremony

The Saif Ghobash Banipal Prize for Arabic Literary Translation was awarded to Roger Allen during the Society of Authors' Translation Prizes 2012 awards ceremony held at Kings Place, central London. Allen won the prize for his translation of Moroccan author Bensalem Himmich's novel *A Muslim Suicide*. The £3,000 award was presented by the editor of the *Times Literary Supplement* Sir Peter Stothard.

When Allen received the award, he thanked the Saif Ghobash family, the Society of Authors and the Banipal Trust and then, to much applause, announced: "Above all, I have the honour tonight to tell you that the author himself is in the audience." His 414-page translation was published by Syracuse University Press in 2011. The central character is Sufi philosopher Ibn Sab'in (1217-1269 CE), who was born in Murcia in Al-Andalus, southern Spain, but was forced to leave for North Africa because of his controversial views. He was later expelled from Egypt and spent his final years in Mecca.

The Saif Ghobash Banipal Prize, first awarded in 2006, is sponsored by Omar Saif Ghobash of the UAE and his family in memory

*Roger Allen speaking at the Award Ceremony, King's Place, London*

of his late father Saif Ghobash. The runner-up was Humphrey Davies, commended for his translation of Palestinian poet and author Mourid Barghouti's *I Was Born There, I Was Born Here*, published by Bloomsbury.

Allen had travelled from Philadelphia for the awards ceremony and two other prize events organised by the Banipal Trust for Arab Literature – a three-hour Masterclass on Arabic Literary Translation attended by 24 keen students, and a discussion event with his author at the Mosaic Rooms, chaired by Professor Paul Starkey, chair of the Trust, and followed by a reception. Bensalem Himmich had travelled from Rabat, Morocco, especially for the events.

In all, eight prizes – for literary translation from Arabic, French, German, Italian, Modern Greek, Portuguese, Spanish and Swedish – were awarded during the evening, the winners being introduced by Paula Johnson of the Society of Authors, who co-hosted the event with the presenter of each award, Sir Peter Stothard.

The judges of the Saif Ghobash Banipal Prize were poet Ruth Padel, novelist Esther Freud, Iraqi poet, novelist, critic and translator Fadhil al-Azzawi, and translator and university teacher John Peate.

Presenting the prize to Roger Allen, Sir Peter Stothard said: "In the view of the judges the most important aspect of this historical novel that takes the 13th-century Sufi philosopher Ibn Sab'in as its hero, is its language. The Arabic original is written in a language not only related to its heritage, but also full of contemplations and Sufi ideas, they accompany the main hero on his long journey across different cities and countries, from Spain to Mecca. And this also opens up remarkable historical, cultural and religious perspectives of the Islamic heritage."

In the judges' opinion "it's hard to imagine anyone in the world besides Roger Allen capable of bringing this serious book to English readers. He has succeeded with his wonderful style not only to turn Himmich's text into brilliant English prose but also to create a real piece of literature."

In announcing the commendation of Humphrey Davies, Stothard observed that he was a former winner of the Saif Ghobash Banipal Prize and that judge al-Azzawi had described him as "one of the masters of translation from Arabic into English. For the judges, "what Humphrey Davies has done once again is to adopt exactly the right palette of both vocabulary and tone in his translation

*The Masterclass with Roger Allen, held at the Arab British Centre, where Banipal has its office*      Photo by Amira Abd El-Khalek

*The panel discussion at the Mosaic Rooms: (l to r) Bensalem Himmich, interpreter Mohamed-Saleh Omri, Roger Allen and Paul Starkey*

all the way through".

The eight Translation Prizes went to six novels and two poetry books. In his lengthy article on the prizes in the *Times Literary Supplement*, Adrian Tahourdin (the TLS's French Editor) leads with Allen's translation: "Most challenging among the novels is undoubtedly Bensalem Himmich's *A Muslim Suicide*."

The novel is set in "turbulent times – the Crusades and the Mongol advance are in the background – but this is very much a personal quest. Poetry, philosophy and Sufism, with its goal of the transcendent, the 'Necessary Existent', are constant presences in this dense and complex novel." Tahourdin adds: "And the many women who cross Ibn Sab'in's path are presented in a style that seems appropriate to the time and place: 'her diaphanous dress was set and showed every details of her luxuriant body'."

During the panel discussion, held the evening after the award ceremony, Roger Allen said that one of the amazing things about *A Muslim Suicide* was the very good impression it gives about an era in relations between two cultures "which is utterly different from our conception about the relationship between the West, and what we'll call the Middle East, now". He spoke of "this enormous variety of intellects and talents represented by this particular culture, this particular moment in the cultural history of Europe which still needs to be rediscovered".

Roger Allen has translated numerous works of modern Arabic literature, and was himself a judge of the Saif Ghobash Banipal Prize in its first years.

Bensalem Himmich, born in Meknes in 1949, is a poet, philosopher, and a distinguished award-winning author of 11 novels, including several historical novels, three of which have been translated by Roger Allen. He has been a Professor of Philosophy at Mohammad V University in Rabat, and served as Morocco's Minister of Culture in 2009 to 2012.

Despite the acclaim for his novels set in the past, Himmich disagreed with the categorisation "historical novel". He told the audience: "I am a prisoner of this category historical novels", and explained that he feels a sense of responsibility writing about characters who are outsiders, or marginal, that he has to "recuperate persons out of history". He added: "I think the best way is to consider the past like the present, and this present, after all, will be a past – this is history, but the label 'historical novel' I don't agree with it."

*Report and photographs from King's Place and Mosaic Rooms by Susannah Tarbush. Additional reporting by Agnes Reeve. For more information about the prize go to www.banipaltrust.org.uk*

# Palestinian Poets in London

To launch *Banipal 45 – Writers from Palestine*, Banipal collaborated with the A. M. Qattan Foundation's Mosaic Rooms in London to host an evening of poetry and discussion with Palestinian poets from the issue Marwan Makhoul and Asma'a Azaizeh. Banipal Editor Samuel Shimon opened the evening by addressing the packed-out audience, recalling how he had dreamed of publishing a magazine completely devoted to Palestinian literature since Banipal's launch 15 years ago.

Asma'a Azaizeh read a selection of poems taken from her first collection *Liwa*, accompanied by Banipal's Agnes Reeve reading Khaled al Masri's English translations.

Marwan Makhoul gave a stirring performance reading his poems, with Raphael Cohen's translations read by poet and translator Stephen Watts. The difference in each poet's style and

*Marwan Makhoul and Asma'a Azaizeh, with the readers of the translations Stephen Watts and Agnes Reeve, and Omar al-Qattan, as he introduces them to the audience*

delivery made the reading captivating and enthralling for the audience.

Omar Al-Qattan (Secretary to the board of the A. M. Qattan Foundation) facilitated a lively and interesting discussion and provided interpretation assistance where needed. The event was a great triumph for all those involved and concluded with the poets signing copies of their own collections, and of *Banipal 45* where their poems have been published.

*Report by Agnes Reeve*
*Photographs courtesy A M Qattan Foundation/The Mosaic Rooms*

*The discussion gets under way after the readings*

*Samuel Shimon opening the evening*

# CONTRIBUTORS

## THE POETS

**Taha Adnan** grew up in Marrakech and moved to Brussels in 1996, where he lives and works and runs the Brussels Arabic Literary Salon. His poems have been translated into French and Spanish. He won second prize at the 2011 International Arab Festival of Monodrama in the UAE.

**Fadhil Al-Azzawi** was born in Kirkuk in 1940. He has published many books of poetry, novels, short stories, criticism, and translations from English and German into Arabic. In 2011 he was Chair of Judges of the International Prize for Arabic Fiction.

**Salah Faik** was born in 1945 in Kirkuk, Iraq. He has seven collections of Arabic poetry and two of English translation, and in 2011 a selection was translated to French. In 2010 his collection *Raheel (Departure)* was translated by Makram Rasheed Talabani into Kurdish. He lives in the Philippines.

**Hussein Habasch** is a Syrian poet of Kurdish origin, living in Bonn, Germany. He has published five collections of poetry in Arabic. Selections of his poetry have been translated into English, German, Spanish, French, Turkish, Persian and Uzbek. He writes in both Arabic and Kurdish.

**Mohamed al-Harthy** was born in 1962 in al-Mudhayrib, Oman. Since 1992 he has published five collections of poetry, some of which have been translated into English, French, German and Malabar. In 2003 he won the Ibn Battuta Award for Geographical Literature for his travel book *Ain wa Janah (An Eye and a Wing)*.

**Musa Hawamdeh** was born in Palestine in the town of As-Samu'. He published his first collection of poems in Amman in 1988. He has won a number of awards including the Jordanian Writers Association Award for non-members, the 'La Plume' prize awarded by the French Fondation Oriani in 2006, and the Terranova Festival Award.

**Heind R. Ibrahim** is an Iraqi poet who has lived in USA since 1998. She studies English Literature at George Mason University in Washington DC.

**Hassab al-Sheikh Ja'far** is an Iraqi poet and novelist, born in Missan, Iraq, in 1942. He has published nine poetry collections and two novels and has also translated several anthologies of Russian poetry into Arabic. He is a member of the Iraq Writers Union's Board. He won the Soviet Peace Award in 1983 and the Owais Award for Poetry in 2003.

**Vénus Khoury-Ghata** is a Lebanese poet and novelist born in Besherri, based in Paris. She has won the Apollinaire Prize for Poetry (1980), the Mallarmé Prize (1987), the Grand Prix of the French Society of Authors (1990), the Prix Supervielle (1998) and the Prix Goncourt de la Poésie (2011).

**Khaled Mattawa** was born in Benghazi in 1964 and emigrated to the USA in 1979. He has published four books of poetry and translated eight volumes of contemporary Arabic poetry. His *Adonis: Selected Poems* (2010) won the 2011 Saif Ghobash Banipal Prize for Arabic Literary Translation.

**Philip Metres** was born in San Diego in 1970. He is an associate professor of English at John Carroll Univ., Ohio, and a translator of Russian poetry. He won the Arab American Book Award for Poetry (2012) and is awarded a National Endowment for the Arts grant for 2013. www.philipmetres.com

**Dunya Mikhail** was born in Baghdad in 1965. She studied English Literature at Baghdad University and has published three collections of poetry. She has lived in Michigan since 1996 and is studying for an MA degree in Oriental Studies at Wayne State University. She was shortlisted for the International Griffin Poetry Prize in 2006.

**Khaled Najar** was born in Tunis in 1949. He has been publishing poems since the late 1960s. He has written for various Arab newspapers and magazines. In 1991 he established Editions Tawbaad.

**Amjad Nasser** was born in Jordan in 1955. From 1976 he worked in newspapers in Beirut, Cyprus and London, and is cultural and managing editor of *Al-Quds al-Arabi*. He has published several volumes of award-winning poetry, travel memoirs and a novel. He has judged many literary awards, including the Lettre Ulysses Award and the International Prize for Arabic Fiction. His works have been translated into French, Italian, English, and Spanish.

## OTHER CONTRIBUTORS

**Ruth Ahmedzai** is a British translator of Arabic, German and Russian into English and an editor. She also translates for a number of charities and NGOs, and is a part-time teacher of Arabic.

**Saud Alsanousi** is a Kuwaiti novelist and journalist, born in 1981. His work has appeared in several Kuwaiti publications, his first novel was published in 2010 and won the fourth Leila Othman Prize. In 2011 his short story *The Bonsai and the Old Man* won first place in Stories on the Air.

**Mohammed Hasan Alwan** was born in Riyadh, Saudi Arabia. He has an MBA from the University of Portland, Oregon, USA. He has published four novels as well as short stories and writes a weekly column for a Saudi newspaper. He was chosen as

# CONTRIBUTORS

one of Beirut39's 39 best young Arab writers.

**Sinan Antoon** was born in Baghdad in 1967 and moved to the USA after the 1991 Gulf War. He is a poet, novelist, translator and filmmaker. Some of his works have been translated into English, Italian, German, Portuguese and Norwegian. He teaches Arabic Literature at New York University.

**Latifa Baqa** was born in 1964 in Sale, Morocco. She won the Moroccan Union of Writers' Award for Best Young Writer. Her short stories have been translated into French, German, Spanish, Italian, and Hebrew, and have appeared in anthologies, including *Sardines and Oranges* (Banipal Books, 2005).

**Mary Ann Caws** is Distinguished Professor of English, French, and Comparative Literature at the Graduate School of City University, New York, and a prolific author, editor, and translator from French. Among her many books is *Surprised in Translation* (2006), a celebration of translators and translation. She is an Officer of the Palmes Académiques (awarded by the French Minister of Education).

**Humphrey Davies** has an Arabic degree from Cambridge University and a PhD from UCLA. He started on his first translation project in 1997 and moved on to modern Arabic literature with a short story published in *Banipal*. He has twice won the Saif Ghobash Banipal Prize for Arabic Literary Translation. The authors whose works he has translated include Elias Khoury, Bahaa Taher, Gamal al-Ghitani, Alaa Al-Aswany and Khaled al-Berry.

**Jana Fawaz Elhassan** is a Lebanese novelist and journalist, born in 1985. She has published her articles and short stories in several publications. Her first novel (2009) won the Simon Hayek Prize.

**Marilyn Hacker** is an award-winning American poet, translator and critic, with many collections of poetry and translations. She served as editor of *The Kenyon Review* and is a Chancellor of the Academy of American Poets. In 2012 she was awarded the International Argana Poetry Prize of Morocco.

**Ibrahim Issa** is an Egyptian journalist, born in 1965. He has been among the most active of Egyptian journalists in protesting against political practices in Egypt. He has won several prizes including the 2008 Gebran Tueni Award, the 2010 International Journalist of the Year Award from the UK's Society of Editors, and the 2011 Index on Censorship Freedom of Expression Award.

**Mohammad Khashan** was born in 1934, in Suhmata, Palestine. He became a refugee in Lebanon with his family in 1948. The memoir he started writing in 2007 has been serialised on various Arab literary websites, such as Kikah.com. He is working on a book of essays on life in Palestine before 1948.

**Herbert Mason** is a writer, translator, emeritus professor of Boston University, and the author of 15 books, including the National Book Award finalist *Gilgamesh, a Verse Narrative*. He is the editor and translator of Louis Massignon's *The Passion of al-Hallaj*, 4 volumes, for the Bollingen Foundation's award winning translation series. His works include novels, poetry, and scholarly studies.

**(Ahmad) Faris al-Shidyaq** (1804–1887) was an Ottoman writer, scholar and journalist, and is considered one of the founding fathers of modern Arabic literature and journalism. He studied in Cairo and Cambridge, wrote most of his works in Paris, and later moved to Tunis and Istanbul. His major works were dedicated to the modernisation of the Arabic language and defending its culture.

**Hussein al-Wad** is a university professor and researcher, born in 1948 in Moknine, Tunisia. He has written several books on classical and modern Arabic literature, notably on Abu al-Ala Al-Ma'arri's *The Epistle of Forgiveness*, and on al-Mutanabbi. His first novel, published in 2010, won the Tunisian Golden Comar Award.

**Jonathan Wright** was a correspondent with Reuters news agency for thirty years, based mainly in the Middle East. His first literary translation, from Egyptian colloquial dialect, was Khaled al-Khamissi's *Taxi* (2009). He has also translated *Azazeel* by Youssef Ziedan, *Judgment Day* by Lebanese writer Rasha al-Ameer, and other works.

---

*The translators in Banipal 46 are:*

Ruth Ahmedzai, Thomas Aplin, Fadhil al-Azzawi, Allison Blecker, Issa J. Boullata, Mary Ann Caws, Raphael Cohen, Humphrey Davies, Robin Moger, Camilo Gomez-Rivas, Marilyn Hacker, Ibtihaj al-Harthi, Ghenwa Hayek, William M Hutchins, Fady Joudah, Khaled Mattawa, John Peate, Paul Starkey, Maia Tabet, Jonathan Wright.

The writers and book reviewers are:

Latifa Baqa, Charis Bredin, Norbert Hirshhorn, Munib Khan, Herbert Mason, Margaret Obank, Khaled Najar, Agnes Reeve, Susannah Tarbush, Stephen Watts, Mona Zaki.

For information on all the translators, writers and book reviewers in **Banipal 46**, and for more on all other contributors, please go to:

**www.banipal.co.uk/contributors/**

*Latifa Baqa*

# "Give Me the Flute and Sing"

"Music is a necessary part of a person's life." This truth was not something a teacher drilled into me in school. I discovered it by myself at home. In the beginning the music came from a large radio located in the sitting room. My mother would turn it on in the morning, and we would listen to Eastern and Moroccan songs, which would keep playing in my head on the road to school until the school bell drowned them out. Next the tape recorder infiltrated some neighbourhood residences, accompanied by plastic rectangles called cassettes, which may seem obsolete today when people get their music through ear-buds. These cassettes introduced us to other types of musical pleasure. Many songs geared toward a wide variety of tastes became part of our lives. In this regard, I still remember, for example, that my sister loved Umm Kulthum's approach to singing while my brother identified with Farid al-Atrash and believed in Bob Marley. I discovered myself in the voice of Fairuz and broke into tears with Jacques Brel when he found fault with fools, weakness and unfaithful women.

I realized early on that singing is an individual pursuit and completely self-centered, even when you sing with a group. Thanks to Jacques Brel I discovered poetry transformed into musical lyrics. He was the only singer who could make me savour the delightful poems embedded in music. He was also the only man I allowed to find fault with women, because of my deep belief that he was a truthful man no matter how macho he was and that he was a handsome man despite his ugliness. A mad artist's creativity remedies all this defects. He is the person who sang "Je suis un homme mort qui est encore vivant".

My relationship with Jacques Brel started the same year as my relationship with Albert Camus and my infatuation with Fairuz. At approximately the same period I read "La Nausée" by Sartre and "Le deuxième sexe" by Simone de Beauvoir. In a class, a few years earlier, we had made the acquaintance of Jacques Prévert and of the boy in one of his poems who stood before the teacher and refused to recite the multiplication table*, at a time when we would not have been able to do that.

Something important occurred when I discovered music and lovely songs because, as Fairuz has said, "Singing is the secret of existence." I felt a tremendous flood of creativity from Western songs, especially French ones. I also liked Arab songs and still do, although one essential objective was, unfortunately, not achieved in them. They were out of sync with the ideas and books I was reading back then, and most did not surprise me the way the scamp Renaud did, for example, by concluding a song with "At the end of a song, we should find a cheerful collapse". All the same, he continued to sing.

In secondary school we became acquainted with Georges Moustaki, who immortalized his lost liberty in "Ma Liberté", and Serge Reggiani, who recounts his sad story with "La femme qui est dans mon lit". We also became acquainted with "La Bohème" of Aznavour, and with Edith Piaf, who regretted nothing. Mireille Mathieu, who had a "Stone" cut, was not as deep, but I liked her and the way she moved her soft black hair. (I wished I had hair like hers.) She screamed at an unseen man, "Je suis une femme amoureuse et c'est mon droit de t'aimer." Then attempting to be wise, she announced, "On ne vit pas sans se dire adieu."

Gilbert Bécaud arrived in a more contentious context when we accompanied him on his tour with his protégée Natalie in the ambiance of the October Revolution, which we stumbled upon in the atmosphere of the College of Arts in

Rabat: the cold and the light rain outside and the warmth created by the gathering of students in the hall and the snack bar, amid heated discussion and the smoke from cheap, black cigarettes till we could almost taste the hot chocolate that Bécaud was drinking with Natalie in Café Pushkin.

"Music is a necessary part of a person's life." There is music that affords you joy, music that plunges you into despair, music that engages with your intellect, and music that addresses your body; there is music that stifles all the avenues of thought, and finally there is music that makes you a writer. Brel inspired me with images, sensations, and writing. I would close my eyes and see him kneeling and imploring that lucky woman:

> Ne me quitte pas
> Je ne vais plus pleurer
> Je ne vais plus parler
> Je me cacherai là
> A te regarder
> Danser et sourire
> Et à t'écouter
> Chanter et puis rire
> Laisse-moi devenir
> L'ombre de ton ombre
> L'ombre de ta main
> L'ombre de ton chien
> Ne me quitte pas

When love and anger fuse together in poetry and music, that is definitely Brel. He used to indict social hypocrisy, preferring his childhood. When I would allow his voice to grow loud and reverberate powerfully throughout our house, that apparently was my revolutionary manifesto that harmonizes exactly with the truth I discovered and announced at the beginning of this confession: "Music is a necessary part of a person's life."

Note:

"Give me the Flute and Sing" is a famous song by the Lebanese singer Fairuz from a poem by Gibran Kahlil Gibran.

*"Page d'écriture", Jacques Prévert, Paroles (Paris: Le Livre de Poche, Librairie Gallimard, 1949), pp.143-143.

Translated by William M. Hutchins